YOUR OLD PAL
MARCUS ALEXANDER HART

GALAXY CRUISE
THE MAIDEN VOYAGE
BOOK 1

Canaby Press, LLC | Sheridan, Wyoming

Copyright © 2021 by Marcus Alexander Hart

Cover design by Marcus Alexander Hart - OldPalMarcus.com
Spaceship model by Jon Lundy - JonLundy.com
Old Pal Marcus logo by Michael Greenholt - MichaelGreenholt.com
Alien League II font by Dan Zadorozny - iconian.com

All rights reserved. No part of this publication may be reproduced, distributed, or transmitted in any form without prior written permission, unless you want to use a short quotation to tell people how great it is.

Thank you for respecting copyright and supporting indie authors!

Canaby Press, LLC
30 North Gould Street | Suite R
Sheridan, WY 82801
CanabyPress.com

This is a work of fiction. Names, characters, places, and events are either a product of the author's imagination or are used fictitiously. Any resemblance to actual persons, human or extraterrestrial, is entirely coincidental.

Galaxy Cruise: The Maiden Voyage / Marcus Alexander Hart
Book 1
Print Edition 3

Amazon ebook ASIN: B08BNP2HYT
Amazon series ASIN: B092MX51QD

Paperback ISBN: 979-8511714394
Hardcover ISBN: 979-8511743073

ALSO BY
MARCUS ALEXANDER HART

The Galaxy Cruise Series
The continuing sci-fi comedy space adventure

The Alexis McRiott Jams
Irreverent, foul-mouthed, supernatural comedy

One Must Kill Another
A paranormal thriller

Find more at OldPalMarcus.com

CHAPTER ONE

The agonizing screech vibrated Leo's skull like a bone saw trying to bore its way out from the inside. The aliens were torturing him. Again.

He had to get away. He had to escape.

His desperate gaze ticked to the single window. The galaxy stretched to infinity outside, cold and bleak and unforgiving. A small, circular pock-mark marred the glass from some bygone impact of ice or rock. The flaw was tiny, but critical. Leo knew if he hit the window hard enough it would shatter. He could escape. Sure, it would be into the void of space where he'd die an agonizing death by asphyxiation, but compared to the alternative, at least that would be quick.

The caustic wail pitched upward. Leo's muscles constricted. His vision blurred. His sphincter clenched. Just when he was on the cusp of permanent detachment from his sanity...

The noise stopped.

And the audience burst into wild applause.

Leo's brain pulled back from the edge of fatal hemorrhaging, letting his eyes slowly return to focus. A hulking alien strutted across the tarnished deck plating, waving his hands at the crowd as he sponged up their praise. Eight beefy tentacles sprouted from his head, each ending in a round, leech-like mouth the size and shape of a trombone bell. Leo leaned into the microphone of his karaoke console and cleared his throat.

"Okay, so... let's hear it for Grund'lay, for that rendition of what was allegedly 'Sweet Caroline'!" He winced at the sound of his own voice in his ringing ears. "It's true what they say, nobody murders Neil Diamond like a Screetoro."

The alien flung his microphone at Leo's head, screeching out words like an angry bugle corps. "Suck it, stubble chimp!"

Leo yelped and ducked the projectile as a roar of laughter erupted from the crowd of gathered... things. A few blue lizards in Hawaiian shirts slurped up cocktails. A party of animate plants devoured a rack of barbecue, spattering sauce on their leafy faces. In a darkened corner, a couple of humanoid felines mewled and pawed at each other like no one was watching. They'd be coughing up hairballs of each other's fur by last call.

Leo sighed as he picked up the microphone and checked the list of names on his console. "All right, the next singer is... oh man, I know I'm gonna butcher this pronunciation. It's like... Kind of a square thing, then two squiggles and what looks like a pregnant seahorse?"

A dark mass the size of a small shuttlecraft slid out of the shadows. It was a rigid and slightly translucent blob filled with a mottled, curry-type substance. Leo didn't recognize the species, but thought it looked exactly like a glacier made of vomit. The alien reached out a short, blobby tendril and accepted the mic.

"Suuuuuuuuuuuu..."

The deck vibrated as a thunderous sound rumbled from deep inside the creature like a didgeridoo mating with a foghorn. Leo flinched and backed away.

"Uh... are you all right?"

"... uuuuuuuuck."

Leo blinked. "Suck?"

"Iiiiiiiiiiiiiiiiiiiiiii..."

"Ah. Okay. I see where you're going with this."

"... iiiiiiiiiiiiiiiiiiiiiiiiiiiiit."

"It. Suck it. Hilarious. Now that we've got that out of the way, let's see what song—"

"Stuuuuuuuuuuuuuuuublllllllllle."

"Oh for crying out loud." Leo crossed his arms and tipped his head back on his shoulders as the glacier droned through its speciest slur. A series of thick, rusty pipes crisscrossed the lounge's ceiling above, each printed with warning labels in every alien language he could identify and several he could not, like the Rosetta Stone of toxic waste. He wondered how hard it would be to take a drink from one and put himself out of his misery.

"Chiiiiiiiiiiiiiiiiiiiiiiiiiiiiimp."

Leo side-eyed the glacier as he leaned into his console microphone. "Yes, thank you. Now let's see what you'll be singing for us tonight." *Please be short,* he silently prayed. *Please be short, please be short.* He tapped a pad and the bar's holoscreens displayed the song. His shoulders slumped. "Ah. Every KJ's favorite eight-and-a-half-minute epic, 'I'd Do Anything For Love (But I Won't Do That).'" He gave the crowd a wave. "Well, I'd encourage you to sign up to sing next, but I have realistic expectations about our average life spans. I hope you all finished those bucket lists!"

The music started and two full verses of lyrics scrolled across the screens before the glacier had worked its way through the first word. Leo muttered to himself as he abandoned his console and dragged himself across the room. "Just get through it, Leo. This is your last night in space. Tomorrow you go home."

He sidled up to the bar and grabbed a stool. Its smooth plastic seat was funnel shaped, sloped toward a large hole in the back. He pulled himself up and perched uncomfortably on its rim.

The bartender noticed him and scuttled over. He was a

Krubb—an insectoid alien with a cylindrical exoskeleton and domed head with a broad mouth. He looked like a trash can with crab legs. In the places where you'd expect handles were two long, skinny arms that nearly reached the deck before hinging at the elbow and coming back up to end in clawed pincers he held curled at his shoulders.

"Whaddya want, hairbag?"

Leo frowned and ran a hand through his shaggy black coif. "Gimme a beer."

The Krubb grunted and pulled a pint of something blue and grainy from the tap. He plunged a claw into a large glass fishbowl on the bar, plucked out a wriggling purple slug, and impaled it on a toothpick. With a flourish of his spindly arms, he dropped the garnish in the drink and slid it to Leo. Leo stared down into the glass, watching a trickle of yellow goop leak out of the bug and swirl into the beverage like an oil slick.

"This is not a beer. This is not even the same genre as a beer."

The Krubb scowled. "If you don't like it you can..."

"Suck it, stubble chimp," Leo grumbled. "I know."

He frowned and slouched back in his chair. His butt slid into the funnel and one cheek fell through the hole at the rear, forcing his knee to jerk up and slam into the bottom of the bar. He hissed and grimaced and awkwardly crossed that leg over the other as if it had all been part of some master plan.

A female voice giggled. "Those stools are usually reserved for beings with tails."

Leo glanced over to see a woman leaning against the bar to his side. She was humanoid in form, right down to the shape of her skull. He could tell, because her head was basically just an oversized human skull. Her orange skin seemed to lay flat on the bone, pierced by five short, claw-shaped horns sprouting upward from her scalp like a tiara. A garland of colorful flowers was woven between them. Leo looked away. He didn't know a lot about aliens, but he knew enough to steer clear of the Ba'lux.

"Thanks for the tip," he muttered.

The girl chuckled. "Could be worse. You could have picked one with genital stabilizer blades." She sashayed closer, seemingly showing off her thin, reedy body, clothed in stylishly tattered jeans and a tank top. She held out a bony fist. "Varlowe."

Leo cringed as he reluctantly met her eyes. Or what passed for eyes in Ba'lux physiology. Two copper-colored domes stared back at him, featureless and unreadable as a pair of soup spoons.

"Leo." He bumped her knuckles. "Leo MacGavin."

"Leo MacGavin," Varlowe said, savoring the words. "Such an exotic name."

"Not where I come from."

Varlowe smiled, baring a mouth full of small, pointed teeth. "It's a rare treat to find one of your people willing to leave the settlement."

Leo glanced out the broad window at a gleaming, blue-green moon in the distance. Eaglehaven was the idyllic world his Earthly ancestors had created to replace the ruined one they had fled. A do-over on a planetary scale. The new cradle of humanity. He sighed longingly. "I made a poor life choice."

"You made a *bold* life choice," Varlowe said. "Most of your people will live their whole lives never daring to step off that little rock. But you did. And I think that's worthy of a toast." Leo flinched as she rested a hot, four-fingered hand on his arm. "Bartender! Get me your finest American champagne."

The Krubb grabbed a bottle embossed with a picture of a mime in a beret hugging the Eiffel Tower. Leo waved it away. "Uh, no. That's okay. I should be getting back to work."

Varlowe glanced across the lounge. The glacier was just ramping up into the third word of the lyrics. "I think you'll be fine. After all..." She gave Leo a knowing look. *"You deserve a break today."*

She peeled the foil off the champagne bottle and began twisting the cage off the cork. Leo eyed her suspiciously. This Ba'lux didn't belong here. There wasn't another orange skull in the room. In the six months he'd been in self-exile on the Jaynkee Spacedock there had never been an orange skull in this room. He cleared his throat nervously.

"So, uh. What's someone like you doing all the way down on sub-level 97-Z?"

"Someone like me?" Varlowe raised a hairless, bony eye ridge. "What's that supposed to mean?"

"Nothing!" Leo cringed. "It's just... you're from a prime world. You're from *the* prime world."

Varlowe set down the bottle and crossed her arms. "And?"

"And, well, this bar is so close to the reactor core it needs a bartender impervious to radiation poisoning." Leo waved a hand at the grungy room, with its stained walls and gurgling pipes. "Isn't the Exhaust Port Lounge a little lowbrow for a Ba'lux?"

"Oh. I see. You think I should be eating goosefish foie gras truffles and watching the Ba'luxi Prime Imperial Lecture Ballet Company over on the *Opulera*."

She thumbed over her shoulder at the window and the rows of ships sprawling into the distance against the dock's gangway tunnels—planetary shuttles, and cargo freighters, and sleek commuter craft glistening in the starlight. But one vessel dominated the rest, dwarfing them all in both size and pure baroque arrogance.

The *Opulera* was the flagship of the Waylade Tour Fleet. An enormous, bulbous teardrop of gray metal swirled with gold and bristling with blade-shaped solar sails extending in flared rows from its sides and top. Leo thought it looked like a robot lionfish with ion burners stuck up its butt.

He returned his attention to his mug, but wasn't brave enough to actually drink from it. "I don't know. I understand your people like that stuff."

A snort of laughter came from Varlowe's nostril slits. "Nobody likes that stuff. Ba'lux culture is so uptight and stuffy and boooooring. We just finished a twelve-day cruise and I can't stand it anymore. So I was excited to hear about this dock bar with authentic American karaoke."

She nodded across the room. Nestled between the decaying tables and chairs was a karaoke setup adorned with disco lights and neon kanji. Images of blue-haired cartoon girls in sailor schoolgirl outfits beamed from its face, holding microphones in one hand and throwing peace signs with the other.

Leo scowled. "I'm sure you were. Everybody up here loves the karaoke booth. You just can't stand its operator."

"That's not true," Varlowe said. "I personally find its operator very alluring."

The orange woman slid her fingers down the back of Leo's arm. A spasm ripped through his body, kicking his legs and inadvertently driving his rump deeper into the funnel of his seat. "Oh, wow. Okay. So, full disclosure. I'm not really looking for... *that*. I'm kinda getting over a heartbreak, so..."

"So that's what brings you to space, eh? Running away from a girl back home?"

Leo cringed at her cutting insight. "Like I said. Poor life choice."

Actually, "poor life choice" didn't begin to cover it. Coming to space had been the single worst decision he'd ever made. If Leo had known then what he knew now, he never would have left Eaglehaven. He wouldn't have subjected himself to the jeering insults of weird aliens with blue scales or purple feathers or embarrassing facial gonads. He'd be safe at home, surrounded by normal people with normal skin not more than a few degrees of saturation off his own brown-paper-bag complexion. But it didn't matter now. Today's paycheck would finally put enough galactic dollabux in his account to buy a ticket home.

Varlowe leaned in with a toothy grin. "Well, I think you'll come to like living off-world. People may be a little standoffish at first, but in time you'll see the truth. *We love to see you smile.*"

She nodded sagely, coaxing Leo to find her deeper meaning. Leo did not.

"Yeah, no. I don't think so." He kicked his bound-up legs, sending his stool into a slow rotation around its base. "Actually I'm leaving first thing in the morning, and I'm never, ever coming back to space under any circumstan—"

Varlowe put a hand on his knee, arresting his spin. "I've studied your people, and I'm deeply passionate about your history and spirituality."

She moved closer, pressing her bony abdomen to Leo's knees. Her head tipped in a way that would have been a sultry gaze through her eyelashes, had she possessed eyelashes or anything resembling eyes. Leo's heart raced as his body completely seized. His mouth opened. No words came out. It closed. It opened again.

"That's... cool?"

Varlowe grasped a fine chain at her throat and pulled a medallion out of her tank top. It was a red circle, emblazoned with a rounded, golden M. "I'm a devout follower of the teachings of the ancient American philosopher, Mickey D." Her other hand clamped around Leo's upper thigh. "And *I'm lovin' it.*"

With a surprised yelp, his entire body spasmed hard enough to flip his chair and throw him to the floor. His nerves jangled as he sprang to his feet and righted the stool, requiring three spastic attempts to balance it on its base.

"Okay, so... As flattered as I am to be part of your..." He rolled his hands, searching for the words. "Alien burger cult... I should really be getting back to—"

"Varlowe!" a voice roared. "What in the name of Queen Akvens is going on here?"

Every head, eyestalk, and visual sensory organ in the room turned toward a Ba'lux elder towering in the entry arch. His broad chest and meaty biceps strained the fabric of his culture's traditional garb, which always looked to Leo like a cross between papal robes and a prom tuxedo. He marched into the lounge, his weathered face tight with rage.

Leo's feet froze to the floor in terror. "Nothing is going on! I was just enjoying a nice refreshing mug of blue sand and—"

He choked as the slab of orange muscle thumped a hand on his throat and hoisted him off the deck without so much as a grunt. The voids of the man's eyes were firmly fixed on Varlowe's. "Why are you canoodling with this rodent?"

Varlowe smirked and crossed her arms. "Who I canoodle with is none of your business. You're not my father."

"Your father is rolling in his grave. This disgusting behavior is unacceptable for the heiress to the Waylade Tour Fleet."

"That's pronounced *president of* the Waylade Tour Fleet," Varlowe said pointedly.

The man huffed. "Unlike you, I worked hard to earn my rank. And as the vice president of the line, I am—"

"Subordinate to the president of the line." Varlowe calmly raised a hand and pointed to the floor. The giant's face crushed in fury, yet he complied, slowly lowering Leo until his shoes touched the deck. He released his grip and Leo coughed air into his empty lungs.

"Okay, I try not to get mixed up in aliens' personal and potentially lethal business, so I'll just excuse—"

Varlowe dropped a hand on his shoulder. "Leo, I'd like to introduce you to Rip Skardon."

"*Admiral* Rip Skardon," the man growled.

"Retired," Varlowe noted. "He's been with my family's cruise line since he left the service."

Leo nodded. "Hello, sir. It's been awful to meet you. Goodbye."

He tried to leave, but Varlowe's grip tightened. "Stay." She spoke to Leo, but her eyes remained locked on Skardon's. "We value your company."

"Well, I don't want to be a bother," Leo said. "Or collateral damage."

Skardon looked Leo's body up and down as if he were planning the best way to disassemble it. "I never thought I'd see the day when a member of the WTF executive board would be caught fraternizing with this kind of vermin." His voice was like hot steam roiling from a furnace on the verge of explosion. "I demand you return to the *Opulera* before you further sully your family's name with this hairy—"

"Oh lighten up, Skardon, before you pop a gel sac." Varlowe plucked the champagne off the bar. "I'm sure you'll love Leo once you get to know him. Why don't you have a drink with us?"

"I will not." Skardon eyed the bottle. "The last time I tasted American swill it made me so sick I nearly died."

"Then we'll make yours a double." Varlowe turned to the bartender. "Hey, can we get some glasses over—"

Skardon ripped the champagne from her hand and roared, "Enough of this nonsense!"

He raised his massive arm and hurled it to the floor. In an instant too brief for any living thing to register, a number of things happened. As the bottle left Skardon's hand, a tiny snap of his wrist caused it to flip in the air, doing a full 180 before it hit the deck. If it had impacted at an angle of just ten more degrees it would have shattered. Or five more degrees. Or one and a quarter. But the bottle landed directly on its cork, completely perpendicular to the floor. The spongy material compressed as it absorbed the entire force of Skardon's enraged throw. In that moment, the carbonated fizz of the beverage rapidly expanded against the stopper, popping it out and launching the glass upwards like a booze-powered rocket.

The bottle blasted straight up and smashed clean through one of the rusted pipes hanging from the ceiling. With a piercing squeal, a cloud of pink gas vented into the room. Skardon looked up at the damage just in time for the falling bottle to clock him on the cranium with a comical *ponk* that folded him like a deck chair.

The singing glacier's eyes rolled to the ruptured pipe. "Gaaaaaaaaaaaaaa…"

"Gas leak!" a lizard screamed. "Let's get the hekk out of here!"

Leo didn't have to be told. He had already bolted three steps toward the exit the instant Skardon's unconscious body hit the floor. But just as he was about to cross into the corridor, a heavy, airtight metal slab fired from the ceiling and slammed into place in the doorway.

"Gas leak detected," a pleasant electronic voice intoned. *"Compartment sealed for guest safety."*

"Safety?" Leo cried. "How is this safe?"

Pink vapor billowed around him, burning his eyes and choking his lungs with the stench of petrochemicals and rotting fish. The sounds of various beings coughing and thrashing in agony filled the cotton-candy cloud.

"... aaaaaaaaaaaaaaaaaas," the glacier said.

"Help!" a voice screeched. "Gahdamn it! Somebody help me!"

Leo blinked his watering eyes and spotted the Krubb bartender on top of the bar, hopping on his tiny, insectile legs. Both long, spindly arms were extended overhead, but he couldn't quite reach the shutoff valve on the ruptured pipe.

"I'm on it!" Leo shouted.

He darted across the lounge and sprang onto a barstool. Unfortunately, it was the barstool designed for tails. The moment his shoe hit the slick plastic his leg plunged through the funnel, dropping one foot through the stool, one foot to the side of it, and his testicles squarely upon its edge. He howled and tried to catch his balance against the bar, but only managed to tumble forward and splash his head into the fishbowl of garnish slugs. He sucked a startled breath, and the burning in his lungs was momentarily extinguished as they filled with briny water.

"Leeeeeeeeeeeeeeeee," the glacier said.

With a spluttering snort Leo jerked upright. The bowl caught on his skull as he lurched back, spilling its contents over his body as it settled over his head like an old-timey diving helmet. He windmilled his arms and tried to catch his balance with one leg firmly rammed through a stool that made it five inches longer than the other.

Each staggering step punched him in the groin as he clomped through the crowd. Some of the aliens were still writhing and screaming, others lay sprawled unconscious on the floor. Leo's hands banged impotently against the fishbowl as he tried to wipe the toxins from his clenched eyes. In a desperate attempt to dislodge the stool, he raised his trapped leg and spun himself around. All he managed to do was take out two cat people and a sentient eggplant before blindly smashing the stool into the window.

With a squeal like cracking ice, the wounded glass shattered and blasted outward as the lounge's atmosphere vented explosively into the vacuum of space. Leo tried to shield himself as bottles and pint glasses sailed through the air and thumped his body on their way out.

"... eeeeeeeeeeeeeeee..." the glacier said.

Leo grabbed a railing around a raised seating area as the howling wind lifted his feet, pulling his body parallel to the deck. With a sharp rip, the stool yanked free of his leg and flung itself through the window, taking his pants and one shoe along with it.

Before he could lament the loss of his trousers, Leo's fishbowl helmet was peppered with mangled flowers. He twisted his head inside the clouded globe to see Varlowe clinging to the edge of the bar, screaming as the rushing air ripped the blossoms from her horn crown. Her thumb slipped, leaving her dangling by three slender fingers. Leo gasped. Freaky alien or not, she didn't deserve to die like this.

"Hold on! I'm coming!" He gritted his teeth and strained as he flexed his biceps and tried to pull himself to the railing. He did not get closer. At all. "Dang, I gotta start working out."

With a shriek that barely carried in the thinning atmosphere, Varlowe lost her grip and flipped end-over-end toward the ravenous, sucking maw of outer space.

"No!" Leo screamed.

He made a desperate grab as her body whiffed past him, but only managed to lose his own grasp. His scream echoed in the fishbowl as he sailed backwards toward certain death.

Just as Varlowe was about to enter the void, a heavy, airtight metal door fired from the top of the window and slammed into place in the empty frame. She hit it face-first with a grisly *thwack*. Half a second later Leo hit it feet-first and dropped on top of her like a pro wrestler throwing a body slam.

"Hull breach detected," a pleasant electronic voice intoned. *"Compartment sealed for guest safety."*

Leo pushed himself upright and gasped for air as overhead vents replenished the lost atmosphere. Across the room, the Krubb bartender hung limply from a claw, still gripping the closed valve in the ruptured pipe. Aliens twitched and gagged, but the toxic pink gas was gone, sucked safely into space.

"... eeaaaaaaaaak," the glacier said.

Leo coughed and rolled off the cruise boss's bony body. "Varlowe!" He lifted her head and looked into her metallic eyes. They were cold and empty, completely bereft of any sign of life. As usual. Leo waved a hand in front of them. "Hello? Are you like... alive?"

With a sharp hiss, the emergency door sealing the exit shot upward, vomiting five armored security troopers into the lounge. Their heads swiveled as the featureless black masks of their helmets assessed the situation. With tensed reflexes, each of them drew a stun pistol and pointed it at Leo's head.

"Freeze, you filthy mammal!" one shouted. "Unhand that woman!"

"Wait!" Leo leaped to his feet and raised his palms as he backed away. "I can explain everything!"

The guards' weapons squealed with building charge. "You've got two seconds!"

Leo was pantless and soaking wet with a cracked fishbowl over his head and confused purple slugs slowly migrating across his face. At his feet was the lifeless body of the president of the Waylade Tour Fleet, bleeding profusely from a broken horn on her forehead. He cleared his throat.

"It's actually going to take much longer than that."

A sizzle of pure electric agony blazed through Leo's body as all five guards fired their weapons.

CHAPTER TWO

The next morning, Leo's joints were stiff from a night spent crammed in a dog kennel between a snoring centipug and a farting lymphound. He had been happy when his captors had hauled him out of his cage, but less happy when they'd stuck a gun in his back and marched him through the public promenades of the Jaynkee Spacedock.

"What's happening?" he asked. "Where are you taking me?"

"We'll be the ones asking the questions, fur turkey!"

The guards shoved Leo down the corridor. Aliens in the concourses chortled and hid their children's eyes as Leo was paraded past them wearing only one shoe and zero trousers. He tried in vain to pull his T-shirt down over his tighty-whities. "Fine! Then ask me a question! Let's clear this up so I can go home!"

"Shut your tooth hole!" a guard barked. "The only place you're going is the *Opulera*." He shoved Leo into the gangway tunnel leading to the Ba'lux cruise liner. "Apparently they want to deal with you themselves after what you did in the Exhaust Port Lounge last night."

"I didn't do anything! I swear!"

Desperate as he sounded, it was true. He hadn't done anything. And that's exactly what he'd tell them. He was just an innocent human rodent minding his own business when a string of comic mishaps led to him standing over the dead body of the wealthy and powerful heiress of the Waylade Tour Fleet.

Oh, he was so screwed.

The guards hustled him all the way to a suite high at the top of the immense ship. The wall between the corridor and the room was an expanse of glass, as was the opposite wall between the room and space, creating the ambiance of an aquarium perched on a windowsill on a starry night. In the far distance, Eaglehaven glittered like a jewel. In the close distance, a meeting was in progress inside the darkened room.

A nervous-looking Ba'lux man stood in front of a large holoscreen, presenting a slideshow. His grim expression and the graph labeled "Waylade Tour Fleet - Financial Report" with its downward plunging arrow told the whole story.

A baroque conference table was circled by high-backed chairs. In one was a sour-faced Ba'lux woman, identified by a gold nameplate as Noxi Kersa, Hospitality Chair. Next to her was a man Leo recognized with a surge of panicked terror.

Retired Admiral Rip Skardon leaned on the table, drumming his three heavy fingertips on the wood. He seemed unscathed by the incident in the karaoke lounge, save for a swollen, champagne-bottle-induced bump over one eye.

The guards shoved open the doors and hauled their prisoner into the dimly lit room. Noxi Kersa gnashed her teeth. "What is the meaning of this interruption?"

Skardon looked from the holoscreen to Leo and his eyes widened. "You! How dare you show your face on this ship after what you did!"

"I don't know what you're talking about! I didn't do it! It was an accident! I'm so sorry! You can't prove anything!"

Leo lurched for the door, but the guards grabbed him and turned him back around.

"I apologize for the intrusion, sir," a guard said. "We got a call down in animal quarantine. We were told to bring it here."

Kersa crossed her brawny arms. "You most assuredly were not. None of us requested that disgusting American."

"Actually, one of us did."

All eyes turned toward the chair at the head of the table as its occupant leaned forward into the light. The slender orange woman wore a gauzy yellow dress under a long cardigan and a green apron. An enormous purple bruise stained the crown of her head, and a blob of hardened blue medi-gel clung to her scalp around the base of a horn.

"Varlowe!" Leo gasped. "You're alive!"

"Yes, I am." She smiled her piranha grin. "Thanks to you."

The twitchy man giving the slideshow gestured at Leo. "I'm sorry, who is this creature?"

"He's a hero," Varlowe said breathily.

"He's a saboteur," Skardon said simultaneously.

"He is no such thing!" they shouted in unison.

Skardon banged a heavy fist on the table. "This terrorist rodent initiated a chemical gas attack upon us and an entire lounge full of innocent travelers!"

Leo cringed as every empty, copper eye turned to him. "Um, okay, that's not *entirely* accurate."

Varlowe leaned back in her chair. "Oh stuff it, Skardon. We both know that isn't what happened."

"Thank you," Leo said.

"When you broke that pipe, Leo was the only one in the room calm enough to take action. While the rest of us were freaking out, he executed a brilliant plan to vent the toxic gas into space." Varlowe glared at Skardon. "Neither of us would have survived without his quick thinking and bravery. We both owe him a blood debt."

Leo considered it and shrugged. "That's not entirely accurate either, but I'm gonna go with that one."

"I owe no debt to this disgusting, hairy thing." Skardon's eyes stayed locked on Varlowe as he spoke to the guards. "Have this criminal disposed of."

Armored hands clamped on Leo's arms, squeezing out a startled squeak.

"He's not a criminal. He's our guest of honor. Let him go." Varlowe waved a hand at the officers. "You are dismissed."

They released Leo with a shove and closed the doors on the way out. Leo stood awkwardly in the dim light, twisting his bare legs. "Uh, you guys don't happen to have any spare pants, do you?"

Kersa ignored him as she turned to Varlowe. "Madame President, for what purpose have you summoned this..." She waved a hand at Leo. "This?"

"*He* is the key to turning our fortunes around," Varlowe said pointedly. She stood up, crossing to the holoscreen presentation. As she passed, she pulled off her knee-length cardigan and handed it to Leo. "Please, have a seat."

Leo stuffed his arms into the sleeves and moved toward the empty chair next to Kersa. She bared her teeth with a low growl. "Okay, yeah. So..." He stepped away from the table. "You know, it's probably better if I just hang back over here."

He quickly fastened the sweater as he ducked into a corner next to a large planter with a decorative purple-fronded palm tree. Lanky as he was, Varlowe's tailored garment barely stretched around him, leaving bulging keyholes of his T-shirt and hairy thigh pushing between the buttons. Kersa held him in her murderous gaze for a long moment before turning away. Leo perched on the edge of the planter and let out a tiny sigh of relief. He sucked it back in hard enough to pop a button when something grunted at his side.

An ornate wooden wheelchair was parked in the shadows

next to the tree. And in the chair was the most ancient Ba'lux Leo had ever seen. She seemed less like a person and more like a deflated pile of orange meat. Her forearms rested on the arms of her chair, the sagging flesh hanging over both sides like soft dough. The domes of her eyes were dull and matte, and the skin of her scalp hung loose around the cracked points of her horn crown, revealing yellowed crescents of exposed skull.

"Oh, hello." Leo gestured to the planter. "I'm sorry, was this seat taken?"

The old lady just frowned and let out a short, wet fart. Leo scooched to the far side of the pot and pressed against the wall. Up at the front of the room, Varlowe strolled past the panorama windows that separated them from space. The dock sprawled into the distance behind her, bustling with traffic. She gestured to the holoscreen and its dismal graph.

"It's no secret that WTF Cruises has been on the decline. Back in the day, we used to be the gold standard of space tourism, but in recent years, we've lost our edge. Our guests have moved on. If we're going to survive, we need to take drastic action."

"For once we agree," Skardon said. "The only way out of this downturn is through aggressive expansion. That's why I've created a plan to build new luxury spaceports across the Four Prime Systems, giving us total dominance of the galaxy's tourism infrastructure." He grinned eagerly. "We'll smother the competition to extinction and ascend to our rightful place as rulers of the deep-space cruising industry."

Kersa pounded the table. "Hear, hear!"

"Pfft, you two are so basic," Varlowe snorted. "Typical Ba'lux, thinking the solution to every problem is balls-out imperialism."

Skardon snuffed and flattened the broad satin lapels of his vestments. "At least we respect our culture. We haven't turned our back on three millennia of custom and tradition for a ridiculous, tasteless fad. Unlike some people."

A chortle of agreement clucked from Kersa's throat as she eyed Varlowe's wardrobe. The president's bony cheeks burned with anger.

"That attitude is offensive and uncalled for," Varlowe said. "Just because they are from a different culture, it doesn't make my ceremonial robes any less valid than yours." She reverently stroked her green apron, tracing her fingers across the round pictogram on its chest. The stark black and white image showed a two-tailed mermaid wearing a crown with a single star at its center. "This is an ancient symbol of my spirituality, and I will not have you disrespect it."

The bespectacled man cleared his throat. "I think we can all agree that our diversity is our strength." He smiled nervously. "But perhaps we should get back to the issue at hand."

"Willijer's right," Kersa said. "We're ignoring the American in the room."

Leo's face flushed hot, as if a bright spotlight had been turned upon him. He shifted his bony butt on the uncomfortable planter. "Oh, uh. I mean, I personally wouldn't wear it, but if the apron makes Varlowe happy, more power to her, right?"

The board members all glared at him, speechless.

"It's talking," Skardon said. "Why is it talking?"

"I'm sorry, I thought you wanted my opinion." Leo's gaze twitched across the scowling faces. "As the American in the room?"

"It's a figure of speech, you rube," Kersa snapped. "It means there's a disgusting, unpleasant, hairy issue that we're all pretending not to notice."

"Ah," Leo said. "That's, uh… well, rude, honestly."

Kersa stood and snatched the presentation remote out of Willijer's hand. He staggered back with a cowardly squeak and returned to his seat. The hospitality chair's brow lowered angrily as she addressed the room. "While it is true that the Waylade Tour Fleet's fortunes have been declining for years, our losses accelerate from a downward trend to a precipitous drop at one key juncture."

She pointed to the spot where the falling red line made a sharp kink between a horizontal slope and a near vertical freefall. Kersa squeezed the remote, and a timeline of events overlaid the graph—one balanced right on the cliff of the plunging line.

Varlowe Waylade assumes control of WTF Cruises.

"Your father's body was barely cold when our cash flow all but vaporized." Kersa glared at Varlowe. "As his heir and successor, the board demands you explain why."

Varlowe crossed to the window with an enigmatic smile. "Okay, so when I took charge I may have diverted a few discretionary funds."

"Diverted a few..." Skardon said incredulously. He banged a fist on the table and thrust a finger toward the screen. "This is a full annihilation of operational capital! Since your father passed we've been running cruises on shoestring budgets! All because of you!" He turned his rage to Willijer. "You're the accountant! How could you not know this was happening?"

Willijer fidgeted and stared into his lap. "It's not that I didn't know. It's just that Ms. Waylade instructed me to..." He licked his dry lips. "Make certain investments."

"Investments my orange arze!" Kersa roared. "This woman has been embezzling from us since the moment she became president!"

"Well, the claws are out today, aren't they?" Varlowe shook

her head. "My great grandfather founded this company. WTF Cruises is my family legacy. I haven't been sabotaging the business. I've been investing in its future."

Skardon gave her a skeptical squint. "So I presume this siphoning of funds is a prelude to your surprise announcement of a network of new spaceports?"

"It is not," Varlowe said flatly. "I told you, expansion isn't the answer. The stars have set on the Ba'lux Empire. We can't expect to survive by continuing to cram our stuffy old culture down the galaxy's throat. Our customers yearn to experience new cultures and explore new ideas."

Kersa's jaw tightened. "And what 'new ideas' are we exploring, pray tell?"

A coy grin spread on Varlowe's face. "Well, that's the American in the room, isn't it?"

"What is?" Skardon asked.

"He is." Varlowe pointed to Leo. "As I said, he's the key to all of this."

Leo noticed everyone looking at him and startled to attention. "What, *me*?"

"Of course." Varlowe sauntered toward him. "My plan for putting the fleet back on top is deeply inspired by my spirituality." She touched the mermaid logo on her chest. "I have heard the call. I have seen the future. I have tasted the pumpkin spice."

Leo blinked. "I have no idea what you're talking about."

"Then let me explain." Varlowe put a hand on Leo's shoulder and turned to the executive board with a beaming smile. "As the first step in my recovery plan, I am proud to appoint Leo MacGavin, hero of the Jaynkee Spacedock, as Waylade Tour Fleet's newest captain!"

The board collectively emitted a wet, savage noise,

somewhere between a gasp and a roar. Leo's cheeks tingled as all the blood rushed out of his head. "What? No! I don't want to be a captain! I just want to go home!"

"This is absurd!" Kersa barked. "That ridiculous creature cannot command a ship!"

"I totally can't!" Leo agreed. "I can't even command a karaoke lounge!"

"We have traditions!" Skardon bellowed. "We have standards! Can you even imagine this pathetic mammalian criminal sitting on the command throne of a proud Ba'lux vessel?"

"I cannot," Varlowe admitted. "Someone like Leo would be utterly out of place at the helm of any ship in our fleet. A square peg in a round hole. Completely unacceptable." She smiled. "And that's why I've been investing in our future."

"So you keep saying," Kersa growled. "Explain yourself."

"Gladly." Varlowe strolled across the room, savoring the spotlight. "Much like Leo's brave ancestors, who left their tiny planet seeking a better life in the stars, we too must leave behind the comfort of what was in order to embrace the promise of what is yet to be." She stood with her back to the window, framed in the dull blue shine of the world below. "The Americans have a phrase that embodies their spirit of independence. Their noble conviction that anyone can achieve their dreams through persistence and hard work. Words that symbolize their belief that everyone, regardless of lineage or circumstance, has the right to life, liberty, and the pursuit of happiness. And today, I bring this notion to the Waylade Tour Fleet." Varlowe's voice turned reverent as she placed one hand on her apron's logo and swept the other toward the window. "Members of the board, I present to you our new flagship, the *Americano Grande*."

A hush fell over the room as an enormous vessel silently glided past the panorama windows. The pointed bow of its hull glinted in the starlight, defiantly unlike any ship the Jaynkee Spacedock had ever seen. Unlike any ship any spacedock had ever seen. The board members just stared, gape-mouthed, unable to form their thoughts into words. Leo said what everyone was thinking.

"It's a boat."

It was a boat. There was no other way to put it. From its elongated hydrodynamic hull to its forty-two stacked decks of stateroom windows, to the swimming pools and sun chairs arranged on its open decks, it appeared to be a twentieth-century cruise ship plucked straight from the oceans of Earth. But in space. And on a massive scale. Enormous clusters of ion-fusion engines clung to its port quarters in art-deco pods, emitting a cool blue glow as it made a stately orbit of the dock.

Varlowe put an arm around Leo's shoulder and whispered in his ear. "What do you think?"

Leo just stared in slack disbelief. "It's the most ridiculous thing I've ever seen."

Kersa managed to croak out the words caught in her throat. "This... this is your 'investment'? This is what you wasted our entire budget on? This..." She pointed at the window, trembling with rage. *"This?"*

The *WTF Americano Grande* slowly came to rest beside the *Opulera* and fired its mooring beams at the dock's bollard ports. A purple vein throbbed in the goose egg on Skardon's cranium as he looked up at the vessel dwarfing the Ba'lux ship.

"Waylade, your behavior has always been erratic, but this is beyond the pale." His voice was low and cold, a layer of ice over a barely contained lava flow of fury. He turned to the others. "The blatant misappropriation of funds to construct this monstrosity in secret, without the consent of the executive board, is not just a step too far, it is a narcissistic, ill-conceived abomination." He rose from his chair to his full, towering height. "Due to her reckless behavior and refusal to act in the company's best interest, I submit that Varlowe Waylade be removed from the board of WTF Cruises immediately."

"Seconded," Kersa said without hesitation. She and Skardon turned to Willijer. He flinched and pulled a tabloyd from his pocket, unfolding the paper-thin screen to its full legal-pad size.

"Yes, well, regarding the, uh... project..." He glanced out the window at the glittering ocean liner. "I don't disagree that the plans should have been submitted to the board for a full review before they were passed on to the construct-o-bots for execution, but according to our charter..." He held up his device, showing a dense block of text. "It is within the president's discretionary purview to initiate confidential projects using company resources as he, she, ze, or bu deems appropriate without due process or transparency."

Skardon fixed him in a lethal glare. "What exactly are you trying to say?"

Willijer adjusted his spectacles. "I'm saying that technically Ms. Waylade hasn't broken any rules. Her actions, though questionable, were within her rights and I can't, in good conscience as a member of this board, vote to remove her."

"It doesn't matter. It's still two to one." Kersa turned to Varlowe. "Pack up your office, Waylade. You're out."

"I think not," Varlowe said dismissively. "Because I vote in favor of myself."

"You don't get a vote in your own dismissal!" Skardon barked.

"Actually..." Willijer swiped at the text on his tabloyd. "It says here she does."

Kersa dropped her face in her palms. "Gah! Who wrote this stupid charter?"

"It appears we require a tiebreaker vote," Skardon noted. "What say you?"

All eyes turned to the corner of the room. Leo shrank back against the potted palm. "Well, Varlowe seems nice, and I do feel that among all of you she's the least likely to murder me. So I vote in favor of her staying in charge."

"Nobody cares what you think!" Kersa snapped.

"But you just asked—"

"I was referring to our emeritus board member," Skardon said. "The sage we call upon to guide us in times like these with her infinite wisdom and fair judgment." He turned to the ancient woman slouched in her wheelchair. "Should Varlowe Waylade maintain control of this company despite her obvious contempt for its board, or should she be removed and replaced by the current vice-president? The choice is yours and yours alone. How do you vote on this matter?"

The old woman blinked the milky domes of her eyes and shook her head. After a long moment she spoke with a voice like a mummy farting dust.

"In all my years as a part of this board, I've never seen such an audacious display of ego. For the president to go over the heads of those meant to steward this company is not only reckless, it's completely mad."

Her breath rattled in her chest as she stared Varlowe down. Varlowe's face remained confidently impassive, but her fingers picked nervously at the arms of her chair. Skardon's grin pulled tight in eager anticipation. The old woman continued.

"You know who else they used to call mad? Her great grandfather, with his crazy idea to put a Ba'lux pleasure palace in a decommissioned battleship and sail it around the galaxy.

Even in splendor, who would want to leave Ba'luxi Prime to slum it on the lesser worlds? People thought he was absolutely loopy." She waved a withered hand at Varlowe. "People think this one is loopy too. And she just might be. Or she might be a visionary like her great granddad. Who's to say if she's qualified to lead us? Who's... to... say?"

Her words trailed off until they were nothing but a troubling rattle in her lungs. Impatience crinkled Skardon's brow. "You are. That's literally what we're asking you to do here."

The elder fingered the control on the arm of her chair and it creaked and wearily rolled to the window. She gazed out at the gleaming new vessel. The space ocean-liner looked proud despite all reason, like a baby that had just loaded its diaper in a public pool. She snuffed through her nose slits. "I want to see how this thing plays out."

Willijer gasped. Kersa growled. Skardon choked out words. "I'm sorry... what?"

The old woman turned her chair to face the board. "The kid thinks this monstrosity is the coming thing. What if she's right?"

"I assure you, she is not," Kersa said.

"But what if she is?" A sly grin spread across the elder's wrinkled face as she gestured at the window. "If this new ship is a success, old man Waylade's great granddaughter will have proven herself a visionary worthy of her lineage. If it's a disaster, her incompetence will be indisputable. I reserve my judgment until the facts are in."

Panic tightened Skardon's voice. "You're not seriously suggesting we send this... *embarrassment* on a maiden voyage!"

"I am." The old woman nodded. "Put it on the next Simishi Riviera cruise."

"But... we can't!"

"We can, and we will."

Skardon's shoulders slumped. "But Mom!"

"Don't 'but Mom' me, young man!" the elder snapped. "Any more sass out of you and I'll take you over my knee and tan your orange hide right here in front of everyone!"

Leo snorted back a surprised giggle. The others gave Skardon a pitying look, and he crossed his arms and sank into his chair without another word.

Varlowe blinked as the ultimatum filtered through the tension. "Wait, are you saying that after four generations of building this line up from nothing, the Waylade family's control of our own business is contingent on the success of a single cruise?"

"It's that simple," the old lady said. "If your captain here can get a ship of happy customers to Ensenada Vega in seven days, you stay president. If you fail, my boy takes control of the company."

"Wow." Varlowe cut a glance at Leo. "Looks like the stakes have been raised."

Leo nodded. "They have. For you. I don't really care either way."

"Fine! We'll do it." Skardon's wounded pride hardened into defiance. "We'll endure one final humiliation under Varlowe's rule. But after her inevitable failure, I will melt that ship down and use its blasphemous hulk to build my first new spaceport!"

He hammered a control pad, changing the screen to a map of the local system with markers on all the planned expansion sites. An icon blotted out the human settlement moon.

"Wait. That's Eaglehaven!" Leo gasped. "You're building a spaceport on my home world?"

Skardon gave him a disgusted snort. "Of course not. That would be absurd."

Leo exhaled. "Oh, good. For a second I thought—"

"That'll be a sewage dump."

"What?!"

"Under my expansion plan, our cruise capacity will far exceed our waste-processing capacity. So we'll need to turn this little moon into a storage facility for unprocessed poo slurry."

"But that's my home!"

"Oh, calm yourself," Kersa grumbled. "You rodents can still live there. We won't need more than eighty percent of the surface." She shrugged. "Plus the oceans."

"You can't do that!" Leo cried.

"I can do whatever I want," Skardon noted. "Once I become president of the company."

"Which you never will," Varlowe said calmly. "Because the *Americano Grande's* maiden voyage will be nothing short of spectacular. The most amazing cruise the galaxy has ever seen! Its captain will see to that." She turned to Leo with a grin. "That is, if he accepts the job."

Leo looked out the window at the placid, blue-green gem of Eaglehaven. He looked at the version on the screen, blotted out by an icon of a smiling poo. He pinched his eyes.

"Oh gahdamn it…"

CHAPTER THREE

Leo spent the next three days in his little rented room on the Jaynkee Spacedock riding waves of despair and denial. After six months of grueling karaoke nights he had finally earned enough for a ticket back to Eaglehaven. But what was the point? In a week the whole place would be neck-deep in alien butt dumplings.

So instead of buying a ticket, Leo bought a shot of hundred-proof methrum. Then another. And he had continued buying them until a steward from the *Opulera* showed up to peel him off the deck, scrub him down, and sober him up.

Now he was slouched in a plush seat on a private WTF shuttle. He stared out the window, numbly watching his home world drift away into the distance. A slender orange hand rested on his arm, startling him out of his trance.

Varlowe was beside him, wearing a sundress and a blue vest emblazoned with a big yellow smiley face and the words "We're rolling back prices!" She gave his wrist an excited squeeze and nodded out the window on her side of the shuttle. "There she is. Isn't she just so beautiful?"

The view blurred as they raced along the vast expanse of spacedock berths, filled with ships of every shape and size. A sleek craft like a cricket bat with wings. A rotating disc ringed with blocky engines. Collections of interlinked orbs. But one vessel stood out from the rest. The *WTF Americano Grande* looked like it had been cut-and-pasted into the scene from a time and place wholly unrelated to this reality. Looking at it, Leo could almost hear the lap of ocean waves and the squawk of phantom seagulls. But more than its design, the ship stood out because of its sheer, unyielding size.

It had appeared large from the boardroom windows of the *Opulera*, but to see it like this, racing up to it from what would have been water level—had the ship been born into its best, most logical life—was like looking at a mountain range with engines. The polished gray chromasteel of its hull stretched to the edge of Leo's vision on every side.

"What do you think, Captain?" Varlowe asked. "Ready to take command of your vessel?"

Leo's stomach plunged into his boots. "Command it? I can't even *see* all of it."

"Don't worry. Before long you'll know every inch of her." Varlowe clapped her hands and sprang from her seat. "Oh! That reminds me. I have to give you your tabloyd."

"I already have a tabloyd."

Leo pulled his folded device from the back pocket of his jeans. Over the years it had permanently taken on the curvature of his right butt cheek.

Varlowe shook her head. "That old thing won't do you any good on board. You need an official WTF tabloyd with your command credentials."

She plucked the crinkled screen from Leo's grip. Before he could argue, she replaced it with an elegant white box etched in gold filigree. He held it in both hands, appreciating its satisfying weight and balance. A bit of blue ribbon stuck out from the front edge, and Leo instinctively gave it a tug. With a soothing purr, the box transformed, separating its lid into long, triangular segments and retracting them in sequence, like synchronized swimmers kicking their legs before plunging into the crystal depths. The retreating lid exposed a sheet of rich purple satin that dissolved upon contact with the air, giving off a fresh lavender scent and revealing the glimmering white, legal-pad-sized page of a top-of-the-line tabloyd. A chorus of warm, ghostly voices sang out from everywhere and nowhere at once.

Welcome to tabloyd. Your world. Flattened.

"Dang," Leo muttered. "That is a next-level unboxing experience."

"I know, right?" Varlowe plucked the device from its cradle and folded it in half three times, turning it in to a stiff, narrow strip. "Even cooler, it can do this." She took Leo's hand and whacked the strip against his wrist. Upon contact it curled up, fitting itself to his arm like a slap bracelet. "That makes it official! Welcome to the WTF family!" Varlowe beamed. Leo frowned. Varlowe frowned. "Leo, are you okay?"

"Yeah, I'm fine. It's nothing. Okay. It's something." He cast a glance out his window and drew a shaky breath. "Just to be totally clear, if I finish this cruise, Skardon won't be able to destroy Eaglehaven, right?"

"Ugh." Varlowe rolled her eyes. "Him and his stupid expansion plans. Don't let him intimidate you. He's harmless."

"Harmless? He's threatening to turn my entire world into Doodie Depot!" Leo's voice trembled with frustration. "This whole thing is crazy! He can't just demolish an inhabited moon because he wants to!"

Varlowe shrugged helplessly. "He can, actually. Galactic eminent domain laws. You know how it is."

"I don't. And I can't believe—" Leo grabbed his armrests as a green light flickered outside the window, sending a shudder through the small craft. "What was that?"

"Edge of the sphere. Nothing to worry about." Despite

Varlowe's vague assurance, Leo's grip didn't loosen. The pilot was bringing the shuttle in low over the deck of the *Americano Grande*, close enough to see the rich, natural wood of its decks. Empty beach chairs and bamboo cabanas fully stocked with liquor stood starkly exposed to space in a surreal parody of the ocean-cruising experience. Varlowe rose from her seat and stretched her back. "Anyway, you don't have to worry about Eaglehaven."

"I don't?"

"Of course not, silly. When we win Madame Skardon's little contest, I'll remain president and your moon will be totally safe." She gazed at him with a smile in her empty eyes. "I promise you, I will never let any harm come to the last children of the planet America."

"Yeah, about that. Contrary to popular belief, the planet my people came from was actually called—"

A thump ran through the craft as it touched down on the deck.

"Oh! We're here!" Varlowe cheered.

Leo peeked out the window. They were parked in the center of a broad sundeck, the shuttle door at least thirty feet from the closest airlock. He assumed it had some kind of telescoping gangway, like some ships he'd seen on the spacedock. If it did, it didn't seem to acknowledge they had landed.

"Let's go check out your new ship, Captain MacGavin!" Varlowe saluted Leo with one hand and dropped the other on the door's release lever, completely failing to notice the *airlock disengaged* warning. Leo sprang out of his seat.

"Stop! The airlock isn't—"

Varlowe cranked the handle and the heavy door swung open with a sharp hiss, revealing the inky sprawl of space. Leo yelped and grabbed the nearest seat before explosive depressurization could blast him into the void. He gritted his teeth and clenched his eyes against the furious stillness. Stillness? He opened his eyes. Varlowe stood just outside the hatch, regarding him with a raised brow. "Are you, uh... Are you coming?"

Leo did not release his vice-grip on the upholstery. He took a tentative breath. The air had notes of paint and industrial sealant mixed with the salty tang of sea breeze, like sitting in a new car parked on a fishing pier. He blinked in confusion. "Space is different than the last time I was here."

Varlowe laughed. "Super cool, right? This ship has its own atmosphere. Its magnetosphere dynamo is a prototype from the Geiko Techlabs, understood only by the top engineering brains in the galaxy." She grinned like a self-satisfied goblin. "I had to back up a dump truck of money, but it's the new ultimate in spacefaring luxury. Come check it out."

Leo cautiously exited the shuttle. The sensation was like stepping out of a closet into the center of a pro football arena. Just a staggering expanse spreading out in every direction. But he wasn't looking at thousands of tiered seats full of spectators. He was gazing at the infinite cosmos. The sheer, humbling scale of it untethered his brain from reality. His knees went weak and he grabbed a deck chair, unsure if it was to hold himself up or just to prove he still existed in the corporeal plane.

"It's very impressive," he squeaked. "In a nightmarish kind of way."

"If you like this, wait until you see the inside!" Varlowe waved a hand and strolled toward a large, open doorway. "C'mon."

Leo let go of the chair and took a hesitant step, then another. His breath came in sharp puffs as he put his hands up to shield his eyes. "Just focus on the door. Don't look at the void."

His pace quickened as he chased Varlowe through the doors,

into a room he would have called enormous, had circumstances not forced him to compare its size to the entirety of outer space.

"Welcome to the Rushmore Concourse." Varlowe raised her arms. "The gateway to the *Americano Grande*."

Leo gaped as his overtaxed brain tried to make sense of what it was looking at. The atrium was a cavernous chamber, cutting through the six decks above in massive oblong circles all the way to a colossal, domed skylight window at the top. Walkways stretched around and across them, glowing with pale blues and cloudy whites like a sky on a sunny day. The bottom level, where he was standing, was a manicured park, complete with patches of green grass and a pond with a fountain. All around its edges were small shops and cafés and reception desks for various cruise services.

But the thing that captured Leo's attention was the towering statue at the back of the Rushmore Concourse. Four enormous heads of gray stone were carved into a faux mountain like larger-than-life deities. He squinted at them. "What am I looking at here?"

"Don't you recognize them? They're four of your planet's most beloved rulers." Varlowe waved a hand at the monument. "They are your champions, my friend."

Suddenly, Leo recognized the faces of John Deacon, Roger Taylor, Brian May, and Freddie Mercury.

"That's Queen."

"Yes, they're all queens," Varlowe chuckled. "This is a replica of an ancient monument celebrating the sovereigns of the American monarchy."

"I don't even know how to start unpacking that."

"I knew you'd love it." Varlowe continued her march through the concourse. "I'll give you the full tour later. First I need to introduce you to your crew."

The words sent a flutter of dread through Leo's belly. His crew. The people he'd be commanding. As captain. Of this ship. Of this enormous, terrifying, apparently stadium-rock-god-worshiping ship. He adjusted his collar and swallowed hard.

Things were suddenly getting real up in here.

He followed Varlowe into a spacious glass elevator. Next to the door was a screen of buttons, each labeled with the name of a deck and its amenities. Varlowe swiped the tabloyd around her wrist at the panel and a new column of options appeared under the heading *Authorized Crew Only*. She tapped the one for *Command Level* and the elevator accelerated upward with a vigor that left Leo's stomach in his boots.

"Your first officer is expecting us." Varlowe sighed. "I admit, he wasn't my first choice, but since you're new to the cruise industry, the board thought they should pair you with someone experienced to show you the ropes."

Leo felt a flicker of relief. "Oh, that's great, actually. I could use all the help I can get."

The elevator slowed to a gut-lurching stop and the doors whooshed open, revealing a broad, circular lobby. To the sides of the lift were a few offices and meeting rooms, and directly across the atrium was a round, armored door. In front of it stood an imposing Ba'lux officer in a crisp, white WTF Cruises command uniform. He didn't look at them when they entered the foyer, as he was preoccupied with a strange semi-spherical device in his massive hands. From his profile, Leo could fully appreciate the bulk of the man's barrel chest and monstrous left arm. His orange face was leathered with age, and the horns of his crown were dull and chipped, as if they'd done their fair share of impaling. Leo took a steadying breath.

Don't jump to conclusions just because he's a Ba'lux. Maybe he's nice.

Varlowe approached the first officer with a breezy wave. "Good morning, Commander."

The man whipped toward her with savage quickness and a predatory snarl, revealing a head that mostly wasn't there. The entire right side was a void of blackened scar tissue, as if someone had taken a giant, white-hot ice cream scooper and dug out half of his skull.

Leo shrieked and bolted back into the elevator. Or at least he tried. He ran face first into the closed doors three times, too terrified to acknowledge their presence.

"Silence that creature!" The officer raised a metal fist. His whole right arm was a twisted mass of mechanical parts, laced with bundles of cable and transparent tubes surging with viscous fluids. "Or I'll silence it for you!"

Leo regained his composure, but his back remained pressed to the elevator doors. Varlowe cleared her throat. "Leo, allow me to introduce you to Commander Rexel Burlock."

The monstrous Ba'lux lowered his cybernetic fist. Leo cautiously inched forward, still gaping at the man's conspicuously incomplete head.

"Um, hi. It's a pleasure to, uh..." He glanced at Varlowe. "I'm sorry, is he all right?"

Burlock growled and palmed the device in his organic hand. He clapped it into the empty void in his head and gave it a quarter turn downward. With a loud *clack* it snapped into a set of sockets embedded in his skull and whirred to life. It was a mechanical prosthetic mirroring the intact side of his face in tarnished gray metal, complete with horns. But where the copper dome of his Ba'lux eye should have been was a round black lens that spun left and right as it found focus.

Varlowe turned to Leo. "The commander is a decorated veteran of the Ba'luxi Prime Imperial Navy who joined the

Waylade Tour Fleet after his retirement."

"Not retirement," Burlock grumbled. "Discharge. I was forced to leave the service."

"Because you died in combat?" Leo asked.

"Because of the gahdamn tabloyd-tapping bureaucrats and their ban on mechanically enhanced soldiers." He muttered under his breath, "Plus, the whole 'war crimes' thing."

Leo paled. "I'm sorry, war crimes?"

Varlowe nudged him forward. "Commander, allow me to introduce you to Leo MacGavin, your new captain."

"Captain? That scruffy thing can't command a ship." Burlock's eye lens twitched. "Is it even housetrained?"

Leo raised a finger. "I prefer *he*." Burlock bared his teeth and growled. Leo flinched. "You know what? *It* is fine."

"Actually, it's not fine." Varlowe fixed her eyes on Burlock. "You will address him as *Captain* and follow his orders. I know your military background has taught you to respect the chain of command, and Leo is your commanding officer."

"Was this approved by Admiral Skardon?" Burlock snuffed.

A storm rolled across Varlowe's face. "Skardon's opinion doesn't matter. *I* appointed Leo, and *I'm* the president of WTF cruises. Do you need to be relieved of duty to review your command hierarchy?"

The first officer spoke with all the warmth of a granite slab sliding down a glacier. "I do not, Madame President."

"Awesome." Varlowe turned to Leo with a smile. "Now that you two are besties, Burlock will introduce you to the bridge crew. I'll be back later to see how things are going."

She punched the button on the elevator pad. Leo gasped. "Wait! You're leaving me? With *him*?"

"Just for a bit. I have to go finish up some last-minute paperwork with the dock master. It shouldn't take long."

Leo squeezed himself between Varlowe and the door. "But shouldn't you finish our tour first? There's a lot of ship I haven't seen!"

"Don't worry, Burlock knows his way around. He'll help you cut your teeth."

The commander flicked his mechanical fingers, unsheathing serrated claws from their tips with an unsettling *schling* of metal on metal. Leo clapped a hand over his mouth. "I'm not sure he understands idioms."

Varlowe smiled and squeezed Leo's shoulder. "Don't be nervous. You're in charge here. You're the *captain!*" The elevator whooshed open and she stepped inside. "I'll be back in time for the Bon Voyage Show. Have fun!"

The doors closed, leaving Leo alone with the simmering cyborg. Burlock stared at Leo for a long, cold minute, blades out, mechanized eye clicking and whirring. Leo rocked back and forth on his heels. "So, I guess you're gonna introduce me to the crew?"

"Is that supposed to be an order?"

"Yes? I mean, if it's not too much trouble."

Burlock mumbled under his breath. "Gahdamn civilians." He flicked his blades back into his fingers and gestured to the huge, circular door. "Command bridge is here. After you, *Captain*."

Leo sidestepped the behemoth, awkwardly maneuvering to keep his back to the wall. A glowing lockpad next to the door read *Authorized Crew Only*. Leo smiled with relief. For once he knew what to do.

"Ah yes. Credentials." He nodded at Burlock. "*Captain's* credentials."

He waved his WTF tabloyd band at the pad, just as Varlowe had done on the elevator. The pad farted an error tone. The door did not open. Leo chuckled nervously.

"Dang. Okay. Maybe it's not turned on?" He tapped the surface of his band and a holographic interface blasted out of his wrist. It was a pudgy pink heart with a single button labeled "dial." As it appeared, the device shouted in a gleeful, childish voice.

"Call Mommy!"

"Oh! I guess this thing has some apps pre-installed on it." Leo shook his arm, but the heart just bobbed behind it like a balloon tied to his wrist. He let out a strained laugh. "Awkwaaard!"

Burlock's eye narrowed. "It looks like you don't have senior staff credentials."

"So it does." Leo yanked his sleeve over the hologram and gave a sheepish nod toward the lockpad. "If you don't mind, could you maybe get that for me?"

"Sure, no problem."

"Thank you."

"While I'm at it, do you want me to wipe your arze after you go poo-poo?"

"Excuse me?"

Burlock clutched the front of his jacket. "Would baby like me to whip out a teat and feed him his din-din?"

Leo's face flushed. "No, just opening the door will be fine."

The first officer straightened his uniform over his strapping chest. "Forget it. No unauthorized crew on the bridge."

"But I'm the captain!"

"That's not what your tabloyd says."

"Varlowe just told you—"

"Admiral's rules. No access without proper credentials."

Leo bristled. "Fine. How do I get proper credentials?"

"Not my problem. Talk to the chief hospitality officer."

"Great! I will. Just one question."

"Yes?"

"Who's the chief hospitality officer?"

Burlock glowered. "Lieutenant Commander Kellybean."

"Right. Okay, cool cool. Thanks. I'll go see her." Leo looked around the empty lobby. "So, uh... one more thing, actually. Where can I find Lieutenant Commander Kellyb—"

Leo squeaked as Burlock thumped a metal hand on his chest and clamped down on his shirt. The Ba'lux dragged him across the room and tossed him through an open door. Leo stumbled into a cluttered office and crashed into a stack of boxes.

"Ah! You must be Captain Leo," a bright voice purred.

Leo whipped around to see a petite young woman standing at a holoscreen interface, gazing at him with reflective yellow eyes. She was a felinoid from the cat planet Gellico, dressed in a pale blue uniform blouse and a crisp khaki skirt. Her fur was silky and white, streaked with light gray stripes that raked back from her face through the chin-length bob of her hair.

Burlock nodded. "Lieutenant Commander Kellybean."

"Thanks for the introduction," Leo grumbled.

The cat woman approached and extended a balled paw. "It's a pleasure to meet you, sir. I've been expecting you."

Leo bumped her fist with his own. "You have?"

"Of course! Before we depart I need to brief you on the status of the hospitality department. We'll have to go over the hotel operations and casino audit, and review the final embarkation plans and customs clearances."

"Dang. You do all of that?"

"If you're keeping score, I also have a level-one engineering certification. You know what they say about my people." Kellybean's tail flicked proudly. "Gellicles can and Gellicles do."

Burlock glowered. "You ladies have fun. I've gotta get to the bridge and prepare the crew for launch."

"Wait, shouldn't I be there for that?" Leo asked.

"You can be there when you can open the damn door."

The first officer marched away without a backwards glance. Leo frowned and slumped against the stack of boxes. "I don't think he likes me."

Kellybean chuckled. "Don't take it personally. He doesn't like anybody."

Her smile eased Leo's jitters. "Hey, before we get to all the other stuff you just said... it looks like my tabloyd wasn't set up right." He pulled the band off his wrist. "Burlock said you could fix it."

"Hmm. Let me take a look." Kellybean took the device from Leo and stuck it into a slot in the top of her desk. The tabloyd appeared in the interface of her holoscreen. "Oh wow, yeah. There's nothing on there. But I can take care of that." She cracked her furry knuckles. "This is perfect. I need to go over the cruise itinerary with you anyway. Have you had a chance to review it?"

"I have not, actually." Leo squirmed. "I'm kinda coming into this at the last minute."

Kellybean nodded at the stack of unpacked boxes. "Same. To be honest, I was surprised to get the call." Her expression sobered. "I didn't expect to ever work for WTF again after what happened on the *Opulera*."

"What happened on the *Opulera*?"

Kellybean eyed him skeptically. "You don't know?"

"I don't."

"Ah. Well. It's not important. It won't happen again, I promise." She forced a smile and turned back to her screen, pulling up a seven-day grid. "Let's get you up to speed on the itinerary, shall we?"

"Seriously though, what happened—"

"Day one. AKA, today," Kellybean interrupted. "After we finish loading in the passengers, we'll do the Bon Voyage Show and then let everyone settle in before your Captain's Welcome Dinner in the formal dining room."

"Okay, but…" Leo's heart clenched. "Wait, 'Captain's Welcome Dinner'? I'm the captain. Do I have to organize that?"

"Don't worry. It's all taken care of. I planned the whole menu myself, from appetizer to dessert. All you need to do is show up and look pretty."

Leo rubbed his stubbly chin. "I can manage that. I think."

The hospitality chief swiped the day-one itinerary onto Leo's tabloyd and moved on to the next block. "Day two. Tomorrow we'll be making our first stop for a beach excursion on Halii Bai, then we'll loop out into deep space to see the Blue Hole. I set up an evening concert on the deck as we cruise by the gravity well. Should be a lot of fun." She transferred it to Leo's device. "Any questions so far?"

"Just one."

"Yes?"

"What happened on the *Opulera*?"

The Gellicle frowned. "Let's just say I left my previous position for personal reasons."

"Is that true?"

"It's not *not* true. But there's no sense in dwelling on the past, right? We have a super fun cruise ahead of us. Check out day three!" Kellybean smiled and turned back to her screen. "We'll be stopping on Nyja for a hiking excursion to the ancient ruins and a wildlife safari. It's the perfect time of year for it. The gazellephants should be in full plumage."

The hospitality chief enthusiastically chattered through pages of tour guide profiles and trail-use waivers and images of weird, feathered pachyderms, clearly trying to put as much distance between herself and Leo's questions as possible. Leo's glazed-over eyes fell to the box on the top of the stack next to him. It was full of awards—trophies and medals and plaques, all awarded by WTF to Kellybean. Underneath them, something was moving.

"Then on day four I've got us set up for a skiing trip on the ice giant Osisi," Kellybean continued. "This one is always a challenge to negotiate, but totally worth it."

She focused on her screen as she droned on, swiping through tables of resort fees and liability policies. Leo kept an eye on her as he carefully reached into the box and pushed aside an MVP award to get a better look at the thing at the bottom. It was a fotoclip in a *WTF Opulera* souvenir frame. Its recorded image still looped, despite the glass being shattered. His eyes shifted from it to Kellybean's back.

"And on day five we'll take a shopping trip to the Sarpong street markets. We'll also be doing a bunch of activities on board for folks who can't breathe a sulfur atmosphere."

She ticked down a list of scheduled trivia contests and guest speakers, but Leo was paying zero attention. He silently pulled the frame from the box. The moving image showed Kellybean and a stout Ba'lux girl, both in WTF uniforms. They held each other close—heads tipped, foreheads touching—as they gently swayed in a slow dance. Their expressions were pure, amorous bliss. The inscription said "Kellybean & Pyrrah 4-eva." The radial crack in the glass was centered on the Ba'lux girl's face.

"Day six is a travel day where we'll do a zero-G shuffleboard tournament, then on day seven we arrive at the pleasure paradise of Ensenada Vega. Boom! Best cruise ever. What do you think, sir?"

Kellybean turned to Leo with a proud smile. He dropped the frame into the box, then jerked out an elbow and casually leaned on the wall in a manner that was not in any way casual. "Well done! Nice work! I love it."

"Thanks! I'll make the final arrangements and get it all locked in. Here you go, Captain."

She snatched Leo's tabloyd from the port in her desk and handed it over. Leo clapped it back on his wrist. "Great! So my credentials are all fixed now?"

Kellybean's brow quirked. "What? No. All I did was upload the cruise itinerary." She waved at the holoscreen. "What did you think all this was about?"

Leo had no idea what it was all about. He had no idea what anything was about anymore. "Sorry. I guess I wasn't clear. My tabloyd can't open doors and Burlock thought you could help with that."

"Ugh. Burlock knows I can't upgrade crew credentials. If anybody on board can it'll be Praz."

Leo blew out a long breath. "I'm sorry, who is Praz?"

"The chief engineer."

"Got it. So where can I find him?"

"In engineering?"

"Right. Obviously. So... I'll just go ahead and..."

He took a hesitant step toward the door. Kellybean's lips twisted in a half smile. "You don't know where engineering is."

"I do not," Leo admitted.

"Sucks to be the new guy, huh?" She grinned and waved a paw. "Come with me."

***

Kellybean led Leo down the elevator and through a labyrinth of plush hallways, then swiped her tabloyd at a secured door to a crew-only area. As soon as they crossed its threshold, the polished veneers of the guest areas gave way to gunmetal gray passageways filled with stout, color-coded pipes and bundles of cable running along the walls and ceiling.

Leo studied the corridors, trying to pick out any landmarks. He had been taking mental notes on their path from the bridge, but his brain had started sloshing over like an overfilled bucket about thirty turns ago. Yet the Gellicle continued to lead him confidently into the bowels of the vessel. The toe claws of her bare feet clicked against the metal grating as they approached a massive black-and-yellow door.

"And here we are. The primary machine room. This area is restricted to engineering crew, but senior staff can unlock everything on the ship." Kellybean smiled and wagged a brow. "Rank has its privileges."

She swiped her tabloyd. With a deck-shaking rumble, the interlocking door slid open, revealing a large, dimly lit control room. Several unattended stations were arranged in a semicircle, quietly humming and blinking. A Ba'lux in a yellow engineering coverall stood over an open console, prodding its circuits with a flathead screwdriver. But Leo barely registered the man as he stared slack-jawed through a huge arc of windows behind him.

The area beyond was a yawning cavern at least twenty decks high and too deep to see the back of. In its center was a massive ball of iron, suspended in midair by six beams of throbbing blue light as big around as sequoias—three above and three below. The sphere rotated in a breathtaking blur of speed, ripping sparks and streaks of furious white lightning off the ends of the support beams at each point of contact. A million gallons of superheated, hyperconductive plasma clung to the orb in a translucent red shell, slowly rotating in the opposite direction.

Leo gaped in awe. He had never seen anything like it, but he instinctively knew what it was. The magnetosphere dynamo.

The prototype Varlowe had bought from the Geiko Techlabs, understood only by the top engineering brains in the galaxy. The heart of the *Americano Grande*, no doubt tended by a corps of genius engineers and expert technicians with unrivaled—

The Ba'lux screamed as a bolt of electricity arced through his screwdriver, blasting him to the deck. Leo snapped out of his reverent trance and crouched next to the smoldering body. "Whoa! Are you all right?"

The engineer spasmed and flailed his arms. "Aagh! I'm fine! Don't touch me!" He scrambled into a corner, eyes wide and shimmering. "Who let you in here? You can't be in here!"

Leo raised a calming hand. "It's fine. I'm the—"

He flinched at the sound of a loud metallic *clang*. Across the room, he spotted a maintenance bot near an armored door. Like most maintenance bots, it was a squat stack of yellow cylinders mounted on six knobby rollers. Unlike most maintenance bots, its front side was smashed completely flat. It backed up ten feet and accelerated full-speed into a bot-shaped dent in the door with a ringing *clang*. It bleeped, reversed, then did it again.

Leo looked at the Ba'lux. "What's wrong with that bot?"

"Nothing!" the man said indignantly. "That bot is fully functional!"

"Then why does it keep running into the door?"

"The door is broken."

Leo regarded the smoke still wafting off the electrocuted technician and frowned. "Not to be rude, but I don't think you should be messing around in here."

He reached out a hand to help him up. The man screeched and swatted him away. "Don't touch me! I've got this under control!"

Leo backed away, palms up. "Okay! Okay. I was just thinking maybe your supervisor should—"

"I don't have a supervisor! I'm in charge here! Me!"

A pained look pinched Kellybean's face. "Leo, I'd like to introduce you to Lieutenant Commander Praz Kerplunkt, our chief engineer."

Leo blinked. "Are you serious?"

"Yes, she's serious!" Praz leaped to his feet and thumped a fist on his badge, showing three yellow chevrons. "I'll have you know I went to a very fancy school for this stuff! Electronicals and whatnot! I know what I'm doing!" He waved his hand at the open console he had been working on. With a spark and a dull *foomph*, the entire thing burst into flames. "Gah! Not again!"

Red lights blinked on as an earsplitting klaxon pierced the air. Praz grabbed a firefoam pod out of his toolbox and doused the panel until it settled into a sizzling, smoking mess. The alarms crackled to silence. The maintenance bot zoomed across the deck and *clanged* into the door again.

Leo grimaced. "Um, does anyone else work here? I hope?"

Praz looked Leo up and down with a scowl. "Who are you? Did the captain send you to check up on me?"

Leo smiled awkwardly. "Actually, I'm the—"

"I knew it! We haven't even left port and he's already spying on me!" Praz pulled out his tabloyd. "Look at the lockpad logs!" He thrust a finger at lines of text on the screen. "Captain! Captain! Captain! He's been in here more times than I have!"

Kellybean shook her head dismissively. "That's impossible. In fact, that's why we're here. His tabloyd isn't registering proper credentials. Can you take a look at it?"

Praz groaned petulantly. "Ugh. I have to do everything around here." He sighed and held out his hand. "Let me see it."

Leo took the band off his wrist and handed it over. Praz unfolded it and swiped at the screen. "Yeah, this is totally screwed up. He's got way more access than he should."

"Wait, *more* access?" Kellybean said.

"Yeah. He's got the credentials of an unaccompanied minor when he should be registered as your pet."

Praz thrust the tabloyd back at Leo. Leo took it with a scowl. "Okay, I'm actually not her pet." He considered it. "Though it would be kind of funny if I was."

Kellybean's brow raised. "How so?"

"You know, because you're a cat and I'm a person."

Praz sucked a breath through his teeth as Kellybean's pupils narrowed to slits. "Are you suggesting I'm *not* a person?"

A knot formed in Leo's stomach. "What? No! I just meant you're a cat person and I'm like a, you know... person person."

"Dang!" Praz gasped. "Your pet is a raging speciest!"

"Me? You're the one who keeps calling me a pet!"

The warmth left Kellybean's voice. "It would be in your best interest to treat me with a little more respect, sir."

"I'm sorry! I didn't mean it how it sounded. I just—"

"Bad American!" Praz rolled up his tabloyd and whacked Leo on the nose with it.

"Ow!" Leo squeaked.

Praz grabbed his canister of firefoam and spritzed Leo in the face. "Bad, bad American! Get out of my machine room!"

"Ack! Quit it!"

Leo stumbled back through the open door into the hallway, choking and swatting at the blasts of puffy gray foam.

"And stay out!" Praz shouted.

The doors slid shut and banged together, followed by the *clank* of its bolts firing into place. Leo spluttered and wiped the dissolving spray off his face.

"Aagh. Damn it." He shouted into the seam of the door. "Hey! Kellybean? I'm sorry. I didn't mean to imply..." He knocked impotently on the thick armor plating. "Hello?"

The door did not open. After a long moment, it became apparent it wasn't going to. Leo licked his lips, trying to get the taste of his own foot out of his mouth. This ship tour had not gone as well as Varlowe had expected. He decided to head back to Mount Rushmore to wait for her. She'd be able to straighten all this out. She actually knew what she was doing.

He tried to backtrack down the endless gray corridors, but instead of finding his way out, he only seemed to get more lost. He passed into a six-sided junction and slowly turned, trying to figure out which path to take.

"Hmm. This doesn't seem familiar." He turned to go back the way he came, and realized he had no idea which of the identical hallways he had just come from. He clapped a palm over his face. "Damn it, Leo."

He trusted his gut and chose a path. After two more turns, he no longer trusted his gut. A minute later he emerged in an unattended cargo area, filled with barrels and auto-crates. The dim standby lighting refused to acknowledge him, leaving the room swaddled in creepy shadows. He turned to retreat the way he had come in. The wall behind him had three identical exits.

He had definitely come from the middle one.

Probably.

"Damn it, Leo!"

Helpless anger raged through him. He was lost. On so many levels. What was he doing here? Not just here in this room, but here on this ship? Here in *outer space*. All he wanted to do was go home. But if he did, seven days from now there would be no home.

Leo closed his eyes repeating the number to himself. Seven days. That's all it would take to save Eaglehaven. After that, everything would go back to normal. He'd been stuck on the Jaynkee Spacedock for six months. Surely he could survive this ship for only seven days. He took a deep, steadying breath and opened his eyes to a spider the size of a grizzly bear.

"Whaaaaaaaaaaa—"

His terrified scream was silenced by a blast of sticky webbing across his face. In an instant he was bound from his shoulders to his ankles. His feet whipped out from under him, throwing him down on the metal grating. His head swam and his eyes throbbed. He felt weightless and wrong and heavy-headed.

He blinked and tried to pull a breath through the mesh wrapped around his mouth and nose. Everything was upside down. No. He was upside down, slowly swinging from a strand of silk slung around a pipe in the ceiling.

The spider scuttled below him, hissing and clicking. From this vantage point Leo could fully appreciate the creature's terrifying scale. Its enormous thorax was supported by four arachnoid legs—scarred and gray, ending in points the size of traffic cones. A second body segment curved upright from the front, armored in overlapping, chitinous plates. Four more limbs sprouted from its sides, hinged like the arms of a mantis.

The spider-thing's elongated face stared at Leo with eight eyes—two large ones, each rimmed along the top by three smaller ones, like hideous eyeball eyebrows. All of them were sunken black pits with a single dot of glowing red peering from their centers. Four clawed mandibles pulled back from the lower part of its face, pushing away mottled gray flesh to reveal rows of jagged teeth sticking out of its gums like porcupine quills.

It let out a sickening, ear-piercing screech. As the noise echoed off the walls, six more spiders gracefully descended from the shadowy recesses of the ceiling on strands of web.

Leo squealed and thrashed as the creatures closed in on him from all sides, but his bindings did not loosen. It was like being wrapped four-inches deep in elastic soaked in glue. His head throbbed and his eyes went fuzzy, partially from terror, partially from the blood pooling in his skull. He gritted his teeth and concentrated on staying conscious. Because he knew if he blacked out, he'd never wake up again. Though, as the chattering spiders crept closer, he thought he might not want to be awake for what was about to happen. Below him, at the edge of his field of vision, a horned, orange scalp entered the room.

"MacGavin?" Burlock shouted. "Where are you? I'm not your gahdamn babysitter."

Leo tried to scream. Tried to cry for help, or warn his first officer to run. But his voice was smothered in the webbing strapped over his jaw. The creatures turned their attention to the Ba'lux as he walked directly into their murder den.

The biggest spider scuttled out of the shadows and screeched in Burlock's face hard enough to jiggle the flesh of his cheeks. The commander didn't even flinch. He just raised a finger and wiped a drop of insect spittle off his prosthetic eye lens.

"Soldier, I can't understand a damn thing you're saying."

The spider lifted one of its limbs, and its pointed tip split along a set of grooves, separating into six spindly fingers. It reached for a metal band around its neck with a round, colorless gem at its throat. The bladelike digits gave the jewel a quarter turn, causing it to illuminate with a pale golden light.

"It apologizes, Commander Burlock," the spider said. Leo shook his clouded head. The creature's mandibles still flexed its hideous mouth, but the screeching was dull and muted, like an argument heard through a hotel room wall. Layered on top was an androgynous voice speaking in a clear, enunciated monotone. "It deactivated its translator to coordinate with hive." The beast pinched its fingers back into a point and jabbed it at Leo. "It must alert exterminator. Ship is infested with invasive rodent."

Burlock's lips curled into a smile as he looked up at Leo, hanging there like a piñata. "Well, well. Seems you've captured yourself a tasty little morsel." He strolled into the room, his boots clicking the deck with menace. "The good news is, it's not an infestation. There's only one of them on board. The bad news is, this rodent is our new captain."

The monster turned back to Leo, its red eye lights twitching in their cavernous sockets. "He is captain?"

"He is." Burlock waved a hand toward Leo. "Why don't you cut him down so we can have a little chat?"

The spider clicked at the six arachnids still hanging from the ceiling. Its collar intoned *"No translation available,"* but the smaller spiders swarmed Leo, grasping him with their chitinous limbs and blasting him with their rancid breath. The world spun and his head throbbed with disorientation. Razor-like fingers slashed at his muzzled face. Leo screamed and the sound echoed off the walls of the otherwise silent cargo bay.

Everything stopped moving. Leo blinked and oriented himself. He was now sitting on a chair, still bound, but with the strands that had been gagging his mouth hanging in a neatly cut mass around his throat.

The biggest spider approached. "It apologizes for error, sir. It has never seen one of your species."

"I've never seen one of your species either," Leo stammered. "Where are you from? Because I never want to go there."

The spider straightened, towering over him. "In galactic-standard Quipp, its planet is known as Dred. Its race is designated Dreda. It is chief security officer of vessel, commanding three hives of drones."

Burlock nodded at the smaller creatures. "They have complete and total loyalty to it."

"To what?" Leo asked.

"To it," the large spider said, tapping a claw on its chest.

"Oh! You're it. Right. Sorry." He shook his head. "It's just, most beings prefer one of the four gender pronouns."

"Concept of gender is irrelevant unless one wishes to mate." The beast leaned in close to Leo's face. "Do you wish to mate with it?"

Leo swallowed hard and flinched away from the hot breath and translated screech. "I, uh... wow. I mean, we just met and..." *You're a hideous monster straight from the blackened nightmare pits of a lunatic's damaged psyche.* "I'm not that kind of guy."

"Then 'it' is sufficient." The spider backed away. "Its name is unpronounceable with most species' mouth parts, so it has adopted appropriate alias. You may refer to it as Lieutenant Commander Marshmallow Hug Dilly Dilly."

"Well. That's a mouthful." Leo shifted uncomfortably in his bindings. "Lieutenant Commander Marshmallow Hug Dilly Dilly, could you do me a favor and untie me?"

The spider turned to Burlock. "Do you wish him released, sir?"

"Hey, *I'm* the captain," Leo said. "Why are you asking him?"

He yelped as Burlock lifted a heavy boot and slammed it on the front edge of his chair.

"Because I've earned Dilly's respect. We fought in the war together. It knows what I'm capable of. But you?" The commander leaned in and his voice went cold. "We both know a rank issued by a civilian is not the same as a rank forged by valor."

Leo blinked. "I, uh... what?"

"Admiral Skardon saved my life on the nightmare planet Rankorrdar. To him, I owe a blood debt. To you, I owe nothing. You're just a little boy-toy who's fallen into the heiress's favor."

"Look, I didn't ask to be—"

"I was assigned to this ship because I know what I'm doing," Burlock continued. "Dilly knows what it's doing. Everyone on this ship knows what they're doing except for one person. Do you know who that person is?"

"The chief engineer seems kind of sketchy."

"It's you, MacGavin." Burlock extended his leg, tilting the chair backwards. Leo sucked a breath as it neared its tipping point. "I think it's best for the mission if you stay out of the way and let me handle things. Do you agree?"

"Well, I don't *disagree*..."

"Then we understand each other." Burlock removed his foot and the chair crashed back down onto its legs, rattling Leo's teeth in his skull. "Cut him loose."

Dilly flicked open the tips of its four front limbs into spindly claws. "Sit still."

Before Leo could react, a whirl of ten-inch blades spun around his body, snipping and slashing. Every reflex told him to flinch, but he was too terrified to move. Three seconds later, the spider backed away, leaving Leo surrounded by a circle of finely-shredded webbing. He sprang out of the chair, his heart hammering.

"Yow, that was..." He pulled a shuddering breath. "I need a drink. And a change of pants."

"And I need to get back to the bridge," Burlock growled. "Dilly will drop you off someplace you can't hurt yourself. I heard there's a bouncy castle in the children's playroom."

Leo gritted his teeth. "Hey, buddy. You may be the one with the experience, and the commanding presence, and the respect of the crew, but don't forget, *I'm* the captain."

Burlock picked a bit of stray webbing from Leo's shirt and gave him a pat on the chest. "For now."

CHAPTER FOUR

Leo breathed in the salty artificial atmosphere as he stood at the rail of an upper-level sundeck, gazing out over a swimming pool below. When he and Varlowe had arrived, the Lido Deck had been an eerie, abandoned ghost town of bamboo cabanas. Now it was packed rail-to-rail with alien passengers, laughing and dancing and reveling in a thrum of party music. From up here, Leo had a perfect view of a large, poolside stage with a green-skinned DJ spinning tunes. Above her, an enormous holographic canopy blinked WELCOME ABOARD, GALAXY CRUISERS!

"Well, don't you clean up nice?"

Leo turned to see Varlowe approaching, devouring him with the shiny domes of her eyes. He suddenly felt naked, despite his excess of clothes. He looked down at himself and gave a tiny shrug. "I kinda do, don't I?"

After the debacle of his orientation tour, Leo had been dropped off in his stateroom with the suggestion it would be best if he never came back out. His instinct had been to flop down on the bed and have a nice little mental breakdown, but he'd been thwarted by a neatly laid-out uniform with a hand-written note.

The clothes make the commander. See you tonight, my captain.
— Varlowe

She wasn't wrong. Putting on the full regalia had been strangely transformative. Like a fresh start. He admired his own reflection in Varlowe's hungry eyes. The crisp white jacket with its snug band collar made his lanky form look broad and elegantly long-necked. Two rows of gleaming buttons ran in a wide V shape down the front, and space-black epaulets rested on the shoulders. A badge was pinned to the chest with the WTF logo above the five white chevrons of command. Even his scruffy black hair looked somewhat regal tucked into his captain's peaked cap—a mountain of unblemished white topping him like a dollop of whipped cream.

Varlowe leaned on the rail at his side, practically drooling. "So, Captain Leo, how is everything going so far?"

Well, the first officer hates me, the hospitality chief thinks I'm a speciest, the engineering chief thinks I'm a pet, and the security chief almost liquefied and devoured my innards.

"Everything's going great," Leo lied. "But there is one problem." He pulled back his sleeve and held up the band on his wrist. "For some reason I seem to have a kid's tabloyd instead of the captain's."

"That's weird. The box had your name on it."

"Maybe there was some kind of mix up. Could you fix it?"

"Of course! I mean, technically no, but..." Varlowe shook her head. "Senior credentials can only be issued at the staffing office on Ba'luxi Prime. I'll have them flash a new tabloyd and express it to the dock at Halii Bai. We can pick it up when we get into port tomorrow."

"Okay, thanks." Leo scratched the back of his neck. "It's just, I can't open doors without—"

Varlowe gasped and squealed as the lights on the deck below dramatically blacked out in sequence. "Shhh! It's starting!"

The DJ's party jams cut off, replaced with a wave of majestic brass and rumbling tympanis. Red, white, and blue spotlights blazed through the darkness. Varlowe grinned ear to ear as a reverent voice boomed from the speakers, drowning out the cheering crowd.

"A long time ago, in a galaxy far, far away, a strange people left their home to seek out new life and new civilizations. Boldly going where no one had gone before. They called themselves... Americans." The music swelled as the holographic canopy over the stage transformed into a rippling red-white-and-blue flag. *"Americans. Huck yeah."*

The crowd laughed and cheered and whistled at the star-spangled banner. Leo looked on in bewilderment. "What is this?"

"It's the Bon Voyage Show, silly. We do them on all WTF cruises. A spectacular shock-and-awe campaign to set the mood for the adventure ahead." Varlowe smiled proudly. "Normally they're produced by the hospitality crew, but this cruise is very personal to me, so I put the show together myself. You're gonna love it."

The flag morphed into a model of the *NASA Star Freedom*. The sleeper ship looked like a row of enormous, titanium-colored tires with a ramscoop generator at one end and six glowing engines at the other. Its pock-marked hull bore the scars of four-thousand years in space. The vessel slowly revolved on its axis as the voice continued.

"Our story begins with the founding fathers of the planet America, and their quest for a new life in the stars."

The ship dissolved as a cylindrical platform rose from the stage, carrying a Gellicle actor. The cat wore a black suit with a tailcoat and stovepipe hat. A beard and fake mole were glued to his furry face. He gripped his lapels and puffed out his chest.

"Four score and seven years ago, the planet America faced an existential crisis. And I, President Abraham Lincoln, had to save my people. With the survival of our species at stake, I called upon the advice of my most trusted advisor." A second platform appeared, carrying a tall Ba'lux man in a red basketball uniform. Lincoln nodded reverently. "His Royal Airness, Michael Jordan."

The Ba'lux raised one arm, lifting a glowing orange sphere above his head. "As Monarch of the Atmosphere, I see only one solution. We must leave the surface of our tiny blue and white and red planet."

"To live in the sky?" furry Lincoln asked.

"Far beyond the sky. We must go dancing... *with the stars*."

They looked up as the canopy over the stage glittered into a panorama of twinkling galaxies and nebulas. Lincoln stroked his beard. "Space. The final frontier. But is it possible?"

Jordan shrugged. "Let us consult our planet's greatest ship builder, Noah."

A third riser lifted, carrying a slug-like man in a nineteenth-century suit with wide lapels and a ruffled white cravat. He consulted an oversized dictionary before snapping it shut with a nod. "I shall construct a great space ark. It shall take me forty days and forty nights."

"Most excellent, Mr. Webster," Lincoln said. "But how will we power such a ship?"

The slug raised a finger. "We must call upon America's secretary of energy!"

Another platform lifted, carrying a Krubb in a form-fitting dress, sequined with a Union Jack pattern. With her cylindrical exoskeleton, she looked like a can of soup in a tube sock. A flowing red wig was fastened to her domed head.

"I'll tell you what I want, what I really really want," the Krubb announced. "I want to fuel this vessel with the planet America's last untapped resource: Our vast reserves of girl power!"

Lincoln clutched his paws. "But will it be sufficient to carry us across the galaxy?"

"More than sufficient, Mr. President. She who controls the Ginger Spice controls the universe!"

Leo gaped at the spectacle, his eyes wide and mouth slack. "Wow. Just... *wow*."

Varlowe clapped her hands excitedly. "I knew you'd like it! I spent hours in the Geiko Archives making sure everything was totally historically accurate."

Leo frowned. "I can see that."

Varlowe's proud expression dimmed. "You don't like it."

"I'm sorry, it's just... Maybe the Geiko Archives aren't the best reference material to work from."

"But they were the ones who made first contact with your people. Their records have been the gold standard of American history for over two hundred years. How can they be wrong?"

Leo leaned on the rail and blew out a long breath. "Okay, so when the Geiko discovered the *NASA Star Freedom* adrift in space it was in pretty bad shape. They studied the ship's computers and published their findings before they even bothered to wake the colonists from cryosleep. Things got lost in translation." He crossed his arms. "To this day, all the galaxy knows about my people is the Geiko's messed-up version of us."

Varlowe's face tightened with humiliation. "I, uh... I didn't know that."

"Nobody outside of Eaglehaven does." Leo shrugged. "It's not a big deal."

"It is, actually. It's not cool that you've been misrepresented for generations. And it's time someone did something about it."

Leo shook his head. "You don't have to."

Varlowe laughed. "Not me, dummy. *You*." She put a hand on his shoulder. "You're the captain of this ship. In command of every aspect of this cruise. This is your chance to introduce the galaxy to your culture and set the record straight."

"Yeah, no. I'm really more of a 'keep my head down and muddle through it' kind of guy."

"Not anymore, my friend." Varlowe gestured to the show. "When you get on stage and sound the ship's whistle, you won't just be kicking off this voyage, you'll be kicking off a new era of respect and understanding for your people."

Leo frowned. "But no pressure."

"It's a ton of pressure. But nothing worthwhile is easy, right?" Varlowe's voice softened. "You can do this, Leo. I believe in you. With both of my hearts."

Leo could feel her sincerity. She really did believe he could, and would, be an ambassador for humanity. Her eyelids closed and her lips puckered over her pointed teeth as she leaned in for a kiss. Leo sucked a breath and lurched back, banging his head on the bulkhead behind him with a dull *thunk*. Varlowe's eyes opened as he sidestepped away, rubbing his skull.

"Okay, well, I won't let you down then, boss! Because I treasure our very professional business relationship!" Leo gave her an awkward salute and backed away. "So, I'd better get down there to blow that whistle, right?"

"Right. Of course." Disappointment tugged Varlowe's lips as she returned the salute. "Make me proud, Captain."

"Will do!" With that, Leo scrambled away to a bank of elevators and rushed into the nearest one. A tall Ba'lux was already inside. Leo spoke to the stranger's back as the doors closed. "Lido Deck, please."

The man poked the button panel, but the lift did not move.

"Emergency stop," the elevator intoned. *"Remain calm. Help will arrive shortly."*

"That will not be necessary," the Ba'lux said.

The sound of his voice put Leo's body on high alert even before the man turned to show his face.

"Admiral Skardon!" Leo pressed himself into the corner and forced a smile. "So nice to see you again. Here. In an enclosed space with no witnesses."

Skardon kept his hands tucked behind his back. "I have to admit, I didn't think you would actually show up." His empty glare was scalding as he sized Leo up. "You have no business wearing that uniform. You should not be here."

"Well, to be perfectly honest, I'd rather be at home." Leo crossed his arms. "But somebody threatened to turn that home into a fiesta of feces. So here I am."

"It's not personal. The planning committee made our expansion plans based purely on logistics. Your world just happened to be in the wrong place at the wrong time."

"That actually doesn't make me feel any better."

Skardon snuffed. "Let me get right to it, MacGavin. I cannot have an American ship with an American captain putting a permanent stain on the reputation of WTF cruises. I want you to resign and abort the cruise."

"Yeah? Well I want you to not drop a deuce on Eaglehaven."

"Done."

Leo blinked. "Done?"

"I'm willing to cut a deal. If you stop this ridiculous voyage before it leaves the dock, your home shall remain untouched."

"Seriously? You'd give up your whole spaceport expansion scheme, just like that?"

"Give up? Oh, stars no. I'll just remove your world from our plan." Skardon smirked. "To be honest, turning Eaglehaven into a sewage dump would only be gentrifying the place."

The admiral pinched the tabloyd on his wrist, pulling a three-dimensional hologram from its face. The vibrant sphere of Eaglehaven spun above his hand, surrounded by the floating red text of an executive order. Above was a menu with two choices.

Demolition order pending. CONFIRM or CANCEL.

Skardon hovered his finger in front of the *CANCEL*. "It's that easy. One tap and your stupid little world is spared." He nodded out the glass back of the elevator at the Bon Voyage Show in progress below. "When you're called on stage, you'll terminate this abomination of a cruise and I'll cancel the order."

"Wow, that's... awesome." A wary smile tugged at Leo's lips. "But what about Varlowe?"

"What about her?"

"If I quit, she still loses the contest. You'll become president and she'll be thrown off the executive board."

"Yes. And?"

"And... well, I don't want that."

"Why not?"

Leo shrugged. "She seems nice."

Skardon pinched his eyes with his fingers. "Are you too stupid to see your options here? You either quit now, forfeiting Varlowe's job and saving your world, or you proceed and fail, forfeiting Varlowe's job and losing your world."

"Yeah, okay, but..." Leo forced himself to stand taller. "What if I don't fail? I could save Varlowe's job *and* Eaglehaven."

Skardon chuckled. "Let us be clear. There is no chance you will succeed. None. You have no cruise experience, no history of leadership, and no idea what you're doing. And the second you fail, I will ascend to the presidency and gain the authority to execute my expansion plan. " He waved at the holographic globe on his palm. "*All* of my expansion plan. Unless you decide to walk away now."

Leo looked at his home world literally resting in this man's hands. His chest tightened. The orange creep did have a point. Successfully commanding this ship all the way to Ensenada Vega was a long shot. He didn't want to screw over Varlowe, but he also didn't want to doom humanity to a Hershey-squirt holocaust. The choice was unfortunate, but it wasn't hard.

He cleared his throat. "You know, I really should get home. Water my plants and whatnot."

"I thought you might see it that way." Skardon tapped the elevator panel, canceling the emergency stop and allowing the car to descend. The doors opened on the Lido Deck and he waved a hand. "Go scamper off and save your little monkey planet."

Leo didn't look back as he rushed out of the lift and into the mass of passengers crowded on the deck. Shame burned him like acid, but at the same time a weight had been lifted. For the first time since he'd arrived, he felt like he could take a breath. Of course, that breath was soiled with Skardon's condescending mouth farts, but it was a breath nonetheless. And Varlowe would land on her feet. Even if she wasn't president, she'd still have the WTF fortune, right? She'd be fine. Probably.

He made his way to the stage to perform his first and final official duty as captain of the *Americano Grande*.

Patriotic music swelled in a deafening crescendo as the show's narrator boomed from the speakers. *"Theirs is a story of hope. A story of dreams. A story of America."*

Leo looked up to see a kick line of Krubbs in football uniforms waving American flags while four Gellicles with pompadours and rhinestone-encrusted jumpsuits bowed to a throne where a Ba'lux woman in a long blue robe swaddled a Mr. Potato Head with a golden halo. He didn't even want to know.

The alien audience went wild with applause as Kellybean pranced onto the stage. She smiled and raised a paw toward the troupe of performers. "Yeah! Let's hear it for the stars of our show, the American Eagle Outfitters!"

The roar of the crowd continued as Leo slipped backstage. He hustled over to Burlock, already in position for his introduction. The first officer's mechanical eye twitched as he looked Leo up and down. "Nice costume."

"It's a uniform," Leo muttered.

"It's a uniform when you earn it with merit. It's a costume when it's a gift from your sugar mama. But your boudoir role-playing is none of my business."

Leo's face blossomed red, but he didn't argue. It didn't matter what Burlock thought of him anymore. None of it mattered anymore. He was going home. "Let's get this over with."

The performers bounded past as they exited the stage, waving at the audience with high energy and plastered-on smiles. Leo looked out over the teeming crowd of passengers and steadied himself as Kellybean continued her welcome spiel.

"Are you all having a good time?" The aliens cheered in reply. She put a hand to her pointed ear. "I can't hear you! Is this the greatest party orbiting the planet Jaynkee?" The audience, conditioned by lifetimes of emcees' rhetorical questions, cheered louder. "Yeah it is! But we didn't come here to party over Jaynkee, did we? Who's excited to go to Ensenada Vega?" The crowd squealed and stomped their feet. "Well then let's bring out our commanders to get us underway!" She swept a paw toward the wings. "It is my honor and privilege to introduce our first officer, Commander Rexel Burlock!"

The crowd applauded as Burlock strode onto the stage in crisp, measured steps. He snapped to a stop next to Kellybean, raised his mechanical arm, and gave the audience a respectful salute. Kellybean continued.

"Commander Burlock served over thirty years in the Ba'luxi Prime Imperial Navy before joining the WTF family. He's tough on the outside but on the inside he's... Even tougher, actually. Let's hear it for the commander!"

Burlock's lips curled into the slightest hint of a smile as the crowd let out a deafening roar of approval. Kellybean's showy voice took on an air of gravitas.

"And now, ladies and gentlemen, both and neither, let's all give a warm welcome to WTF's newest addition. The senior officer of the *Americano Grande*, Captain Leo MacGavin!"

A thunderous wave of noise rolled off the audience and crashed against the stage, vibrating Leo in his boots. He took a deep breath, steeled himself, and strode onto the platform. But he wasn't more than three steps into the spotlight before the energy of the crowd began to change. The whistling stopped. The clapping thinned. By the time he had made it all the way to Kellybean and Burlock, the sea of passengers had fallen totally silent. Leo looked out at the bulging eyes and slack jaws and leaned into the microphone.

"Um, hi. Welcome aboard. I hope you're all—"

"It's an American!" a voice shouted. "The captain is an American!"

A murmur rippled through the crowd, spattered with outbreaks of laughter.

"He sure is," Kellybean said brightly. "A real live *person person*."

She gave Leo a withering stink eye.

"I said I was sorry," Leo grumbled. "Jeez."

"Wait, it's really the captain?" a slug in a muumuu shouted.

"Yes, *he's* really the captain," Leo corrected. "Although—"

"Of this ship?" another passenger yelled.

Leo nodded. "Yes. But—"

"Like the actual *captain* captain?" someone called out.

Leo's shoulders slumped. "Look, if you'd just let me—"

A rumble of panic swept across the deck. Burlock stepped to the microphone. "Your attention, please." The audience fell silent, as if crushed under the boom of his voice. "I assure you, this ship and everyone on it are safe in my hands. You can think of MacGavin here as more of an..." He looked at Leo and shook his head. "Ornamental captain."

"Oh! I get it!" the muumuu slug cackled. "He's the mascot!"

The crowd exhaled a sigh of relief, rippled with laughter.

"A stupid American mascot for a stupid American ship!" a teenage Gellicle mewled. "That's hilarious!"

An old Ba'lux hunched over and scratched at his armpits like an ape. "Oooh ooh! Captain American want a cheeseburger!"

Leo scowled. "Wow, that is so speciest."

Kellybean's professional smile wavered as she eyed the abusive crowd, but her voice remained light. "How about we get this voyage underway, huh?" She flicked her hand and a long, thin chain with a polished wooden handle descended from above. She glanced to Leo. "Before you sound the ship's whistle, is there anything you'd like to say to our guests, Captain?"

Leo wiped his clammy palms on his pants as he looked out over the crowd. Thousands of aliens surrounded the stage, but only one caught his eye. Out in the throng, Skardon raised his arm, displaying the demolition order. He lifted a finger and poised it above the *CANCEL* button.

Leo's heart thundered as he drew a deep breath. "There is, actually." He picked at his coat buttons. "Okay, so... I didn't ever plan to be the captain of a cruise ship. And I appreciate that this is like, a really big honor, but I can't—"

"Shut uuuuup!" a high voice bellowed. Leo spied a tipsy Krubb woman with a cocktail in each claw. "Stuff a corn dog in it, American slob!"

Laughter roared across the deck. Even Burlock snorted a

chuckle. Leo's teeth clenched and his cheeks burned. He was trying to quit. He was trying to do exactly what they all wanted if they'd just stop crapping on him for two seconds. His head pounded and his vision went red and fuzzy at the edges. Burlock stepped to his side, his eyes still fixed on the crowd.

"Stop embarrassing yourself and go home," he muttered. "Nobody wants you here."

The words stung, but Leo knew they weren't true. There was one person who wanted him here. And only one. He looked up at the first-class sundeck to see Varlowe flash a proud piranha grin as she gave him two bony thumbs up. His stomach plunged. Was he really going to do this to her?

He was. He had to. For Eaglehaven.

"Before I say what I have to say, I just want to thank the president of WTF for believing in me." His throat tightened. "And I hope she'll forgive me for—"

"Oh for the love of..." Burlock pushed Leo aside and leaned into the mic. "On behalf of the crew and our idiot captain, bon voyage."

He yanked the chain and an earsplitting horn sounded, blasting a vent of roiling steam through the artificial atmosphere. Explosions of confetti and pyrotechnics arched over the crowd as everyone burst into raucous cheers.

Leo's eyes widened and his face flushed. "Wait! We're not leaving! I'm officially calling off—"

His microphone cut out as the DJ resumed her jams, blasting the audience with a wall of party hits. Leo shouted hopelessly against the deafening celebration as the ship's engines rumbled to life and pulled the *Americano Grande* away from the dock for its maiden voyage.

"No! Stop!" Leo shouted. "I quit! Listen! I quit!"

Nobody heard him. Nobody even looked at him. His pulse

spiked and his adrenaline surged, pulling his vision into a blurred tunnel. The multitude of passengers before him narrowed to a group. To a cluster. To a single person.

Skardon bared his teeth and stabbed the *CONFIRM* button on the hologram. A new heading appeared.

DEMOLITION CONFIRMED.
PENDING PRESIDENTIAL APPROVAL.

Leo's view constricted to the model of his home as enormous craters opened in its face and filled with lumpy brown sludge.

His entire world now rested on his success.

Eaglehaven was doomed.

CHAPTER FIVE

An alarm rang through the ship—bold and authoritative but stopping just short of being panic-inducing. It echoed down the long expanse of the Riviera Deck concourse, lined on one side with shops and restaurants, on the other with broad panorama windows. Every thirty feet, a large round, airtight door was set into the exterior bulkhead between the panes of glass. At each hatch, a member of the hospitality staff in a bright yellow safety vest addressed a group of bored, irritated passengers.

Kellybean smiled as she adjusted her vest. Everything was going according to plan, and she was going to make sure it stayed that way. She only had seven days to prove herself to Admiral Skardon, and she wasn't about to blow it. She turned to the tourists gathered around her door and put on her assertive hostess voice.

"Good afternoon, one and all. At Waylade Tour Fleet Cruises, passenger safety is our highest priority. So on behalf of the captain and the senior staff, thank you for reporting to your assigned muster stations for this short safety briefing."

"Not short enough," a man groused. "I've heard this blasted speech a thousand times."

The elder crossed his bony arms over his chest. He was a Geiko—a bipedal lizard with a long, tubular body, short arms and legs, and a stubby tail. His bulbous gray eyes peered from his broad face, and a few withered, pale-orange tentacles drooped from his scalp. He wore a neat golf shirt, rumpled cargo shorts, and black socks and sandals. His orange tiger stripes were faded to a distinguished, rusty gray against the royal blue of his skin.

"I'm sorry. I know it can be a little boring, but please bear with me," Kellybean said patiently. "It's important for all guests to review our safety procedures, even if you've cruised with us a few times before."

"A few times?" a woman hooted. "Little miss, I'll have you know we were cruising with WTF while you were still waiting for your whiskers to come in!"

Kellybean turned to a second hunched blue lizard. Unlike her mate, this Geiko was not resigned to aging gracefully. Her scalp tentacles were plump with collagen injections, and her stripes were airbrushed a screaming shade of fuchsia that suggested she was barely out of puberty. The cosmetic ruse was so blatant it was actively insulting to the intelligence of onlookers.

"I don't doubt it, ma'am. But these muster drills are required by the Intergalactic Convention for the Safety of Life in Space and—"

"We should be exempt from this nonsense," the man griped. "We're not just some lousy tourists, you know. We're Platinum Elite Class!"

The couple simultaneously raised their arms and flicked fingers at the tabloyds on their wrists, pulling up holographic identicards like badges of honor. According to their stats, Horman and Clermytha Gwapwaffle had logged enough miles on WTF cruises to have flown to the galactic core and back. Twice. Each.

"And we do value your loyalty," Kellybean said with appropriate reverence. "As our most honored guests, we want to keep you safe in the unlikely event of an emergency. So let's quickly review—"

"Move it! One side, dirtsuckers!"

The assembled passengers yelped and stumbled as an enormous creature shoved his way through them like a slow-motion wrecking ball. He was a Nomit—a race of giants, built like hunched-over boulders with two elephantine legs and four arms. A huge, bodybuilder-sized pair bulged from his shoulders and a smaller, actuary-sized pair sprouted from his ribs. All four were loaded with musical instruments. A battered drum kit banged against the other passengers, knocking them out of the way as he lumbered through the crowd.

Kellybean regarded him with a twitch of her whiskers, taking in his shabby, black-leather biker vest and stained muscle shirt. His thick, grayish-yellow skin looked like a full-body nicotine stain, and had the stench to match.

"Excuse me, sir," she hissed. "We're in the middle of an emergency drill. All guests need to report to their assigned stations."

The Nomit's barrel head turned her way, sizing her up with a pair of perfectly round eyes the size of salad plates. "That's whut we're doin'. 'Cept we ain't guests."

"We're entertainers!" said a synthesized voice.

A skinny robot rolled around the monstrous punk. His boxy body casing was made of discolored beige plastic with a large datacassette deck in the chest. At the bottom was a fork attached to a single tri-star axle with three knobby tires. At the top was a telescoping neck holding a flat, rectangular head, like a cereal box tipped on its face. Two eyes blinked from a screen at its front. His digital brows raised cheerfully through a haze of scan-line distortion.

"We're Murderblossom! The planet Jaynkee's most notorious garbagepunk band!" The robot squinted proudly. "Voted 'Most Difficult To Listen To' three times. In a single week!"

Horman's snout wrinkled. "Never heard of you."

"Then it's 'bout time you did." The Nomit smirked and held up a guitar with two parallel necks—one a stringed bass, the other a keyboard. "Sickie Stobber, master of the double bass keytar and Murderblossom's lead motherhucker." He cocked a thumb at his partner. "Hax. Drums and robot crap."

"I'm a midi interface!" Hax said proudly.

Kellybean scowled. "Gentlemen, please. I need you to quiet down and—"

"Wait, where's the other one?" Stobber grunted.

Hax's head turned in a slow circle on his neck like a submarine periscope. He beeped and pointed a slender plastic hand. "Over there!"

Irritation ruffed Kellybean's fur as she looked past her muster group to a lounge on the opposite side of the concourse. The venue was dark, closed for the shipwide emergency drill, but there was a figure behind the bar, silhouetted against the light of the glass-fronted cooler. Its lockpad had been ripped off and someone was crouched over it, fiddling with the wiring inside. With a *pop* and a bright white spark, the doors unlocked and swung open.

Kellybean gasped. "Hey! Stop that! Before I call security!"

The figure in the lounge plucked a blue beer bottle from the cooler, popped it open, and took a long swig before sauntering out of the shadows and into the light of the concourse. Kellybean gasped again.

The stranger was a Verdaphyte—a lanky assemblage of greenish-brown vines and sticks woven into the shape of a sinewy girl. Long, pink leaves sprouted from her head, shaved down to the bark on one side and arching in a mangled wave across the other. Her root system was bound in a pair of worn leather pants, and a tattered tank top showed off lean wooden arms carved with hearts filled with lovers' initials. Flecks of glitter glinted from the furrows of her brown, barky face as her eyes rolled up and down Kellybean's feline body.

"*Me-yow,*" the plant girl growled. "What's new, pussycat?"

Kellybean's frustration wavered as her heart skipped a beat. The Verdaphyte just stood there, weight slouched on one hip, guitar slung over her back, radiating bad-girl sex appeal like pollen on the breeze. Kellybean blinked and shook her head, chasing off her impure thoughts.

"You're with these two?" she asked, gesturing at the other punks.

"Reluctantly." The girl raised her bottle to her brow and gave a salute. "Jassi Kiktrash, guitar goddess and Murderblossom's lead motherhucker."

"*I'm* Murderblossom's lead motherhucker," Stobber spat.

"You're delusional," Jassi snorted.

"Please don't argue," Hax said. "You both display equally deplorable leadership skills."

"This is ridiculous!" Clermytha Gwapwaffle huffed. "We came on board to relax, not to listen to squabbling ruffians." She grabbed her husband. "Come on, Horman, let's go."

She turned to leave, but Kellybean pounced in her way. "Wait! I'm not finished drilling you on the lifeboat."

"You can drill me on the lifeboat." Jassi wagged a brow salaciously. "Or in the lifeboat. Or under it. I'm not picky."

"I don't get it." Hax cocked his head and his eyes went fuzzy as his datacassette shuttled back and forth. "Oh! Innuendo! How cheeky!"

Horman hitched up his pants and snorted. "Now listen here! I paid a lot of dollabux for this cruise, and I'm not going to have you waste another minute of our time with this tomfoolery!"

Kellybean's tail thrashed in irritation. The ship had barely left the dock and she was already losing control. She took a breath and forced a smile onto her face. "I do apologize for the rude interruption. As I was saying, in the unlikely event of an emergency, an alarm tone will sound. At that time, all passengers must report—"

"Wait!" Hax gasped. "Where's my drum?"

"Yer drums are right here, ya dope." Stobber shrugged his shoulders, rattling the snares and ringing the cymbals of the five-piece kit tucked under his massive arms.

"No, my bass drum. It's missing!"

"I have all the others. How many hucking drums do you need?"

Hax's eyes turned sad. "But you just got me that drum! I haven't even played it yet! I'm not going to evacuate and leave it here to die!"

A nervous titter ran through the guests.

"Nobody is evacuating. Or dying!" Kellybean narrowed her eyes at Stobber. "Also, there's no cargo allowed. Each lifeboat only has space for its designated passengers."

Stobber snorted. "Well we ain't leaving without our gear, so I guess we're gonna have to figure out who gets left behind to make room."

Hax scanned the tourists, landing on Horman and Clermytha. "These two are the best candidates. They've already exceeded their biological expiration dates."

"How dare you?" Clermytha fluffed her bloated scalp tentacles. "I've barely hit my prime!"

"By my estimate you've hit several primes." Hax tipped his head. "The most recent likely being eighty-nine or ninety-seven."

Horman's long hands balled into fists. "You take that back you mechanical—"

"Stop it!" Kellybean mewled. "Do you people want to learn how to use a lifeboat or do you want to die frozen and gasping for air in the vacuum of space? Your choice!"

The group fell silent. Jassi chuckled and swigged her beer. "Cooperation or death? Dang, kitty is hard core."

Kellybean's eyes widened. "No! I meant... gah!" She raised her paws to the alarmed guests. "Everything will be fine. This ship is perfectly safe. Please remain calm."

"Remain calm?" Clermytha squawked. "You just told us we're all going to die!"

"In all my years of cruising this is, bar none, the worst safety briefing I've ever heard!" Horman wagged a finger at Kellybean. "I'm lodging a complaint with WTF corporate!"

"No no, that won't be necessary," Kellybean whimpered. "I'm sorry I raised my voice. Please just—"

"Come on, Clerm." Horman grabbed his wife's hand. "I need to take my medicine."

"Wait! Don't go!"

The two Geiko stormed off. Kellybean wilted as her muster group followed them, muttering and griping under their breath. Jassi hung back, slouching against the lifeboat hatch.

"Rough crowd." She tipped her leafy head toward the lounge. "Wanna get a drink?"

"I don't drink on duty," Kellybean seethed.

Jassi nodded. "So, straight to bed then?"

Kellybean roared and stomped away. If she never saw Jassi Kiktrash and Murderblossom again it would be too soon.

CHAPTER SIX

Conversation and laughter filled the Rushmore Concourse as guests mingled at the various cafés and booked shore excursions at the hospitality desks. The cruise was well underway, and everybody was pumped up for seven days of fun and excitement.

Except for one person.

Leo slumped on a bench near the elevators, bile gnawing his guts as he remembered the hologram floating above Skardon's wrist. In his mind he could still see Eaglehaven slowly rotating, surrounded by the text of the executive order.

DEMOLITION CONFIRMED.

PENDING PRESIDENTIAL APPROVAL.

He had screwed up. Screwed up epically. More epically than any human had ever screwed up. Skardon had handed him the safety of his home world on a silver platter, and he'd fumbled that platter onto the floor and then taken a dump on it.

He had regrets.

"Hey, Captain. Shouldn't you be on the bridge?"

Leo looked up to see Kellybean standing in front of his bench.

"I should be." He raised his tabloyd band. "But I can't get the elevators to take me to the command level."

"Still didn't get that worked out, huh?" Kellybean rolled her eyes. "C'mon. I'm heading up there anyway."

She stepped into a lift and held her tabloyd to the panel,

unlocking the restricted levels. Leo joined her and the doors slid shut behind them. Decks whooshed by in awkward silence. Kellybean fidgeted with her claws. Leo put his hands in his pockets.

"I owe you an apology," they said simultaneously.

"You? For what?" Leo said. "I'm the one who said you weren't a person. And I'm sorry."

"Thanks, but I know you didn't mean it that way." Kellybean looked away guiltily. "I can be a little oversensitive about that stuff. A lot of beings out there really don't consider Gellicles people. The galaxy can be pretty prejudiced against mammals."

"You don't say," Leo snorted.

"Preaching to the choir, right?" Kellybean half smiled. "When I saw how the passengers mistreated you at the Bon Voyage Show, I realized you and I are a lot alike. Two warm-blooded fur-bearers out to earn the respect they deserve."

Leo scratched his shaggy hair. "I guess you're kinda right."

"I'm totally right. And we're going to show everyone on this ship that we're a force to be reckoned with."

"Ah. I'm not a 'force' as such. I'm really more of a light-to-moderate pressure."

"Enough of that. Nobody's going to respect you if you don't respect yourself." The elevator pinged and opened its doors. Kellybean strode confidently into the command lobby with Leo trailing behind. "You're the captain. You're in charge here. Don't let anyone push you around just because you have nipples."

"Uh... okay. Good pep talk." Leo nodded. "Weird, but good."

"You've got this, sir." Kellybean put a paw on Leo's shoulder and looked into his eyes. "Now go show 'em who's boss."

She swiped her tabloyd band at the door to the bridge and it whirred open. Leo gazed through it into the command center, taking it all in for the first time.

The bridge was a broad, shallow space rendered in deep blues and purples with a wall of enormous windows bulging across its front, overlooking the bow of the ship. A field of stars stood motionless outside the glass, stretching to infinity in every direction.

Three officers were stationed within three pods of controls. A leafy green woman in a circular pod to his left, a feathery purple man in one to his right, and a scaly blue girl at the navigation console to the front. Between them all was a large swivel chair with blinking panels in its armrests. Kellybean ushered Leo inside and called out, "Commander on deck!"

The three aliens looked to her with confusion.

"We know," the plant woman said. "He's been here for an hour."

She nodded at the captain's chair, where Burlock was looking quite at home. He turned to Leo and scowled. "MacGavin. What are you doing here?"

"Oh. I'm sorry, I thought I was supposed to..." Leo took a half step back, but Kellybean put a paw on his back and nudged him forward. "I'm here because I'm the captain."

The purple man looked to Burlock in confusion. "I thought you were the captain."

"No, it's me. For real." Leo tapped the five chevrons on his badge. Everyone continued to look at him blankly. "But I guess it is weird you're just meeting me now for the first time, isn't it?"

"It's almost like we don't even need you here," Burlock said.

Kellybean glowered at him. "But now that he is here, I'm sure the *first officer* will be thrilled to introduce the *captain*."

Leo nodded. "Right! Because I'm the boss of you."

A growl sounded in Burlock's throat. "Don't ever say those words in that order again."

"But... I'm your commanding officer."

"Technically. And precariously."

"But accurately," Kellybean said brightly. "So now that we've got that sorted, I'll leave you boys to it." She turned her back to Burlock as she headed toward the lobby. On her way out she silently mouthed a message to Leo. *"Force to be reckoned with."*

She patted him on the shoulder and swished out the door, leaving the captain alone with his crew. He smoothed down his uniform and forced confidence into his voice. Nobody would respect him if he didn't respect himself, right? Mammal power!

"Okay, Burlock. Let's have some introductions."

The commander bristled as he rose from the captain's chair and crossed to the woman. She was a Verdaphyte—like a bundle of supple green vines dressed in a sharp white uniform. Her face was soft and dewy as a fresh melon, and shoulder-length sprays of small yellow blooms sprouted from her scalp. Burlock rested a hand on her console. "Over here we have MonCom."

Leo smiled. "Nice to meet you, MonCom."

The woman raised a petaled brow to Burlock. "Is he serious?"

"MonCom is her position," Burlock snuffed. "The lieutenant is responsible for monitoring and communications."

"Of course, yes. Duh," Leo said. "And your name is?"

"Monica Comfit."

"I bet your friends call you MonCom for short though, am I right?"

"You are not," Comfit said frostily. She went back to her work, poking at the dozens of controls on her panel.

"Okay, cool. You just..." Leo waved at the console. "Keep doing that." He turned to the station on the right side of the bridge. The officer there was vaguely gorilla shaped, with short legs and large, muscular arms. The Screetoro was covered in downy purple feathers, and eight stalks ending in round, leech-like mouths curled from the top of his broad, squat head. Three eyes with rectangular pupils stared from the center of his face. Leo gave him a nod. "And who do we have over here?"

"Quartermaster," the Screetoro trumpeted.

"A very important position! And what is your name?"

"That is my name, sir. Lieutenant St'ondo Quartermaster, Senior EngTech."

"Ah. Right. You're the guy who... teaches English?"

"He's an engineering technician," Burlock said impatiently. "Quartermaster is our liaison to the primary machine room."

"What is 'English'?" Quartermaster asked.

"Oh, nothing," Leo said. "Just an old Earth language."

"What is 'Earth'?"

Leo smiled. "I'm so glad you asked. Earth is—"

"And finally, we have the helm." Burlock turned his back on the EngTech and motioned to the console in front of the windows. "And in case you can't figure it out, her *position* is helm and her *name* is Lieutenant Narleen Swoochatowski."

The girl chuckled. "Dude, I'm out of the service. It's just Swooch now."

Leo eyed the young lizard lounging in the seat behind the navigation console. She was a teenage Geiko, with scaly blue skin tiger-striped with vibrant yellow. Her long body stretched like a paunchy sausage between her stubby legs and tail at one end and her broad face and half-lidded gray eyes at the other. Thick, uneven tentacles sprouted from her scalp and hung down her back like canary-streaked dreadlocks. She wore a wrinkled hoodie over her wrinkled uniform.

Burlock frowned and straightened up, as if trying to balance out the officer's slouch. "The lieutenant is a decorated war hero, and the youngest pilot to ever serve in the Geiko Prime Supernova Strikeforce."

"Wow, I've actually heard of them," Leo said. "The most elite battle squadron in the Four Prime Systems. You people are legendary."

"It's not as hard as it looks." Swooch languidly slapped a hand on the steering yoke. "You just push the stick where you want to go and hit the button that goes *pew pew*."

"It's so much more than that," Burlock said. "Piloting a Strikeforce Stingjet takes nerves of steel. Only the best of the best can pass the simulation test, let alone fly one in combat."

"Eh, you get the hang of it pretty quick when folks are shooting at you." Swooch shrugged. "Or, you know, you die."

Leo gaped in awe. "Legendary."

Burlock nodded at him. "Now that you've had your little meet and greet, sit down and stay out of the way."

He pointed to a vacant console at the back of the room as he returned to the command chair. Leo crossed his arms. "Actually, I think I'll take that seat. Since I'm the captain and all."

"So you are." Burlock's jaw clenched as he rose to his feet. "You have command of the bridge, *sir*."

Leo sat down gingerly in the captain's chair, pulling in his elbows so as not to bump the control panels. The seat had three tiered sets of armrests, each covered in hundreds of blinking buttons and switches and toggles. Sitting within them, Leo felt uncomfortably like he was being hugged by a Hammond organ.

Burlock settled discontentedly at the ops console to the rear of the bridge. "All right, Captain. What are your orders?"

"Orders?"

"Yes, orders. Giving orders is what the person in the big chair does."

"Oh! Right. Orders!" Leo looked around for a clue. Comfit and Quartermaster were both busy with their endless panes of controls. "Everybody just, you know, carry on with what you're doing here."

"You got it, bro," Swooch said. "I've already laid in a course for Halii Bai. You just chill. We got this."

"Awesome," Leo said, with a bit too much relief. "Thank you."

He took a calming breath. Each member of the crew went about their duties. They all seemed so experienced and competent. Maybe this whole captaining gig wouldn't be so hard after all. He cautiously settled back in his seat and a blaring alarm ripped through the bridge.

"I didn't do it!" he yelped, leaping from his chair. The others barely flinched.

Burlock gave Leo side-eye. "Comfit, report."

The MonCom's green fingers danced across her screens. "Sensors indicate imminent collision with an ice-belt object."

Swooch glanced at her console. "Nah, we're cool. The belt is still half a million miles out."

"It's a breakaway. A rogue iceberg is headed straight for us."

Leo squinted out the window. Outside was nothing but tranquil space. "I don't see it."

Quartermaster looked at him incredulously. "Um, yes. The object is over fifty thousand miles away, sir."

"Oh. Okay." Leo chuckled. "So when she said 'imminent' she didn't mean like, '*imminent* imminent.'"

Comfit raised a brow. "Sir, do you have any idea how fast we're going right now?"

Leo's eyes ticked to the window and the stationary stars.

"Yes?" he wagered.

Burlock ignored him. "Quartermaster, switch the view to Perception Mode."

The Screetoro flicked a control and an electric sizzle wiped from one side of the glass wall to the other. As it did, the pinpoints of stars stretched into hot white streaks, blurring past the ship at impossible speed. Leo yelped and tumbled back into his chair, gripping the cushions. The blur of infinite cosmos widened his eyes and crippled his brain.

"Holycrapholycrapholycrap," he stammered. "Fast. Fast fast so fast too fast fast fast."

Burlock rose from his seat, gazing at a moon-sized hunk of blue ice hurtling toward them, growing larger every second. The tumbling menace reflected in the placid domes of his eyes. "Helm, evasive maneuvers."

Swooch adjusted a handful of sliders. "Not happening, bro."

"Lieutenant, that is an order."

"Yeah, I hear ya. But it's not happening." Swooch pushed the sliders up and down again. "I'm putting full juice to the nav thrusters but they're giving me jack cheese here."

"There's been a malfunction," Quartermaster confirmed. "Something's leeching power from the navigation system. I'm seeing transmission glitches all over the grid."

"Glitches?" The word squeaked from Leo's mouth, high with lingering terror. He looked away from the streaking stars and cleared his throat. "How are there glitches? I thought this ship was brand new."

The EngTech frowned. "This vessel was hastily put together by unsupervised bots. Engineering is still working out the bugs."

"Didn't they take this bucket on a shakedown cruise?" Burlock muttered.

Swooch snorted. "I think you're on it, buddy."

"I second that. There's no way these systems have been field tested." Comfit glowered at her panel. "Sensors should have picked up the incoming object much sooner. It's like I'm looking through mud here."

Leo nodded. "Okay, so to recap, we're going really fast, we can't turn or see, and we're about to hit an iceberg."

"Correct, sir," Comfit said. "What are your orders?"

Cold sweat beaded on Leo's brow. "I'm, uh... open for suggestions."

"I suggest you get out of the way." Burlock's mechanical arm whirred as he pointed to the MonCom. "Comfit, launch a full tactical sim, 20K aperture."

"Aye, Commander."

She flicked at her panels and a three-dimensional hologram bloomed to life between the captain's chair and the helm. It was a model of the *Americano Grande*, its long, slender ocean-liner hull flanked with four enormous pods of glowing blue engines bulging from its aft quarters. A rendering of the iceberg tumbled toward it, surrounded by blinking figures and dotted lines showing vectors and spin rates and trajectories and dozens of other stats Leo couldn't identify.

Quartermaster eyed his controls. "I'm diverting power from non-essential systems to the port thrusters. I can get you a ten-second burn."

"It's not enough." Comfit swiped her leafy hand up her panel as if flinging data across the room. The hologram updated, drawing a dotted line that curved from the bow of the ship to the outside edge of the iceberg. "The turning radius is too wide. The hull will clear, but the port engine pods will take a direct impact."

"That sounds bad," Leo said.

"It'll set off an antimatter fusion cascade, sir. Hundreds of casualties."

"Okay, so, definitely bad."

"What are your orders, sir?" Quartermaster asked.

"I, uh..." Leo stared at the jagged ice rolling toward them. His adrenalin burned. His muscles tightened. His mind emptied.

"Orders!" Burlock snapped. "Say something!"

The commander's shout knocked an idea from Leo's brain. Not a good idea. Not even a full idea. Barely an image...

"This reminds me of something from my ancestral planet," he stammered. "It was an ocean-going ship, but it was a lot like this one."

"I was thinking the same thing," Comfit said bleakly.

"You know about my people's ships?"

"Well, just one. I saw a holodrama about it once. This is just like the *Titanic*."

"Wait, what? This is nothing like the *Titanic*."

Comfit blinked. "A luxury liner. Maiden voyage. Iceberg. It's literally exactly the same."

"How did they avoid the collision?" Quartermaster asked.

"They didn't," Comfit said. "The ship was destroyed and most everyone died."

Burlock snorted at Leo. "This is your idea? Suicide?"

"Gah! No!" Leo pinched his eyes. "I wasn't talking about the *Titanic*! I was talking about the polar icebreaker ships. They could plow through arctic ice." He gestured at the ax-blade of the holographic ship's hull. "The bow is pointy. If we hit it full-speed, straight-on, we'll smash right through the iceberg."

"That's insane. We're not doing it." Burlock raised his voice over the continued scream of the warning klaxon. "Helm, take evasive action. Let's see how many casualties we get from clipping an engine."

Leo's stomach plunged at the commander's blasé attitude toward collateral damage. Swooch glanced at Leo. "Evade or attack? It's your call, Cap'n."

A shock of nervous energy ran through Leo's body. It was his call. He was the captain. The ship was in his hands. And he had no idea what to do. Every instinct told him to shrink back. Give up. Let Burlock take over. But a tiny Gellicle voice in his mind said this was his chance to prove himself. To save the ship not with experience or know-how, but with his unique knowledge of old Earth. His chance to use the history of the very people the aliens disrespected to rescue them all from certain death.

Leo would be a force to reckon with. Or die trying.

He thrust a finger at the mass of deadly ice. "Swooch, I order you to hit that iceberg!"

"You got it," Swooch drawled.

The Geiko pumped the pedals and spun the yoke. The nose of the vessel turned toward the center of the ice.

"Brace for impact," Comfit said with commendable serenity. "Brace for impact."

The iceberg tumbled toward them, filling the entire wall of windows. Leo grabbed the back of Swooch's seat and clenched his teeth as the gap between the bow and the ice grew smaller and smaller. Then... impact! With a half-second screech of rending metal, the front of the ship was obliterated by ninety-thousand tons of ice. The windows shattered and the deck shook as every console in the room simultaneously burst into pyres of yellow flame, devouring the bridge crew. Leo wailed in horror as the flames rolled over his body.

He continued screaming.

He screamed some more.

"Deactivate tactical simulation," Burlock said calmly.

Comfit leaned over her flaming panel and tapped the screen. The holographic model of the ship and iceberg blinked out, taking the flame and destruction with it. Leo sucked a breath and gaped at the intact bridge and the tumbling ice, still miles off the bow outside the window.

"How? What?" He trembled as he clutched his chest. "Gah!"

"I'm sorry," Comfit said. "Did you not know we were in a holographically augmented tactical simulation?"

Leo flailed his hands through the space where the hologram model had been. "I thought that's what this thing was! I didn't realize it was a whole..." He flung his arms wide. "Gah!"

Burlock's teeth ground as the actual iceberg raged ever closer. "We wasted our simulation run on the monkey's asinine idea. It's do or die time."

"Power is diverted to the thrusters," Quartermaster reported.

"Swooch, do you feel lucky?" Burlock asked.

The Geiko wagged her brow. "Getting lucky is what I do, brah." She clutched the flight controls as her bulbous lizard eyes studied the tumbling ice. "Might wanna hold onto something."

With that, she stood on the pedals and swung the yoke in a smooth, broad motion. The jury-rigged thrusters ignited in sequence, rolling the vessel to the side. Leo grabbed the back of Swooch's chair as the wall of ice slid to one side of the window, revealing the safety of open space beyond.

"Bow is clear, but engines are not!" Comfit cried. "Brace for impact!"

"Nah," Swooch muttered. "I got this."

She kept the ship snug against the cratered surface of the ice just as its rotation revealed a deep scar carved in its side. With a swish of her wrist, Swooch slotted the engine into the gap. The ice lit up like a salt lantern as the blue burners traced the length of the channel, the outer edges of the pods barely missing the jagged walls. After an eternal second, the engines cleared the end of the gash and the iceberg rolled away behind them.

"We're clear!" Comfit shouted. "No damage! No injuries!"

"No problemo," Swooch said with a grin. She glanced at Leo, who was still clutching the back of her seat with white knuckles. "Sorry your way didn't work out, bud."

Leo just stood there, pale-faced and sweating. "This way was good too."

"Excellent flying, Lieutenant," Burlock said. "Comfit and Quartermaster, way to stay cool under pressure." He turned to Leo. "As for you, Captain..."

Leo looked down, humiliated. "Yeah, I'm sorry. I'll do better next time."

"If we'd followed your orders, there wouldn't be a next time."

"I said I was sorry."

Swooch spun lazily in her chair. "Don't sweat it. So you're not good at command. That's fine. There's a bunch of other stuff the captain's gotta do."

"There is?"

"Sure! Like plan the Captain's Welcome Dinner."

"Oh, that," Leo mumbled. "Kellybean said she's got that all taken care of."

"Maybe you should go double check," Quartermaster said.

"Yeah, it's probably best if you give it an official inspection," Comfit added. "You know, as captain."

Leo looked at the three bridge officers, but none of them would make eye contact.

"Right. For sure. That's super important. So I'll go and, uh... take care of that." He gestured at the command chair. "Unless you want me to stick around and—"

"That won't be necessary," Burlock said. "We've got things under control here."

"Yeah. Okay." Leo's cheeks prickled with humiliation as he scurried to the exit. He stopped in the lobby and turned to the bridge. "So, I guess I'll just pop back up here after dinner then?"

The doors closed in his face as Burlock settled into the captain's chair.

CHAPTER SEVEN

Leo hustled down the broad concourse of the Aloha Deck, taking deep breaths of the cool evening air. It was actually the same air it had been all day, but the ship's artificial day-night cycle added a crispness to it as the ambient lights slowly went low and blue.

He tried to put the iceberg and their brush with death out of his mind as he scurried toward the main dining room. The day had been a total disaster so far, but he still had one chance to end it with a win. At the Captain's Welcome Dinner, he'd be hosting the WTF executive board. This was an opportunity to convince the bigwigs that he was, as Kellybean insisted, a force to be reckoned with.

Maybe he'd even convince himself.

Leo reached the intimidating double doors of the ship's most formal dining room and placed his hands on the polished brass handles, shaped like a pair of capital Fs standing back-to-back. He mustered his confidence, closed his eyes, and pushed his way into the posh eatery.

He opened his eyes. He blinked. He blinked again.

It was not what he was expecting.

The decor was... busy. Walls of dark wood and brick were hung heavy with a mismatched assortment of tchotchkes. One sported street signs and surfboards and an oversized novelty rack of billiard balls. Another, an electric football table and a gigantic Levi's jeans logo and several tarnished funeral urns. Just junk everywhere, lurking in the dim lighting of the hanging, Tiffany-style lamps. Each table was covered in a garish red-and-white striped tablecloth.

A few alien servers bustled around the tables of the empty restaurant, laying down place settings. Each of them wore a red-and-white shirt and suspenders dotted with colorful buttons and pins. A tabby Gellicle girl smiled at him from behind a lectern. "Welcome to WTF Friday's! In here, it's Friday once a week."

Leo gaped at the cluttered room. "I'm sorry, what am I looking at here?"

"This is a faithful recreation of the most upscale eatery on the planet America."

"There is no planet America."

The Gellicle's tail drooped. "Sorry, that was insensitive. I meant 'the *former* planet America.'"

Leo pinched his eyes. "No, I mean—"

"Captain! Welcome!" A barrel-chested Geiko in a white chef's coat and hat sidled up to the lectern, pushing a serving cart with a domed tray on top. "Master Chef Wabbo Fiero." He held out a blue fist and Leo politely bumped it. "I'm so glad you're here. I want to show you the American-style appetizer I've whipped up exclusively for your guests at the Captain's Table. Feast your eyes!"

He whisked the cover off the tray, revealing what looked like a bloated, spiny starfish covered in chili and smothered in cheese. The creature slowly wriggled its limbs, sucking a wheezing breath as it crept across the plate. Leo jumped back with a gasp.

"Olé!" the chef said proudly. "The traditional dish of your people! Nachos!"

"No. Just no," Leo stammered. "That's messed up."

"Messed up? Hmph." The lizard chef looked down his snout

at Leo. "Fine. If you're going to be a pedant about it, yes, we were out of gouda cheese so I used muenster."

"Wow, that is not even close to the problem."

Chef Fiero slammed the lid back over the wriggling, cheesy abomination. "My family has been cooking authentic American recipes since before you were even born! I think I know a fair bit more about the food of your people than you do! Good day, sir!"

He stomped away toward the kitchen with his cart. The hostess shook her head. "So rude."

"I know, right? What's with that guy?"

"No, you're rude. A seventeen-star Goodyear chef offers you a delicacy of your ancestral world and you throw a hissy fit? What's that all about?"

"It wasn't a hissy fit. It was more an expression of primal horror," Leo muttered. "I don't know what that thing was, but it was not from the planet Earth."

The hostess looked at him like he was a moron. "Right. It was from the planet America."

Leo sighed and groaned at the same time. "Look, my people came from a planet called 'Earth,' and on that planet there was a country called the 'United States of America.'"

"That's not what the Geiko Archives say."

"I know! The Geiko Archives are nonsense!"

The hostess blinked. "So... you guys don't eat nachos?"

"Gah! Forget the nachos! That wasn't even nachos! That was a nightmare cheese beast!"

Leo rubbed his temples. He didn't know anything about commanding a ship, but he did know about human history. Maybe he could just let Burlock do the heavy lifting on the bridge and he could be more of a cultural ambassador, like Varlowe said. He could use his position as captain to teach the galaxy the true story of the planet Earth.

He held his chin high and puffed out his chest.

"Let me see the menu for my Captain's Dinner. The chef and I are gonna have a little chat."

***

An hour later, the formal dining room bustled with passengers in their finest attire—tuxedos and gowns and ceremonial robes and bedazzled sweatpants. They mingled and laughed among the candy-cane striped tables and garage-sale junk, reveling in what they imagined was the apex of American elegance. At the front of the room was the Captain's Table.

Actually, it was two tables shoved together to accommodate his large party.

Leo sat at the center of one of the long sides, straddling the seam between tables. Admiral Skardon sat opposite him, flanked by Willijer the nebbishy accountant and Kersa the lady yes-man, all of them in regal Ba'lux formalwear. Sitting alone on his side of the tables, Leo felt like he was being interviewed. Or maybe condemned. He forced an uneasy smile. "So, are you all enjoying the cruise so far?"

"It's carried on longer than I expected it to," Skardon said pointedly.

Leo remembered the admiral's ultimatum and cringed. "My 'welcome aboard' speech kinda got away from me."

"Pity. If things had gone differently we all could have been home by now."

Leo's stomach plunged with regret, but before he could reply, a dusty voice croaked behind him. "Where's the food? I'm starved."

A motorized wheelchair rolled up at his left elbow, containing the wrinkled, doughy heap of Madame Skardon. The admiral's face tightened. "Mother. What are you doing here?"

"Whatsa matter? Ashamed to be seen with your old mom? Afraid I'm gonna pull out your baby pictures?"

Skardon scowled. "I just didn't realize you'd been invited."

"I almost wasn't. Luckily I ran into the Waylade kid and she told me about it."

"Yes. That is lucky," Skardon grumbled.

Leo glanced at the empty bentwood chair to his right. "Speaking of which, where is Varlowe?"

Willijer adjusted his glasses and nodded over Leo's shoulder. "Fashionably late, as usual."

Leo turned in his seat to see Varlowe gliding across the dining room. For once, her flawed studies of Earth culture had not betrayed her. She wore a black satin gown that hugged her form, complementing her narrow body in exactly the way a department-store vest or coffee-shop apron didn't. Its sleeveless tailoring highlighted her slender, elegant arms. Her thin lips were dark and glossy, and her bony eye sockets were airbrushed with a design like black swan wings. Tiny, sparkling white jewels clung to her tiara of horns, making it seem like a... well, like a tiara.

She actually looked, in a Ba'lux kind of way, pretty.

"Sorry I'm late," she said breathily. "Getting ready took longer than I expected."

Leo hopped up to pull out her chair. "It was worth the wait." A prickle of blush warmed Varlowe's cheeks, and another rose in Leo's to match it. "Welcome to the Captain's Dinner, Madame President."

"Thank you, Captain." She slid into her seat. "You're such a charmer."

Leo sat down just as a tuxedoed Verdaphyte waiter swept up to the table with a smile on his leafy face.

"Good evening to our most esteemed guests. Now that you've

all arrived, we'll get started with the appetizer." Three more Verdaphytes swooped in and set down a series of covered silver trays. "It's an authentic American dish Chef Fiero has prepared exclusively for you. His famous seven-layer nachos!"

The servers whipped the covers off their trays, revealing huge, heaving piles of starfish smothered in cheese and onions. They tumbled and slid over each other, spreading out across the table like a bucket of dumped fish. Leo lurched back in his chair and hissed under his breath. "Damn it, Fiero! I said no nachos!"

"What's wrong with nachos?" Willijer asked.

"Yeah, these look delicious," Madame Skardon agreed.

"No, Mother," the admiral said. "Your doctor has you on a strict diet, and—"

"Ah, stuff it. My doctor's a tool."

The head waiter grinned as his team backed away with a bow. "Bon appétit!"

Kersa picked up a long fork with two prongs. "Hmm. Looks surprisingly edible for American food."

She brutally stabbed a starfish. The appetizer squealed and shot a jet of blood like she'd impaled an artery.

Leo lurched back in his chair. "Ack! You killed it!"

Varlowe snickered. "Killed it. Aww. You're such a gentle soul." She grabbed her own fork and plunged it into a starfish like a serial killer slaughtering a babysitter. The creature let out a high, piercing wail as its blood pooled on her bread plate. With a twist of her fork, she pried off a leg and popped it in her mouth. Her pointed teeth made short work of the spiny flesh, and her eyes closed in ecstasy. "Mmm! Oh! That's so good."

Leo looked on in horror as the wounded delicacy struggled to escape before she could rip off another limb. Skardon stabbed at his plate, trying to get a fork into one of the scuttling appetizers. Willijer pried his screeching meal apart with a pair of dining forceps, flicking droplets of blood across the tablecloth. Madame Skardon snatched hers off the table with her bare hands and tore into it like it was a bread roll, spilling gore down her wrinkled chin.

"Stop! Stop it!" Leo squealed, reeling back in his chair. "What is the matter with you people?"

Kersa spoke through a full mouth, glancing at the others in confusion. "Why is it so upset?"

"Why am I so..." Leo clutched at his ears. "Can you not hear your dinner screaming?"

Varlowe chuckled. "Leo, they're not screaming. They're fruit."

Leo's eye twitched. "Fruit?"

"Fruit," Willijer confirmed. "That noise is their seed pods decompressing." He balled his napkin and pressed two fingers against his twitching meal. The edges of its wounds rippled with escaping gas as it seemed to cry out in a whistle of excruciating agony.

"But why do they move?"

"Nutritropism," Varlowe explained. "They're not sentient. They crawl until they find somewhere suitable to put down roots."

Leo waved at the red flecks of carnage dotting the table. "And the blood?"

"That's blood," Kersa said condescendingly. "You've never seen a fruit that bleeds?"

Varlowe pushed her maimed appetizer toward him. "You really should try it. And be quick about it, they're no good once they start clotting."

"No, I'll pass. But thank you."

"I don't understand." The smile faded from Varlowe's face. "Is something wrong? I know Kellybean vetted the menu to make sure it was all genuine American food."

"Yeah, her idea of what we eat may be a little... flawed." Leo powered through his nausea. "So that's why I worked with the chef to revamp tonight's dinner. Fiero was stubborn at first, but ultimately I think he was happy with what we came up with."

Willijer gave him a skeptical look. "Wait, are you saying *you* planned our dinner?"

Leo's hesitant smile turned real as he found his confidence. *Force to be reckoned with.*

"I sure did. As captain of the *Americano Grande*, I am proud to share a down-home meal straight from the kitchens of Eaglehaven." He nodded to three Nomit waiters hovering near the kitchen. They descended on the table, clearing away the appetizer trays with one set of arms while depositing a new set with the other. Leo spread his hands in a flourish. "I present to you, a true, authentic food of my people."

The waiters whipped the covers off the trays, revealing plates piled high with food. Leo's dining companions collectively gasped and lurched away from the table.

"What is that?" Madame Skardon choked.

"Worms!" Kersa roared. "You dare insult us with a meal of worms?"

"Worms and gonads!" Willijer gagged. "Covered in Krubb cerebral fluid!"

Leo's brows lowered in confusion. "What? No! It's spaghetti and meatballs!"

Varlowe's lips contorted around the word. "Spuh-get-tee?"

"Yes! It's a traditional noodle dish from my ancestral home world. As an honorary ambassador of Eaglehaven, I wanted to share it with all of you."

Skardon sneered as a waiter set a plate in front of him. "But it's visually appalling."

"And the smell is nauseating," Kersa added.

"And…" Willijer pointed a fork at his food. "Gonads."

"Oh stop whining," Varlowe said. "Our people have been shoving Ba'lux cuisine down the galaxy's throats for two thousand years. It won't kill you to try something new."

She put a warm hand on Leo's. For once he didn't pull away. "Thanks, Varlowe. I know this may be a little weird for all of you, but I think you'll like it once you taste it."

"Ah, what the hekk." Madame Skardon gave a limp shrug. "Nobody lives forever."

"That's the spirit," Leo said. "Well, it's the spirit adjacent."

The old woman jabbed a fork into the mass of pasta and scooped some into her mouth. All around the table, curiosity beat out skepticism as the Ba'lux gave it a try. Leo took advantage of the uneasy silence to take a mouthful of noodles himself. They tasted surprisingly accurate. Despite the chef's claims, the kitchen had not at all been stocked for "American-style" cooking. But Leo had worked with him to find acceptable substitutions using the alien ingredients on hand. This wasn't spaghetti and meatballs like his mother made, but it was the closest any non-human chef had ever come. He swallowed and gave a satisfied nod.

"Hey, that's pretty good." He grinned and looked up from his plate. "How is everyone enjoying their bwaaa!"

He recoiled at the sight of the Ba'lux trying and failing to eat spaghetti. Willijer's jagged teeth were knotted in strands of pasta, the limp ends hanging down and dribbling sauce over his chin. Kersa sputtered and coughed as she tried to pull a clump of mangled noodles out of her throat. Madame Skardon's dentures were packed full of gray meatball remains. Even Varlowe struggled to slurp down a noodle, carefully working her lips in an attempt to keep it off the blades of her teeth. It was like watching a bulldog eat a garter snake.

Leo sighed. "Maybe this was not the ideal choice of entree."

"On this we can agree." Skardon threw his napkin on his uneaten meal. "I refuse to sit here another minute while you desecrate our bodies with this abomination you call dinner. I'm leaving."

Kersa gagged and spit a wad of pasta onto her plate. "Hear hear! This is the worst meal I've ever had on a WTF ship."

"I'm sorry," Leo said. "I didn't know this would be so much trouble. I just thought we could all have a nice dinner together and I could teach you something about my people's culture."

"Nobody cares about your stupid culture!" Skardon tapped his chest. "Our customs are proudly steeped in millennia of tradition. Yours are an obscure fad, embraced only by fanatics and cultists."

He thrust an accusing finger at Varlowe. She calmly blotted her mouth, careful not to smudge her lipstick. "As usual, you're wrong. Wrong and dumb. Always assuming everything Ba'lux is superior to everything human."

Leo raised a hand. "Look, let's not fight about... wait, did you say 'human'?"

Varlowe bit her lip. "Sorry, did I pronounce it wrong?"

"No, that was right, actually. I'm just used to everyone calling us 'Americans.'"

Kersa huffed. "Because that's what your stupid race is called!"

Willijer nodded at Varlowe. "She is correct, Madame President. Haven't you read the Geiko Archives?"

"I have," Varlowe said smugly. "But apparently none of you have bothered to look at the original source material from the *NASA Star Freedom*. I dug through some of it this afternoon."

Leo blinked. "Wow, really?"

"Really. And I wish I'd done it earlier. Turns out the humans have affected our society more than any of us realize."

Madame Skardon snuffed. "Like how?"

"Like, before you were even born, the human units of measure became the unifying galactic standard, replacing dozens of other planetary metrics." Varlowe turned to Leo with the grin of a proud student brownnosing a teacher. "They were that good. Right, Leo?"

Leo frowned. "Technically our system wasn't adopted, only our words. When the unifying committee created the revised measures they named them after our units because they thought we were too dumb to learn new vocabulary."

"Ah. I did not know that." Varlowe winced. "Okay, bad example. But there's a ton of other stuff galactic-standard Quipp has borrowed from human language."

"Oh, it has not," Willijer groused.

"It kinda has, actually." Leo sat forward in his chair. "Look at idioms like 'cold turkey' and 'cool as a cucumber' and 'go bananas.' All of them came from humans."

"Right? It's crazy," Varlowe agreed. "We all say these things, but when you stop and think about it, half of those words are total gibberish. What even is a 'banana'? Nobody knows."

"I know, actually," Leo said. "It was a yellow—"

"This is nonsense," Kersa snapped. "The purity of galactic language has not been corrupted by the Americans. Speak no more of this vulgarity."

Varlowe leaned back in her chair with a mischievous grin. "You want to talk vulgarity? Fine. I can go vulgar as huck."

A collective gasp rose from the diners.

"Excuse me?" Madame Skardon hissed indignantly.

"You know, huck," Varlowe repeated calmly. "Like, 'I don't give a huck,' or 'Go huck yourself.' Or, 'Everything is abso-hucking-lutely hucked up.'"

Skardon pounded a fist on the table. "Silence! I did not come here to listen to your profanity!"

"It's not technically profanity." Varlowe grinned eagerly. "It's actually kind of a funny story. When the Geiko anthropologists studied the *Star Freedom's* databases, they came across an old literary controversy. An author named Mark Twain had written a book that repeatedly used a term the humans considered offensive. But if you review the source material, it's obvious the vulgar word wasn't 'Huck,' but was in fact—"

"I don't care!" Skardon roared, launching to his feet. "I will not sit here another minute, being fed disgusting food and forced to listen to obscene conversation."

"Hear hear!" Kersa snarled, leaping from her chair.

"Wait, I'm sorry," Leo squeaked. "Look, there's a lot more to my culture than swearing! Let's talk about music, or art, or—"

"I've heard enough," Madame Skardon croaked. "This is the most indecent, offensive Captain's Welcome Dinner I've ever attended." She wagged a finger at Leo and Varlowe. "You two should both be ashamed of yourselves."

The Skardons and Kersa stormed away as Willijer rose to his feet. "I must say I am in agreement. This has been… unpleasant." He adjusted his collar. "Good night."

He followed the others through the red-and-white tables of guests and toward the tchotchke-covered exit of WTF Friday's. Leo slumped back in his seat and raked his hands through his hair, blowing out a long breath. "Well, that could have gone better."

Varlowe giggled and waved a hand dismissively. "It went fine. If they don't want to learn the true facts of human history, it's their loss."

Leo admired her confidence. "You really read the *Star Freedom's* files?"

"Yes. Kind of." Varlowe crossed her hands in her lap. "I admit, I didn't get through much of them."

"Well, it's a lot more than most non-humans ever do." Leo fidgeted with his fork. "And I want you to know I appreciate the effort."

Patches of pink warmed Varlowe's bony cheeks. "Well, there was quite a bit I didn't understand. I could really use a subject matter expert to explain things more clearly."

Leo smiled. "I think that could be arranged. Maybe we could get together tomorrow morning."

Varlowe rested a warm hand on his arm. "Or maybe we could just stay together now."

Leo met her eyes. Before they had been the empty copper glare of an alien. Now they were the affectionate gaze of a friend. He gave her hand a pat. "Sure, why not?"

CHAPTER EIGHT

The stunning blue-and-gold orb of the planet Halii Bai rose like the morning sun outside the windows. A majestic and dazzling start to the second day of the *Americano Grande's* maiden voyage to Ensenada Vega.

Leo watched the spectacle from a private seating nook tucked at the back of a concourse cocktail bar. Since he'd arrived there, the nightlife sounds of glassware clinking and guests chatting had risen and ebbed away. A second wave of noise had taken its place, crew scurrying with vacuums and bus trays. Then it had gone silent except for the soft, ever-present drone of the Fiesta Deck's tropical background music. Now the lounge was showing signs of life again as the morning crew were beginning to arrive and prepare for the mimosa crowd.

Leo slouched in the corner of a plush sofa, uniform still on but boots off, feet up on a low table littered with glasses and tumblers. His butt ached from sitting. His eyes were bleary and his throat was dry. But, for the first time since coming onboard, he actually felt good.

"And so a lot of what happened wasn't the humans' fault, but a lot of it was," he said. "In the end, it didn't matter. The Earth had to be abandoned."

Varlowe's soft voice croaked at his side. "I didn't see any of that in the *Star Freedom's* records. None of the files had anything later than the Earth year 2014."

Leo nodded and shifted his arm. It had gone from pins-and-needles to total numbness hours ago, but it was still draped over Varlowe's narrow shoulders. At some point she had snuggled herself against his side and put her head on his chest. Her high heels were thrown on the floor and her bare feet were curled under her body. One side of Leo's uniform was damp with sweat where the furnace of her hot-running Ba'lux physiology had nested.

"Yeah, the *Star Freedom*'s library systems got pretty corrupted on the journey. To be honest, it's amazing anything on that ship worked at all by the time it was discovered. The Americans got really lucky."

"Americans?" Varlowe asked. "Don't you mean Earthlings?"

"No. Americans, actually. The United States of America was a country on the planet Earth."

"Country?"

"A geopolitical boundary on the planet's surface."

Varlowe shifted, poking Leo's chest with her horns. "I don't get it. The whole planet wasn't under a single government?"

"Nope. Different parts of our world had completely different rule, as well as different climates and cultures and languages."

"Weird. Every planet I've ever been to is totally homogenous with one single defining characteristic."

Leo nodded. "Well, humanity's lack of unity kind of bit us in the butt. When the Earth went sideways it was a free-for-all. The countries that were able built exodus ships, and they built them quickly and badly. Most didn't even make it out of the solar system. The ones that did set a course for Proxima Centauri."

"Is that a planet?"

"A star. But it had a planet that scientists thought might possibly be Earthy enough for humans to live on. The trip was supposed to take about two-hundred years, so they put the ships on autopilot and everyone went into cryosleep."

Varlowe yawned and stretched. "So what happened when they got there?"

"They didn't." Leo's words should have felt more grim, but time had worn the tragedy smooth and benign. "After all the colonists were in stasis, the different ships' computers stayed in contact. We know for sure that catastrophic failures destroyed the *Wan Hu*. And the *Saint-Exupéry*. And *Spacey McSpaceface*."

"That's terrible. How many of the sleeper ships actually survived the exodus?"

"As far as we know, only the one from America. But the *Star Freedom* suffered its share of failures too." Leo imagined the enormous ship, rocketing through the void with a hundred thousand people asleep at the wheel. "When it got to Proxima Centauri it didn't slow down or wake up the crew. It just kept right on going. For like, four thousand years."

"Until the Geiko found it drifting at the edge of the Four Prime Systems," Varlowe said, fitting the piece into her mental puzzle.

"Yep. Their anthropologists scraped the data from the ship's computers and dropped my ancestors on a refugee moon above the planet Jaynkee. And you know the rest."

Varlowe sighed. "I had no idea how little I knew about your people. Thank you for enlightening me."

"Thank you for listening. And for caring in the first place."

"You're a good teacher."

"And you're a good friend."

They sat in sleepy silence for a long moment, strangely comfortable in each other's presence. Finally, Varlowe spoke.

"Leo, do you think I'm ugly?"

He snorted at the unexpected question. "I, uh... what?"

Varlowe's body tightened. "Ugh, okay. I don't mean like, 'Do you think I'm pretty?' I mean like, 'Do you think I'm a monster?'"

"No, of course not. Why would you say that?"

"It's just... when I was looking at your records, I saw folk tales and horror movies. Monsters with sharp teeth and horns and inhuman eyes." Her voice lowered. "Monsters who look like me."

Leo shifted uncomfortably. "Humans have a long history of fearing things that are different from ourselves. But we're not like that anymore. We're much more accepting now."

"Then why do you call the rest of us 'aliens' even though you're technically the aliens here? Why don't any of you ever leave Eaglehaven and mingle with us?"

The questions settled heavily on Leo's chest.

"Okay, so maybe we're a bunch of terrified xenophobes." He shrugged. "But admitting you have a problem is the first step to recovery, right?"

Varlowe rubbed her sleepy eyes and pulled away. Leo's body tingled from the sudden absence of her weight and heat.

"So you don't think I'm ugly?"

Leo turned to her with a smile. "I promise, I don't think you're... yeeaagh!"

He scrambled back, nearly flipping over the arm of the sofa. Varlowe frowned. "I'm getting mixed messages here."

Leo gaped in horror. Varlowe's skin had gone pale and yellow under her smudged makeup. A web of blue, swollen veins corrupted her face. Sweat dripped down her long neck.

"What happened?" Leo stammered. "What's wrong?"

"Nothing's wrong. What are you—"

A violent blast of green foam choked from Varlowe's lips. She clapped a hand over her mouth and her eyes went wide. "Whoa. I don't feel so—"

Her head tipped back and she collapsed onto the sofa.

"Varlowe!" Leo sprang to his feet and shouted at the bartender. "Doctor! Call a doctor! Now!"

***

Leo ran down the Fiesta Deck concourse, barely able to keep pace with the enormous spider-beast strides of the first responder. Lieutenant Commander Marshmallow Hug Dilly Dilly pushed a medical gurney that looked eerily like a high-tech coffin—white and blue with a hinged lid of blinking bio-readouts stretching from Varlowe's shins to her collarbones. Leo trotted alongside, pale and frenzied.

"It's gonna be okay, Varlowe. Hold on," he said. Varlowe groaned and rolled her head on the pillow as Dilly pushed her through a pair of broad doors and out onto the open deck. Leo blinked in confusion. "Why are we outside? Shouldn't we be headed to the infirmary?"

Dilly shook its head. "We do not have facilities to treat this on board. Doctor has hospital on planet standing by to receive patients."

The word stuck in Leo's ear. "Wait, *patients*? As in, plural?"

Before the Dreda could answer, they plunged into a crowd of passengers in sunglasses and beach gear, all moving toward the spacedock's gangway tunnel for their shore excursion.

"One side!" a gruff voice shouted. "Move, gahdamn it!"

Commander Burlock bullied guests out of his way, clearing a path for three Dreda drones pushing more clamshell gurneys.

An older woman followed behind them, shouting into a tabloyd on her wrist. "That's right, three patients inbound from the *Americano Grande*. Prep your staff for a fun-filled day of bioflushing!"

The woman was from the aquatic planet Simishi, and was dressed in a white lab coat over her medical-blue wetsuit. Well, what the Simishi called a wetsuit, which was the opposite of what a land-dweller called a wetsuit. Her pear-shaped body was wrapped in a formfitting one-piece garment that circulated a quarter-inch of water over her skin at all times, complete with a glass bubble encasing her head like a fishbowl. Her face was green and vaguely humanoid, except for the gill slits in her cheeks and her narrow orange eyes, set in bony lumps on the sides of her head like a front-facing hammerhead shark.

She scowled at the crowd of gaping tourists and gestured at Dilly. "Yo, legs-for-days. Get rid of the lookie-loos, will ya?"

"As you wish," Dilly said.

The Dreda reared up, extending its pointed forelimbs as it scuttled toward the guests with a menacing screech.

"Please step back," its collar intoned calmly.

With a collective shriek of terror, the crowd broke up and ran for cover. Dilly and its drones fanned out, establishing a perimeter as Leo pushed Varlowe's gurney up to the Simishi. "Hey! Are you the doctor?"

"Ah! You must be the captain. Doctor Ebba Waverlee, at your service." She pinched his cheek with her gloved, webbed hand. "Hairless Gellicle?"

"No! Human."

The doctor shrugged. "Eh, I'll figure it out. Mammals all work basically the same." She noticed Varlowe's gurney. "Stars and gas, another one?"

"Another *what*? What's happening?"

Waverlee glubbed a bubble in her helmet and checked the readouts on Varlowe's bed. "Food poisoning. The worst cases I've ever seen." She waved a hand at the other gurneys. Willijer, Kersa, and Madame Skardon were in the diagnostic clamshells, looking pasty and grim. "Looks to me like they had something that didn't agree with them last night at dinner."

"At dinner?" Burlock's eye narrowed as he turned to Leo. "At the *Captain's* Dinner?"

Leo's stomach plunged. "It couldn't have been at dinner. I ate the same food and I didn't get sick."

The doctor shook her head. "Well, you would be immune to it, wouldn't you?"

"Would I?"

"You would. Whatever this is, it only affects Ba'lux physiology."

Burlock suddenly noticed the conspicuous absence among the board members. "Where's Admiral Skardon? Is he all right?"

"Admiral Skardon is fine," a voice boomed. "Because Admiral Skardon was the only one sensible enough to refuse the captain's tainted offerings."

Leo turned to see Skardon, glaring smugly in the third person. He stood tall and proud in his formal robes, showing no hint of the sickness that gripped the rest of the board.

Burlock gave him a sharp salute. "You are wise and wily as always, sir."

"And you're predictably obsequious."

"I am merely respectful of my blood debt."

The admiral glanced at the commander's mechanical arm. "I trust the implants are still serving you well."

"They are." Burlock's eye lens twitched. "I'll never be able to repay you for them, sir."

"No. You won't." Skardon waved a hand. "Go help the hospitality staff escort the guests to the dock for their shore excursion. You are dismissed."

"Yes, sir!"

Burlock turned on his heel and marched off to the gangplank tube. Waverlee tapped on the gurney readouts and shook her head. "I don't get it. All of our menu items are screened for hazardous ingredients. Somebody would have to royally screw up a recipe to get a mess like this."

Kersa moaned and coughed up a foamy belch. "It was the American! He made a special dinner to poison us!"

The doctor turned to Leo. "Did you?"

"No! I mean, yes." Leo pinched his eyes. "The first part, not the second part."

Waverlee choked a bubble. "You served a meal to the bigwigs without giving it a toxicity analysis?"

"Of course he didn't," Varlowe said. "Give him some credit. He's not an idiot."

"Well, I uh... I mean, it was kind of a last minute..." Leo clutched his hair. "It was spaghetti! Who can't eat *spaghetti*?"

"Apparently we can't," Madame Skardon hissed. "I should have known better than to eat American food."

"I did try to warn you," the admiral said dryly.

The elder opened her mouth to reply, but all that came out was a churning growl from her belly followed by a venting of gasses that made Leo's eyes water.

"I didn't mean to hurt you," he stammered. "I swear, it was an accident!"

Skardon chuckled airily. "Oh! Simply an accident." His brow lowered and his voice went dark. "The captain is responsible for the lives of everyone on this ship. Your ignorance isn't just an inconvenience, it's an active safety hazard." He leaned in, close enough for Leo to feel his hot, stale breath on his face. "You can't afford any more *accidents*, MacGavin."

Leo nodded. "There won't be any more, sir. I promise."

"He promises! Well, that makes me feel better. How about you?" Skardon turned to the gurneys. Willijer groaned from his throat. Kersa groaned from the other end in a way that almost certainly ruined her sheets. Skardon put a hand on the lid of his mother's bed. "Mother, I demand you remove this creature from command for the safety of this ship."

"No!" Leo gasped! "You can't!"

"She can," Skardon said wickedly.

"No, she can't," Willijer said. "According to the charter, she doesn't have the authority to remove a captain."

"Maybe not." Madame Skardon turned her milky gaze on Varlowe. "But I do have the authority to remove a president."

Varlowe's eyes widened. "But... the contest! You said if Leo can get the ship to Ensenada Vega in seven—"

"I wouldn't have even been at that blasted dinner if you hadn't invited me." The old woman cringed as her stomach gurgled. "This is your fault as much as his. You're both too dangerous to leave in charge."

"We're not dangerous!" Leo said. "Just extremely unlucky!"

"Madame Skardon, we had a deal!" Varlowe's bed flashed alerts as her pulse rate and adrenalin levels spiked. "You can't just call it off and make your son president!"

"Who said I was going to?" The old lady snorted. "You may have turned your back on Ba'lux tradition, but I have not. If we lose our honor, we've lost everything."

Leo blinked. "So... you're not removing Varlowe from the presidency?"

"I most certainly am."

"Ha," Skardon barked.

"But I'm not promoting my boy."

"What?" Skardon squeaked.

"I'm not going back on my word. At the end of this cruise, the winner of the contest will be president. Until then, there will be no president."

"Are you serious?" Varlowe moaned. "You can't just leave the company without a leader!"

Willijer raised a pale finger. "Actually, according to the charter—"

"Shut up, Willijer!" Varlowe and Skardon snapped.

The admiral turned to the old lady. "Mother, I implore you—"

"I don't want to hear it. You two cast your lots on whether or not the American could captain, so let him captain. From now on, the contest is all on him."

Leo felt the heat of everyone's gaze burning through his uniform. A uniform he had never wanted less than he did in this moment. He tugged his collar. "I, uh... hoo. Okay. No pressure."

"It's sink or swim time, bucko." Madame Skardon groaned and waved a hand. "And Burlock says there's a problem with the engines you need to take care of."

Panic curdled Leo's belly. This was his challenge? This was how he had to prove himself? He didn't know anything about fixing engines. Images of Eaglehaven swirling down a toilet bowl assaulted his frenzied mind.

"Right. Yes. I can totally fix engines." He muttered under his breath. "I'm sure there's like, an instruction manual or something..."

A sharp tone pinged from Doctor Waverlee's tabloyd. She glanced at it and nodded. "That's the Halii medevac crew. They're ready on the dock." She slapped a palm on a clamshell. "Let's go! Move 'em out!"

Skardon went with his mother as the medical staff began maneuvering the gurneys into the gangway tunnel to the Halii Bai Spacedock. When they were out of earshot, Varlowe reached up and took Leo's hand in her sweaty palm.

"Don't worry, Leo. You've got this."

"I don't. I so don't," he stammered. "Varlowe, I can't do this without you backing me up. I don't know what I'm doing. And Burlock will eat me alive. I'm going to screw this up and—"

Varlowe put a hot finger on his lips, silencing him. "You won't screw this up."

"How can you be so sure?"

A weak smile crossed her foamy lips. "Because if you do, we are both well and truly hucked."

CHAPTER NINE

Kellybean peered out the window of the shuttle as it came in low and slow over the colorful town of Port Ardoba. It touched down in the transit plaza and the doors opened, exhaling the stale, spacedock air and inhaling the moist, tropical atmosphere of Halii Bai.

She took a deep breath and steadied herself. There was a lot riding on this shore excursion. She had to show the admiral he was right to put his confidence in her. Everything had to go perfectly. And it would. She wouldn't let him down.

Not again.

The smooth wooden planks of the boardwalk were pleasantly warm on the pads of her paws as she strode into the bustle of the plaza. Tourists from all worlds mingled with the locals at shops and cafés. As a whole, the Halii people were tall and fit, with deep, eggplant-purple skin and symmetrical bands of glowing yellow and green bioluminescence wrapping their limbs and sketching out the features of their faces. It was as if their species had evolved specifically to attend blacklight raves.

Lined up along the edge of the plaza were a dozen brightly colored huts—one for each of the cruise lines that serviced the port. All were busy with herds of tourists from the ships currently docked in orbit. Her own herd was gathered at the Waylade Tour Fleet hut as she arrived, flashing a bright smile.

"Hello, *Americano Grande* adventurers! I'm Hospitality Chief Kellybean, and I'll be your guide on today's excursion to the tropical paradise of Halii Bai! I'm so happy you all chose to join me today! Before we get started, I just need to check you all in. Please have your optical organ ready."

The tourists pulled back sunglasses and excess mucous membranes and she quickly scanned their retinas with her tabloyd, ticking them off her guest list. They all seemed polite and enthusiastic. The perfect group for a perfect excursion. As she scanned in a Krubb family, a voice croaked behind her.

"Does this tour include a box lunch?"

"I told you it does," a second voice grumbled. "We paid for the box lunch, so it'll have a box lunch."

Kellybean's fur ruffled at the sound of the familiar, raspy voices. She turned to find a pair of elderly Geiko eyeing her suspiciously. Her mouth smiled. Her eyes did not. "Mr. and Mrs. Gwapwaffle. So lovely to see you again. I trust you're having a nice cruise so far?"

"Don't try to distract me. I know your tactics," Clermytha barked. "Is there a box lunch or not?"

"I assure you there is," Kellybean said patiently. "The service will be provided on the hovercoach ride back from the beach."

"It better be. If I don't eat I get cranky."

"Too late," Horman muttered.

"Don't worry, ma'am," Kellybean said. "I promise you're in for a good time. Let me just scan you in so we can get started."

"Scan me in?" Clermytha snorted. "But we're Platinum Elite!"

The old blue lizards once again raised their arms and swiped up their glittering holographic identicards. Kellybean rolled her eyes. "And we do value your loyalty," she said by rote. "But it's important we scan everyone for your safety and security."

"Bah! I know you're just checking our tickets," Horman said. "Back in my day we had a thing called trust. If you said you belonged on an excursion, folks believed you!"

"The whole industry is going downhill." Clermytha turned to Kellybean. "When we took our first cruise on the *WTF Sophisticate* there was still some glamour in it. Nowadays they let species into the formal dining room who don't even have necks, let alone neckties. And another thing..."

Kellybean's tail twitched impatiently, but she continued smiling as Clermytha vented a backlog of grievances against WTF that predated her birth. She knew the woman didn't actually want someone to fix these problems. She just wanted someone to listen to them and acknowledge her anger. Hospitality 101. The old woman's voice became a buzzing drone as Kellybean sighed and quietly weathered the word storm.

She hoped her tour would go better than her muster drill.

***

The Fount of Doboo sat on a tranquil, grassy hill on the edge of Port Ardoba. Its ancient, cut-gemstone statue depicted the supreme deity of the Halii people with arms outstretched, a natural spring flowing water from his raised hands as a representation of his divine power to cleanse the world of evil. The imposing devotional and its crystal reflection pool were the most sacred site on the planet.

Jassi slouched against the statue with her gnarled feet soaking in the pool. She wore nothing but a short skirt, pink bikini top, and oversized sunglasses as she lay with her leafy arms and legs sprawled spread-eagle, basking in the sun. She groaned and writhed languidly against the warm stone.

Hax looked on with worry in his digital eyes. "Not to be an ol' fuddy duddy, but I don't think you should be doing that here."

Stobber slouched in the shade of a nearby tree, obnoxiously slurping and smacking his fleshy lips as he took bites off a melty yellow disc in his hand. "Doin' what? Eating?"

"Not eating." Hax pointed a plastic finger. "What Jassi's doing."

Jassi peered over her shades. "I'm also eating."

"Are you?" Hax asked, eyeing her exposed body.

"It's called photosynthesis. Look it up, ya ignorant tape deck."

Stobber leered at her. "Not gonna lie, you flashin' yer coconuts at the sun is better than eating compressed fertilizer bars. That shix is disgusting."

"You're one to talk about disgusting food." Jassi tipped her head toward his sweaty snack. "The huck are you even eating?"

"It's gouda," Stobber said defensively. "I stole it from the ship."

"You stole an entire wheel of cheese?" Hax asked. "Where did you find that?"

"Kitchen. I broke in with fake credentials." Stobber proudly tapped the tabloyd wrapped around one of his smaller wrists. "Hacked the access routines myself."

Jassi leaned on her elbow. "You're full of shix. You couldn't hack your way into an open manhole."

"Huck you. My code is smooth as liquid nipples and you know it."

Hax rolled between them. "Please don't fight. We're supposed to be having fun!" His eyes smiled. "Why don't we go take the sightseeing tour?"

Stobber gnawed off another hunk of cheese. "I ain't takin' no stupid tour."

"Sounds like the worst idea ever," Jassi agreed.

"Come on. It'll be great! Look." Hax pushed the play button in his chest and his datacassette rolled, replacing his eyes with a slick promotional video. *"Experience the best of Halii Bai with this all-inclusive WTF excursion! Start with a scenic tour of historic Port*

Ardoba, followed by a trip to a beautiful volcanic beach in our exclusive climate-controlled hovercoach. Authentic sights and sounds await as you—"

Stobber poked Hax's stop button. "I've heard enough."

The robot's eyes reappeared and blinked. "So you're going?"

"No hucking way I'm going. Why don't you go by yourself? It'll get you out of my arze for a while."

"But I'll be lonely!" Hax turned to Jassi. "Will you come with me?"

Jassi patted her sun-baked belly and splashed her rooted feet in the sacred fountain. "Bro, I'm bingeing so hard on sunlight and water I'm about to go into a food coma here." She shrugged. "Besides, that shix ain't free. We don't have the scratch to afford one of those fancy cruise trips."

"Aww." Hax frowned and looked down the hill toward the travel plaza below. He spotted the WTF excursions hut and cocked his head. "Hey, why don't we ask the nice kitty if we can just tag along?"

Jassi perked up. "Kitty?"

"Kitty!" Hax pointed. "It looks like that lady from the lifeboat drill is leading the tour."

The lounging plant jerked upright and lifted her sunglasses, peering down at the plaza. She immediately picked out Kellybean's silky white fur in the crowd. Her eyes lingered on the Gellicle's broad hips and petite frame, dressed for a casual adventure in khaki shorts and a formfitting WTF polo.

"I'm in," Jassi said.

"Yay! Together forever!" Hax cheered. He turned to Stobber. "Are you sure you won't join us?"

The Nomit stuffed the last clod of cheese in his mouth and sneered. "Join you in what? You ain't going on that tour unless they accept payment in ladyboners."

"Pfft, whatever." Jassi swung her legs out of the fountain and stuffed her wet feet into her boots. "You're just wussing out because you know you can't hack the ticketing system to get us on the list."

"I could if I wanted to."

Jassi nodded. "That's code for 'I can't and I suck Krubb nuts.'"

"Aww, that's too bad." Hax pouted. "I wish Stobber was as good at hacking software as you are at hacking hardware."

"I know, right?"

"The huck you turds talking about?" Stobber said. "I'm twice as good."

Jassi shrugged. "If you were, you'd get us tickets instead of wussing out like a little bish."

"Like the littlest bish in the galaxy," Hax agreed.

The Nomit crossed his arms. "I'm not an idiot. I see what you two are doing here."

Hax cocked his head. "Is it working? Or do we have to berate you for another cycle?"

Stobber ran a meaty hand down his face. "Gahdamn it." He unfolded his tabloyd and swiped at the screen. "What do you shixheads want in your box lunches?"

***

"And don't get me started on the towel animals on the beds," Clermytha whined. "We used to get exotic things like centipugs! It takes real skill to fold a towel into all those little legs! But now you're lucky if you get a triger. Three legs! It's a disgrace."

Kellybean blinked and snorted. She suddenly realized she had no idea how long she'd been listening to the old lizard rant.

"I sincerely apologize for..." She waved a paw. "Whatever it is that's bothering you. I promise, I'll have my staff do everything they can to make this cruise exceed your expectations."

Clermytha stuck up her snout and harrumphed. "I'll believe it when I see it."

Kellybean gave up and turned to the rest of the group, still patiently waiting to get underway. "Okay, now that everyone's all checked in, let's begin our tour, shall we? First, just a couple of safety rules. I'm going to ask everyone to choose a buddy, that way—"

"Yay for buddies!" a digital voice cheered. "I brought two!"

The hospitality chief turned to see an excited robot rolling up to the excursion hut, followed by a sweaty Nomit and a Verdaphyte girl with...

Kellybean's brain locked up at the sight of her. It was the same girl from the muster drill, but... wow. On the ship she'd looked limp and scraggly, but here, in the bright sun, she was lush and green and absolutely aglow. And significantly more naked. Kellybean's tail fluffed as she pinched her eyes closed and shook her head. She knew better. That girl was trouble. And so were her friends. She had to get rid of them before they ruined everything.

"I do apologize, but we won't be able to take on any last-minute guests," she said with a tight smile. "This excursion is for pre-paid ticketholders only."

"That shouldn't be a problem." Jassi raked back her pink scalp foliage. "We've got tickets."

"No, you don't. I just checked everyone in. You weren't on my list."

"Check again," Stobber said. "People make mistakes."

"I don't."

"Check anyway," Stobber insisted.

Kellybean glowered and pulled up her guest roster to prove them wrong. The list updated and her breath caught.

"That's... odd." Her yellow eyes flashed as she glanced at the smirking Nomit. "It appears you three *are* on my list. In fact, you're suddenly on *all* of my excursion tours for the rest of the cruise. As special guests of the captain, no less."

Stobber grinned. "Oh yeah, me and him go way back. He's always ready to do me a solid." He looked to Jassi with a satisfied grin. "You must really appreciate having a bandmate who's so connected."

"He's gonna be connected to life support if he doesn't shut up," Jassi muttered. She turned to Kellybean. "Don't mind him. His mother huffed a lot of sealant when she was pregnant."

Horman scowled. "Is this a blasted sightseeing tour or a coffee klatsch? I paid to see the planet, not to stand in the travel plaza all day arguing about tickets!"

"Yes, of course." Kellybean cleared her throat and reset her tour-guide smile as she addressed the group. "Welcome, one and all, to WTF's exclusive Halii Bai shore excursion. We're going to have a lot of fun today!"

As she said the words, she silently prayed they'd be true.

CHAPTER TEN

Leo walked at a staccato pace down the gunmetal gray corridors toward the primary machine room, trying to stay a step ahead of Burlock while at the same time letting him lead the way through the unfamiliar labyrinth. The rest of the bridge crew followed behind. Comfit, Quartermaster, and Swooch may not have been the best team Leo could have assembled to troubleshoot the faulty engines, but they were currently the only people on board willing to take orders from him.

He wiped the sweat off his upper lip for what felt like the thousandth time. His heart hammered so hard he was sure the others could see it through his uniform. With Varlowe in the hospital down on the planet, the fate of the cruise was entirely on Leo's shoulders. Not to mention the fate of her job and of his entire home world. And he had no idea what he was doing. None. His only chance was to keep his chin up, project confidence, and bluff his way through the rest of the voyage.

Burlock swiped his tabloyd at the machine room's lockpad, opening the door with a deck-shaking rumble. Inside, a few engineers sat slouched at their consoles, gazing at their screens with heavily lidded eyes. They were shelled slugs with long, skinny arms and legs, and round, sloth-like faces. Leo recognized them as sedentary beings from the planet Lethargot, pronounced with a silent T like French snails.

Leo self-consciously swaggered into the room, followed by his bridge crew. They all gaped at the electronic carnage before them. The console Praz had set on fire during Leo's last visit was still charred and blackened, with a crusty dribble of dried firefoam clinging to its sides. Since then, two wall panels had joined it in similar states of disrepair. But at least the rogue bot was no longer repeatedly smashing into the doors. It was now strewn across the deck in pieces. The largest of which still had a long-handled ax buried in it, which raised a lot of questions Leo didn't want answered.

Comfit's face wrinkled in disgust. "This place is a dump."

Quartermaster blew out a long breath and shrugged. "Well, what do you expect on a ship run by an American?"

"Wow, I'm right here," Leo grumbled.

A Ba'lux head jerked up from under a console, cheeks smudged with grease. Praz Kerplunkt launched to his feet and tripped over a toolbox, spilling its contents across the floor. "What are you people doing here? You don't belong here! This is my room!"

"And I love what you've done with it," Leo said diplomatically. "But there seems to be a problem with the engines, so we came down to take a look."

Praz guiltily spread his arms, trying to hide the entire machine room as if it were an unwrapped birthday present. "This is my area! I'm the boss here! I'm in charge and I've got everything under control!"

As if to offer a counterargument, the cratered, bot-smashed door fell out of its track and crashed to the deck. Comfit looked to it, then to Praz.

"Do you, though?" She gestured to the sleepy slug techs at the consoles. "You don't seem to have a lot of backup here."

"They're Lethargots," Praz said. "They're nocturnal. They work better at night."

"Then why don't they work the night shift?" Leo asked.

"Because they don't get along with the Solarjellies."

"Your night crew is Solarjellies?" Comfit raised a brow. "As in, the Solarjellies that literally lose cellular cohesion at night and have to sleep in buckets?"

"Don't you criticize my scheduling!" Praz waved his arms at the room. "Can't you see how busy I am here? It's like I have to do everything myself!"

Leo rolled his eyes. "All right, are we going to fix the engines or what?"

"We are." Burlock stepped in front of him. "We'll need to run some high-level diagnostics and work from there."

"Right." Leo maneuvered back in front of Burlock. "That's totally what I was going to say." He gestured at two consoles. "Get to work with the tappy tappy and the beepy beepy."

Comfit and Quartermaster shared a pained glance, but did as they were told.

"I can confirm the engines aren't damaged," Quartermaster reported. "Their structural integrity is nominal, but something is putting an unusually high power drain on them."

Burlock turned to Comfit. "Do we know what that is?"

"No, sir. Whatever is leeching energy is crippling internal sensors. It'll take the system days to isolate the problem."

"That's gonna make driving a real challenge," Swooch noted.

Burlock nodded. "We'll have to do a manual inspection."

"I know that! I was just going to say that!" Praz turned to his crew. "Up and at 'em, boys! Get out your manuals and start inspecting them!"

The Lethargots didn't look at him. Some were snoring. Burlock shook his head. "We'll handle the inspection ourselves."

"Our tabloyds are equipped with a diagnostic scanning app," Quartermaster said. "We just need to sync them to the latest system schematic and we can start a panel-by-panel analysis."

"Ugh, that'll take forever," Swooch grumbled.

"It will. So let's quit moaning and get started." Burlock pulled his sleeve back from his tabloyd. "Sync up."

He flicked a finger on the device around his wrist, activating a blinking blue light. Praz and the bridge crew swiped on their bands and more blue lights appeared. Leo swiped on his and a cartoon heart sprang from his arm.

"Call Mommy!" his tabloyd shouted.

"Gah!"

Leo swatted the kiddie app away as the other four tabloyds simultaneously intoned *"System schematic synced."*

"Wait, hold on," Leo said. "My thing didn't do the thing..."

He poked at his band. The cruise itinerary appeared, advancing through activities with each increasingly frantic swipe. Swooch gave him a pat on the shoulder. "Dude, you know you can sit this one out if you want."

"Because I'm the captain?"

"Yeah, let's go with that," Quartermaster said.

"You can help by not helping," Comfit added.

"Enough chatter," Burlock barked. "Everybody split up and start scanning."

The crew acknowledged the order with a sharp "Yes, sir" and started to step away.

"Wait!" Leo cried. "I give the orders around here!"

Comfit sighed. "And what are your orders, sir?"

Everyone looked to Leo, awaiting his command.

"Uh, right," he muttered. "Everyone split up and start scanning."

"Don't tell me what to do, American!" Praz shouted.

The rest of the crew didn't say it, but it was etched in their expressions as they went to work. For some it was defiant, for others pitying, but the sentiment was ubiquitous. Leo swatted the floating itinerary off his arm and held his chin high as he marched through the broken-off door into the dynamo chamber. He needed to put some space between himself and his crew. Partially because he was angry at them, but mostly so they wouldn't see his imminent emotional collapse and ugly cry.

His boots clanged against the metal steps as he raced up a spiral staircase and onto a high catwalk. The magnetosphere dynamo screamed its ghostly wail below as it spun at preposterous speeds, lashed by enormous pylons of pure energy. It was like a force of nature created by mortal hands, but Leo was too overwhelmed by his own drama to be impressed. He leaned on the rail, gazing into the sphere as Madame Skardon's words echoed in his mind.

"It's sink or swim time, bucko."

Leo didn't know how to swim. He didn't know how to do anything. He was in over his head and everyone knew it. But he couldn't give up. He also couldn't fix an engine. But he had to do *something*.

He trudged down the catwalk, eyeing a dizzying array of plumbing and wiring, dotted with gauges and meters and little sparking things and windows into chambers of percolating goo in various colors. He had no idea what any of it did. How was he supposed to know if it was broken? Everything seemed to be in place and—

His toe cracked against something hard, drawing a pained hiss through his teeth. He staggered back and looked down to see a waist-high metal cylinder standing on its rounded edge, blocking the catwalk. A pulsing yellow light glowed from rings etched around its circumference.

"Hmm. Weird."

He crouched to get a better look. A circular hatch in the disc's side was open with a thick mass of cables pulled taut from its innards and clamped to a power junction on the wall. A small readout on top of the cylinder flashed a repeating error.

Surge detected. Core corrupted. 15% efficiency.

Leo's first instinct was to call the others. There's no way Praz would know what to do, but maybe one of the bridge crew could deal with this. But as soon as he had the thought he shoved it aside. The blinking message was crystal clear, even to him. This thing had something to do with power. And it was broken.

And he found it.

A manic giggle of joy and relief escaped his lips. He found it! He found the problem with the engines! All by himself! It was sink or swim time, and he was Michael hekking Phelps.

Leo was aglow with self-confidence as he grasped the release latch on the wiring clamp and immediately lurched back with a hiss and a whiff of singed meat.

"Hot!" he gasped, shaking his scorched fingers. "Hot hot!"

He took off his captain's cap and put it over his hand, then gave the release a sharp poke with his shielded digits. The heat seared the white fabric, but the latch popped open and the wiring harness retracted into the cylinder like the end of a tape measure snapping into place. In the same instant, its illuminated rings went dark and the lights in the dynamo chamber brightened. Before Leo's eyes had adjusted to the change, the force of the retracting cables sent the disc rolling toward the edge of the catwalk.

"Ack! Stop!" He made a grab for it, slapping a hand on both flat sides as it rolled under the railing and teetered over the edge. Pain sizzled through his palms. "Ow! Right! Hot!"

Reflex yanked back his arms, and the cylinder plunged from the catwalk into the roiling ball of the magnetosphere dynamo below. Leo watched it splash down in the superheated plasma shell with a heavy ripple.

"Well, that could have gone better."

Everything in his body tightened as he pulled a breath and waited for the inevitable explosion, implosion, meltdown, or whatever lethal reaction was about to transpire. But the magnetosphere core swallowed the object without so much as a sizzle or jet of black smoke. It was just gone.

"Oh my gosh!" a female voice gasped. "What did you do?"

Leo whirled around to see Comfit approaching from one side of the catwalk with Quartermaster behind her. He tried to back away, but Burlock and Swooch rushed up from the other side.

"I, uh... okay, listen," Leo stammered. "I can explain..."

"I can't believe this." Comfit tapped at her unfolded tabloyd, her mouth hanging open. "The glitch is gone!"

"Look, I didn't mean... come again?"

"I was just trying to brute-force a system sweep and suddenly everything came online at once. Full power to the engines and all systems. As soon as internal monitoring was up I could isolate the problem to this sector, but only the residual traces of it."

Quartermaster checked the schematics on his device. "I can confirm that. The abnormal power drain was coming from this junction, but now it appears to be working normally."

Swooch smiled and slouched against the rail. "Daaang, Captain Fix-it. The rest of us were just derping around and you went right at it. How did you know to come up here?"

Leo blinked. "Oh, uh. You know..." *I ran away from you guys before I could have a breakdown.* "Just instinct, I guess."

"It looks like there was a malfunction in the main cross-lateral power junction." Quartermaster's mouth stalks wheezed in disbelief. "These components are so complex, it would have taken me a month to isolate the problem, let alone troubleshoot it." He turned to Leo. "Seriously, how did you do this?"

I have absolutely no idea, Leo thought.

"I just tried some... normal techie stuff. No big deal."

"It is, actually," Quartermaster said. "There's enough voltage here to spontaneously ignite organic material if handled improperly."

"Really?" Leo fingered the scorch mark on his hat. "I mean, yes. I knew that. Of course I knew that." He noticed skepticism creeping into the Screetoro's three eyes and forced himself to stand tall. "But I'm willing to take personal risks for the good of my ship and its crew."

Comfit's expression went soft. Her voice was an awestruck whisper. "So brave!"

Leo puffed out his chest. "I guess it was, wasn't it?"

Burlock just stood there, glaring, arms crossed and mechanical eye twitching. "Well the important thing is that it's fixed. I'll report in to Admiral Skardon."

"Yes, you do that." A broad smile spread on Leo's face. "And be sure to mention exactly who fixed it, and how quickly and expertly the job was done."

The commander's teeth ground. "My report will state the facts accurately, *sir*."

"Well, that's just five gallons of awesomesauce." Leo put on his burned captain's hat and swaggered in a slow circle, orbiting his first officer. "I guess now you can see that I'm pretty valuable around here, am I right?"

"I have to admit, I'm impressed," Quartermaster said.

"More than impressed, honestly," Comfit added breathily.

"You're the shizzle with the technizzle," Swooch drawled.

Leo turned to Burlock. Burlock said nothing.

"I'm sorry, do you have anything to add?" Leo asked.

Tensed servos whined in Burlock's arm as his whole body trembled. "I do not."

Leo smiled and waved him off. "Okay then, you're dismissed. I'll see you up on the bridge. Don't keep my seat warm."

Burlock stomped off, his face boiling a murderous red, followed by the rest of the crew. Leo leaned on the rail, smiling ear to ear and basking in the glow of his accidental triumph. But despite the swell of victory, he couldn't help but wonder exactly what that thing was that he had disconnected and subsequently destroyed. He looked over the railing at the thrashing plasma storm of the magnetosphere dynamo.

Eh, it was probably nothing.

CHAPTER ELEVEN

Kellybean stood alone in the shade of the private WTF cabana overlooking the clear water of the Haliiloa Sea. She'd finished ushering her excursion group through their tour of historic Port Ardoba, herded them onto the hovercoach, and set them loose on the beach. In two hours she'd load them back onto the coach, feed them their box lunches, and escort their happy, sun-weary bodies back to the ship. In the meantime, all she had to do was breathe the fresh, seaside air and relax.

She leaned on the rail and gazed over the black dunes nestled in the cone of the extinct volcano. Her family of Krubb tourists played in the crystalline surf, scuttling like trash-can-shaped crabs on their tiny legs. A Screetoro couple on their honeymoon rubbed sunblock on each other's mouth-stalks for significantly longer than necessary. But she barely registered them. They were all harmless.

She was keeping an eye on the troublemakers.

Jassi, Stobber, and Hax had found a set of broad paddles and were batting a ball back and forth. Stobber lobbed it to Hax. Hax volleyed it to Jassi. Jassi hit it as hard as she could into Stobber's face. He shouted and cursed at her before picking up the ball and passing it back to Hax. Hax paddled it to Jassi. Jassi spiked it into Stobber's face again. He roared and charged her like an enraged rhino. She raised her paddle in both hands, ready for a brawl. Hax rushed between them, arms out, always the peacekeeper.

Kellybean rolled her eyes. At least if they were fighting each other they weren't bothering anyone else. She still couldn't believe someone on her staff had actually hired Murderblossom to perform on this cruise. Hopefully their music was better than their interpersonal skills. That girl Jassi was the rudest, most disrespectful plant she'd ever met. Why were the hot ones always such jerks? She shook her head. It didn't matter, she had a job to do, and she wasn't going to be distracted by—

"This is an outrage!" a brittle voice roared. "I paid good money for this trip!"

Kellybean recognized both the voice and the complaint. Not far from her cabana, Horman Gwapwaffle stood on a floating dock next to a small passenger boat, jabbing his finger at a muscled Halii man below, who was wading waist-deep in the shallows. Clermytha was by her husband's side, arms crossed and shaking her head, tag-teaming his gripes. Kellybean sighed and muttered to herself. "Time to get back on the clock."

She hurried down to the waterfront to find a collection of rusty tools spread on the dock. The Halii had the boat's engine compartment open and was pointing into it, trying to explain something to the Geiko in his native language.

"Hello, friends," Kellybean said calmly. "Is everything all right over here?"

"Hardly!" Horman snapped. "This con man won't take us on our sightseeing cruise. We bought tickets! I have them right here!"

He swiped his tabloyd, producing a WTF excursion ticket for a private sea cruise. The most expensive add-on available for this port, paid for entirely in frequent cruiser points. Kellybean turned to the local in the water. "What seems to be the trouble, sir?"

"Habbo shinda molt bolt," he replied.

Kellybean cringed and said the only phrase she knew in Halii. "Zimba nok Quipp?"

The man gave a hesitant nod and pointed at the engine. "Um... Boat not. Go. Engine is..." He scratched his head with a tarnished wrench, searching for the foreign word. "Hucked."

"I see." Kellybean turned to the two Geiko. "I'm sorry, folks. It looks like our tour partner here is having some technical difficulties. But don't worry. I'll give you a full refund, plus additional WTF travel vouchers for your inconvenience."

"I don't want vouchers!" Clermytha howled. "I want to go on a sightseeing cruise!"

"What kind of a shoddy operation are you running here, missy?" Horman turned on Kellybean, wielding his complaining finger. "I'm reporting you to the management! Unlike Gellicles, the Ba'lux care about customer service!"

Kellybean's ears flicked back, hot with rage. Her smile wavered at the edges into a toothy sneer. "Again, I do apologize, and I'll be happy to do whatever it takes to make you—"

"Gah damn, are these two motherhuckers up your arze again? Give it a rest, ya wrinkly prune-munchers."

Kellybean gasped. The Gwapwaffles gasped. The Halii blinked, unfamiliar with most of the words. Everyone looked over Kellybean's shoulder at a Verdaphyte girl, slouching with her hands on her hips.

Clermytha's jaw trembled with outrage. "How dare you speak to us that way, you... bark-skinned trollop!"

Horman hitched up his pants and fumed. "I've got half a mind to take a belt to you, girly!"

Jassi snorted and cracked her knuckles. "Try it and see how that works out for you, gramps."

Kellybean sprang between them and hissed at Jassi. "Get out of here! I've got this under control!"

"Do you? It looks like you need some backup."

"I do not," Kellybean said firmly. "I was just going to give the Gwapwaffles a refund, plus travel vouchers, and also a free VIP dinner in the ship's most exclusive restaurant. Doesn't that sound great?"

"Bah!" Horman growled. "We want our gall dang boat tour!"

The Halii nodded. "Yes. Boat is hucked."

Kellybean winced. "So you've said." She turned to the couple with a tense smile. "I'm sorry, there's nothing I can do here. The boat is having mechanical trouble."

Jassi snorted a chuckle. "Wait, is that what all this bishing and moaning is about? Pfft. Step aside, moth balls."

She shoved her way past the tourists and stepped off the edge of the dock, plunging into the sea, boots and all. Water glistened off the arch of her lithe, verdant body as she surfaced and flicked her wet pink scalp leaves back over her head. The heat of Kellybean's frustration spiraled with the heat of her libido in a way that only made her angrier.

Gah damn this rude, stupidly hot girl!

Jassi waded to the boat and scratched at her exposed belly. "Lemme take a look at this." The Halii moved aside as she peered at the engine. "Well, shix. There's your problem right there. The torsional pivot spring is locked up."

Kellybean blinked. "You know how to fix boats?"

Jassi grabbed a huge pipe wrench from the dock. "I spent my seedling years in a spaceport repair shop. Machines are all basically the same when you get down to it." She slotted the long wrench into the engine, wrapped both hands around it, and pulled. Supple, vine-like muscles flexed down her lean arms and through her exposed torso. Kellybean's whiskers twitched hungrily. With a creaking of rusted metal on metal, the wrench moved. Belts jerked. Pistons trembled. Then, all at once, the engine roared to life. Jassi yanked the enormous wrench free and tipped it over her shoulder as the aquajets churned the water to foam around her sodden skirt.

"You fixed it!" Kellybean said. "That's amazing!"

Jassi shrugged. "Meh."

The Halii smiled and closed the compartment. "Thanks you for removing huck from engine." He climbed onto the dock and grinned at the two Geiko. "Tour is ready for much boat fun!"

"Well, it's about time." Horman adjusted his fishing hat. "You see? The squeaky wheel gets the grease."

Clermytha turned to Kellybean. "I trust our inconvenience still entitles us to all the perks you've promised."

"Yes, of course," Kellybean said wearily. "As always, your satisfaction is my number one priority."

The old woman patted Kellybean's arm. "That's a good kitty. Maybe I won't report you to the Ba'lux after all."

With that, the Halii guide escorted the Gwapwaffles onto his boat and puttered away from the dock. Jassi hauled herself out of the water and shook herself off. Kellybean averted her eyes and bit her lip. "Hey, thanks a lot. I really appreciate the help."

Jassi swept her wet leaves off her face. "Good. Because I was trying to make you all appreciative and indebted to me." She grinned and thumbed toward the boardwalk bars. "What do you say we go grab a drink and talk about how you can express your gratitude."

Kellybean smirked and shook her head. "I don't drink on duty. Also, I'm not allowed to fraternize with the guests."

"I'm not a guest," Jassi noted. "I'm an entertainer. Totally different."

It was a gray area, Kellybean couldn't deny that.

Jassi slapped her own wet backside. "And you know you want to knock a few leaves offa this."

Kellybean couldn't deny that either. But she was here for a reason. She couldn't let Admiral Skardon down. "I'm senior hospitality staff. You're technically my subordinate. It would be inappropriate." She straightened her back and smoothed out her uniform polo. "So, thanks again for fixing the boat, but I've got to get back to work."

"Come on, one drink." Jassi moaned. "I won't tell if you don't."

"I have to work," Kellybean repeated. She pointed a claw at Jassi. "Stay out of trouble."

With that she turned and darted away before she could change her mind.

***

The sun dipped low over the rim of the volcanic wall as Kellybean waited on the dock. She checked the time on her tabloyd. Twenty minutes until the hovercoach was scheduled to depart. The shore excursion had been a little rocky in parts, but overall she was happy with her performance. Now all that was left to do was round up the guests, get them on the coach back to Port Ardoba, then herd them down gift-shop alley for some last-minute shopping. She sighed happily. From here, the rest of the excursion was an easy downhill slope back to the ship.

A gurgling, puttering sound got her attention, and she straightened up and smiled as the tour boat returned to the dock. The Halii guide helped Horman and Clermytha out of the craft and onto dry land. Kellybean hardly recognized them. There was something weird about their faces.

They were smiling.

"Hello, and welcome back!" she said. "It looks like you two had a good time."

"Oh, we did." Clermytha patted the Halii's firm bicep. "This foreign boy talks gibberish, but he knows where the pretty scenery is."

"Thanks you much great," the guide said.

Horman snorted in agreement. "We've taken this tour twice before, and I gotta say, this was a vast improvement." He thumbed at the boat. "The last time the engine was too loud to hear yourself think. This time it was smooth like butter."

"Your little green friend needs her mouth washed out with soap," Clermytha said, "but she did a great job fixing this tub."

Kellybean raised a brow. "Believe me, I'm as surprised as you are." She waved a paw at the gleaming chromasteel hovercoach parked next to the boardwalk. "Go ahead and make your way to the bus. We'll be departing just as soon as I round everyone up."

"Sounds good," Horman said. "I'm ready to get back to the ship for a nap."

"And I'm ready for my box lunch," Clermytha said. "We get them on the ride back?"

"You most certainly do," Kellybean assured her for what felt like the ninetieth time.

"That's wonderful." Clermytha smiled. "I can't wait."

The two Geiko headed off toward the coach and Kellybean sauntered across the beach, locating her guests and reminding them of their imminent departure. There was really only one group she was looking for. Murderblossom was missing. Which meant Murderblossom was causing trouble.

Panic wrenched her gut as a child's scream cut the air. Then another. Kellybean's ears flicked up. It was coming from behind a tall black dune.

"Oh crap. Oh no. What are those jerks doing now?"

She dashed to the top of the dune. On the other side was a broad gash in the planet's surface, venting a geyser of warm gas from the long-dormant volcano. Like the other geothermal vents in the area, it had been fenced off for safety. But the largely symbolic barrier did nothing to keep out a half-dozen Halii children, none of them more than ten years old.

Kellybean watched in horror as one of the purple kids ran full speed toward the plume of volcanic gas and dove in headfirst.

"No!" she screamed.

Her paws slipped and she tumbled down the sand. She dashed over and hopped the fence, but she was too slow. Before Kellybean could stop her, another Halii child flung herself into the vent.

"Stop!" Kellybean shrieked. "What are you—"

The first kid fired from the pit like a rocket, sailing straight up with a joyful screech. The second kid was right behind, arms and legs spread as she launched upward on a warm gust. Right behind her was a clunky plastic robot.

"Wheeeeee!" Hax cheered. "Look at me! I'm Superbot!"

Kellybean gaped as another body was flung to the sky. Jassi threw out her limbs and came to a hovering stop ten feet above the ground. Her skirt and scalp leaves fluttered violently as she hung there, arms and legs splayed against the updraft like a stationary skydiver.

"Oh, hey kitty," she called out. "Wanna get high with us?"

"What in the worlds is going on here?" Kellybean shouted. "Did you tell these kids to jump into a volcanic vent?"

"Pfft, no. They told us to."

A tiny girl put a hand on Kellybean's hip. "Gas jumping! You little! Okay fun!"

Kellybean looked from the girl back to the bodies shooting out of the hole in the ground. Hax fumbled awkwardly, dipping and lurching like a malfunctioning elevator, but the children flew like birds, maneuvering their arms and legs to sail in swirling formations through the gas. In all her trips to this beach, Kellybean had never seen anyone do this. The grace and agility on display was mesmerizing.

Jassi rolled in the air. "The kid says you're cool. Jump in!"

"I... I couldn't," Kellybean said. "In fact, you guys need to come down. It's almost time to go."

"Aww, c'mon," Jassi pleaded. "How often do you get a chance to fly with a bunch of freaky purple kids?" She reached out a hand. "I won't let anything bad happen to ya. Trust me."

Kellybean's lips pursed. In her experience, people who said "trust me" were not to be trusted under any circumstances. But there was something in Jassi's eyes that made Kellybean want to jump in and fly with her. The way her skirt flapped scandalously around her green thighs also didn't hurt.

"Okay," Kellybean conceded. "But just for a minute."

Another kid raced past her and dove into the hole, plunging into the pit before firing back out. It looked easy enough. Kellybean took a steadying breath, ran toward the cliff, and grabbed her knees as she hurled herself into the gassy abyss.

She did not soar. She did not fly. She did not even float. She dropped like a stone into the dark, warm crevice. The pink gas stung her eyes, but she could see dense twists of spiny, berry-covered brambles clinging to the sloped walls as she plummeted into the bottomless chasm. She opened her mouth to scream, but before she could make a sound, two woody hands grabbed hers and heaved her arms out to her sides. Her vision blurred as she was thrown upward, spinning around and around until she burst into the light. She blinked and got her bearings, finding herself serenely floating high above the pit, her paws in Jassi's hands.

"How... What..." Kellybean stammered. "What happened?!"

Jassi smiled as the two of them drifted, slowly pivoting around each other.

"You can't keep your limbs tucked in or you drop," Jassi said. "I didn't know you were gonna cannonball. Bold choice."

Kellybean laughed, despite herself. "Sorry, I don't really know how to dive. Gellicles don't swim."

"This is way better than swimming anyway."

The wind rippled through Kellybean's fur in a full-body massage of exquisite weightlessness. Her worries and stresses blew away on the warm gas, leaving her in steamy serenity. The moment was like a blissful dream. Nothing seemed real except for the rough, barky hands in her paws. She squeezed them tight.

"It is pretty good," she admitted.

Jassi grinned. "You glad you trusted me?"

Kellybean gazed into her eyes. "It's not the worst choice I've ever—"

"No! No!" a child shouted. "You big! No okay!"

"Ah shut yer hole, ya filthy little grape."

Down below, Stobber wrestled his massive body over the low fence. The children crowded around him, trying in vain to push him back as he plodded toward the vent on his elephantine legs.

"No okay! No okay!" they repeated. "You big!"

Hax spun across the fissure and shouted down to Stobber. "I think they're trying to say that you exceed the maximum weight for this attraction."

"Whatever," Stobber said. "I'm not just gonna hang back and let you shixheads have all the fun."

With a bellowing cry, the Nomit ran full-speed toward the pit. Three children grabbed onto his arms, clinging like anchors in a desperate attempt to stop him. But he plowed on like an idiotic juggernaut. He ran off the edge of the cliff and plunged straight down. A second later, the three kids fired out of the hole. Stobber did not.

"Stobber!" Hax cried.

"You hucking imbecile!" Jassi added.

The gas did not even pretend it could lift the Nomit's massive weight. He screamed as he hit the chasm's sloped side and flipped end-over-end. Prickly briar vines ripped from the walls and wrapped his body, slowing his descent until he smashed down on an outcropping of rock.

"Oh my gosh!" Hax squeaked. "Are you okay, buddy?"

"I'm fine. I'm not a wussy." Stobber thrashed against the brambles, tearing his clothes and knocking his tabloyd off his wrist. It bounced once on the narrow rock shelf before plunging into the bottomless gorge. "Damn it! Somebody fly down there and grab—"

He yelped as a swarm of bulbous yellow insects blasted out of the pit. The children pointed and screamed. "No okay! Run! Glomps!"

Their terror infected Kellybean. "Wait, what? What are glomps? Hey! Stop!"

The kids did not stop. They launched themselves out of the buoyant gas and hit the ground running, screaming at the top of their lungs. "Glomps! Tiggy wonk! Glomps! Tiggy!"

Jassi looked to Hax. "What are they saying?"

"Let me see..." Hax's eyes blinked out as his tape shuttled. "Ah, here we are. Volcania Glomponosta, commonly known as 'glomps' or 'gas glomps.' Indigenous insect. Natural habitat, volcanic vents. Best known for their role in the fertilization cycle of baisenberry brambles. Harmless unless disturbed."

"What if they are disturbed?" Kellybean shouted.

Hax blinked. "Then not harmless."

Stobber wailed as the storm of glomps turned in the air and pelted against his body. Each fat insect exploded upon impact, letting off a splash of bright yellow venom.

"Aagh! That smarts!"

He grabbed at the craggy walls and hauled himself toward the surface. A rock broke free in his enormous hand and another spray of insects buzzed from the cliff face and swirled through the gas. Jassi jerked as they peppered her bare belly. "Ow! Damn it!"

"Jassi!" Kellybean gasped. "Are you—"

A cluster of glomps pelted against her fur. Each impact was like being snapped with a thick rubber band. The sticky venom burned like drips of hot wax. And there were thousands more of them buzzing murderously through the chasm.

"Let's get the huck out of here!" Jassi shouted.

She swung herself under Kellybean and angled her body against the gas. Before the Gellicle knew what was happening, they slipped beyond the boundary of the updraft and dropped a few feet to the ground. Jassi's boots hit the dirt and she caught Kellybean in her arms and set her lightly on her hind paws. It was the most chivalrous thing anyone had ever done for her, but before Kellybean could acknowledge the moment it was ruined by a flurry of stinging insects splattering against her face.

"Ow! Son of a..." she hissed.

Hax's tires squealed against the ground as he backed away from the pit clutching one of Stobber's large hands. The other big hand clutched the edge and the smaller ones desperately swatted against the swarming glomps. Stobber howled in pain as they bombarded his bramble-scratched skin, but he hauled himself up and ran after the girls.

Kellybean and Murderblossom crested the dune with a million angry glomps at their back. Everyone on the beach looked up in horror at the thunderous buzz of insects swarming into the sky and blotting out the sun.

"Glomps!" a Halii bartender screamed.

"Tiggy!" the tour boat captain cried. "Glomps! Tiggy wonk!"

Kellybean didn't understand the native language, but the meaning was clear enough. All over the beach, Halii ran for cover in cafés and shops, slamming heavy shutters behind them as the venomous yellow swarm surged over the black dunes.

The glomps assailed the Screetoro newlyweds, drawing out an earsplitting sixteen-mouth scream. More bulbous insects bombarded the Krubb family, bursting against their hard exoskeletons like bright yellow paintballs.

"Get to the hovercoach!" Kellybean screamed.

She swatted the bugs away as she raced across the sand, herding her tourists toward the bus. Horman and Clermytha clutched each other's hands as they climbed on board, followed by the rest of the group. Jassi and Hax shoved Stobber's oversized body through the narrow door and Kellybean pounced in behind them.

The driver slammed the door and Kellybean fell into her seat, gasping for breath. The shell of the bus vibrated as thousands of glomps hammered its outside like a gooey yellow hailstorm.

She swiped the custardy venom off her arms and face, and realized it no longer burned. The toxin was apparently fast-acting and temporary. But it didn't matter. The damage was done. All through the bus, tourists wailed and clawed at themselves, too traumatized to realize they were unharmed. Kellybean took a deep breath, stood up, and addressed the sticky, sobbing crowd.

"So, who's ready for their box lunch?"

CHAPTER TWELVE

Hours after the *Americano Grande* departed Halii Bai, Leo had retired to his stateroom to prepare for the evening's activities. Next up was an outdoor concert by legendary Geiko crooner Swaggy Humbershant, Jr. The old man played a program of classic, velvet-throated standards the seniors enjoyed nostalgically and the youngsters enjoyed ironically.

Swaggy worked on a lot of levels.

Leo finished buttoning the coat of his dress uniform, admiring his reflection in the full-length mirror. He gave himself a confident wink and a set of pistol fingers.

"Lookin' good, Captain MacGavin!"

He was excited to attend the concert in his official capacity as the captain. Because, for once, he felt like the captain. Ever since he'd fixed the power drain on the engines, the bridge crew had started taking him more seriously. Even Burlock had reluctantly backed off. He grinned and straightened his hat. Today had really turned around since the debacle this morning.

As soon as he thought it, the image of Varlowe—yellow-skinned and sweaty and bulging with veins—torpedoed his good mood. He hadn't heard a word from her since the medics had wheeled her off the ship. Guilt chewed at his gut. Varlowe had trusted him and he'd poisoned her. Accidentally, but still… He was worried.

He frowned and pulled back his sleeve, revealing the white band of his tabloyd. A wheel slowly spun on its face. Ugh. It had been failing to connect to the tab network for hours. Maybe he'd have better luck if he went outside.

He tapped on the device as he crossed out onto his enormous private balcony. Cool, exterior air tingled on his skin, but the wheel continued spinning. Nuts. He blew out a long breath and tipped his head back to gaze out at the night sky.

He froze. Eyes wide. Mouth open.

Space was broken.

That was the only explanation. The usual velvet-black expanse pricked with twinkling stars had become furious, boiling chaos. Angry blue gas churned and spiraled in a storm thousands of miles wide. Electrical disturbances the size of continents raged across its face, whipping off breathtaking tendrils of sapphire lightning. And in the center of it all was a circle of blackness. Leo's brain tried to tell him it was a planet, but it wasn't a planet. It wasn't made of dirt or rock. Some deep, primeval part of his psyche told him it was made of nothing. Just a hole in the very fabric of reality, slowly devouring the storm as it coiled into its nightmarish mouth.

Looking at it made Leo's throat feel raw and blistered. Some tiny collection of synapses at the edge of his consciousness wondered why it would do that. The seed of curiosity took hold, pulling him back from the brink of madness.

Leo realized he was screaming. Just standing there, limbs slack, eyes wide, staring at the sky and screaming in primal terror. He clapped a hand over his mouth and turned to run back inside, but before he could move, an enormous spider crashed down in front of him. Leo wailed and clutched his heart. "Gah! Dilly! What are you doing here?"

"It is head of security, sir. Its duty is to keep guests and crew safe."

"But what are you doing *here*? On my balcony?"

"It heard you screaming."

"And..."

"It came to help," Dilly said without emotion.

Despite its assurances, the sudden appearance of a nightmare beast with slavering mandibles and razor-sharp teeth was not helping Leo's sphincter-loosening horror. He thrust a finger at the sky. "What's happening? What is that?"

"Is Blue Hole, sir. Sightseeing attraction. Is harmless."

"Harmless?" Leo repeated, as if trying to convince himself. "But... what is it?"

"Unstable, electrically charged accretion disc orbiting supermassive gravity well."

"So... it's a black hole?"

"No, is blue hole."

"What's the difference?"

Dilly's glowing eyes blinked. "Is blue."

Leo scowled, unsatisfied with this answer. He'd add this to his ever-expanding list of things to ask Varlowe. She'd know all about it. She knew everything. If he could just get in touch with her. He cleared his throat. "Hey, could I borrow your tabloyd? I have to make a call."

"You cannot make calls from dead zone."

"Okay, but I really need to..." Leo squinted. "I'm sorry, did you say 'dead zone'?"

"Around Blue Hole. Anomaly disrupts deep-space comms. We can only contact ships within visual range."

"I see. And how many of those are there?"

"Zero. Blue Hole is millions of miles outside shipping lanes. Too dangerous for most vessels."

"So, to be clear, you're telling me we're in the middle of nowhere, completely alone, and we can't call for help if there's a problem?"

"Why would there be problem?"

"No reason," Leo said. "Just obvious historical precedent."

His tabloyd beeped with a sharp emergency tone. He tapped it and a holographic comm bubble appeared, containing the fishy green face of Doctor Waverlee. "We've got a problem, kid!"

"Oh, do we?" Leo sighed. "How completely unexpected."

"Infirmary's flooded with patients. I got heart failures and hemorrhaging out the wazoo. All of them from the concert."

"Why? What's causing it?"

"How should I know? That's why I'm calling you! Figure it out before I run out of beds!"

Leo's heart raced. This was so not fair! He fixed the engines! Couldn't he have the rest of the day off from emergencies?

"Okay, I'll check it out." He swiped away the bubble and turned to Dilly. "What's the fastest way from here to the outdoor—"

He screamed as the Dreda snatched him up and scrambled over the balcony's railing. He continued to scream as the security chief scampered vertically across the ship's enormous glass and metal side. Leo's breath choked at the sight of the endless void sprawling out below him. But even as terror numbed his senses, he heard a noise thundering through the bubble of atmosphere clinging to the ship. It grew louder as they neared the outdoor concert, turning into a deafening wail of electronic tones and percussive hammering and agonized screaming.

Dilly raced up the side of the gunwale and launched over the rail like a hungry puma. It came down on its four back legs, dropping the captain on his own two. Leo staggered away, clamping his palms over his ears against the blistering cacophony. Dozens of alien tourists were gathered on the deck—their levels of discomfort aligned with their unique physiologies. The daintiest among them clutched chairs with their eyes rolled back in pain, the hardiest cupped their hands to their mouths and booed at the stage.

Leo's vision swam as he tried to focus. Strobes popped and spotlights circled around three beings that could loosely be called a band. The drummer was an obsolete robot hammering snares and hi-hats in a rhythm that was shockingly off-beat for a machine. At his side was a huge Nomit in a shredded tank top molesting a double bass keytar. His thick, yellow-gray skin was crisscrossed with fresh scratches, like he'd been scrubbed with steel wool. In front was a plant-girl guitarist in leather pants and a tattered denim vest—buttoned once across her chest with the rest open to expose the twisted vines of her abs. Sappy sweat flicked off her body as she screamed lyrics into the microphone.

"Leaves of three! Let it be! You won't be lichen what you're gettin' if you huck with me!"

Even with his hands pressed over his ears, the performance was still a buzz saw to Leo's brain.

"Music is too loud," Dilly said calmly.

It jabbed out two arms, firing off streams of webbing at the stacks of speakers flanking the stage. One knocked out a cable, silencing a few woofers. The second went wide and connected with a junction panel. Dilly squealed as a power surge raced down the strand and blasted it backwards into a bulkhead.

Leo dodged around the spider's crumpled body as he rushed to the control booth at the rear of the deck. It was an elevated platform with a curved roof and glassed-in walls, loaded with audio-holo gear. He bolted up the stairs, wrenched open the door, threw himself inside, and slammed it behind him.

As soon as it was closed, the booth dulled the savage song to a thumping roar. Leo pulled his trembling hands from his ears as his brain came back online. Kellybean stood at a massive board of sliders and dials, wearing pointed earphones on her pointed ears. She gazed out at the source of the weapons-grade noise, dreamily twisting a long, pink leaf around her finger.

"Kellybean!" Leo barked.

The Gellicle reflexively spun and dropped into a crouch, pupils narrowed and claws out, hissing through her fangs. Leo screamed and lurched into the back wall. Kellybean gasped and straightened, smoothing down her puffed fur.

"Captain! Sorry, you startled me."

Leo rubbed his smashed skull. "The music! Turn it down before heads start exploding!"

"What?" Kellybean pulled off her headphones and sucked a surprised breath. "Oh! Oh no!"

She yanked back a slider on the console until the booth's windows stopped rattling. Outside, the guests blinked and shook their heads as the audio assault subsided. Dilly clattered to its feet, looking embarrassed but unharmed.

"I'm sorry, sir!" Kellybean cried. "I didn't realize how loud they were!"

"How could you not know?"

"I, uh..." Kellybean held up her headphones sheepishly. A coiled cord hung from the bottom, connected to nothing. "I forgot to plug in my headset. I'm so sorry! I didn't have time to set up properly. This isn't like me! I know you don't want to hear excuses for poor performance, but—"

"It's okay."

Kellybean's ears flicked. "It's... okay?"

"It's okay," Leo repeated. "People make mistakes. After the day I've had, I'm not going to chew you out for one little mishap."

"Well, that's really kind of you. But... there was more than one mishap. Several more, actually."

Leo sighed. "Do I even want to know?"

"It'll all be in my report," Kellybean said guiltily. "But the short version is, I had to give the whole excursion group refunds and laundry vouchers after my tour got attacked by exploding insects." She shuddered. "That's why I was late. It took two hours to clean their slime out of my fur."

Leo noticed a crusty yellow stain on Kellybean's elbow. "Looks like you missed a spot."

"Ugh. Thanks."

She lifted her arm and licked it clean with her little pink tongue. Leo blinked. "You know, you could take a shower."

"And get wet?" Kellybean's nose wrinkled. "Gross."

Before Leo could respond, the Verdaphyte girl's blistered voice scraped at the windows. "Leaves of three! Let me be! Kiss my roots and suck my seeds!"

Leo looked across the deck at the band, continuing to desecrate the very concept of music. "Look, I don't want this to turn into a performance review, but... why exactly did you hire this band?"

"I didn't. Someone on my staff did."

"To open for legendary crooner Swaggy Humbershant, Jr.?"

"Uh... no." Another guilty look flashed in the Gellicle's eyes. "Murderblossom was actually only contracted to play one late-night show in a tiny little lounge way down on the Piñata Deck. But I kinda..." She turned the pink leaf in her hands. "Gave them a promotion."

Leo crossed his arms. "Okay, now we've gone beyond mishaps into straight-up poor life choices."

"I have some regrets," Kellybean admitted. "I hadn't actually heard them play before I offered them this gig. But I owed them a favor." She fidgeted. "Well, I owed Jassi a favor."

"Which one's Jassi?"

"The guitarist. Down on the planet she really saved my tail with a couple of high-maintenance Platinum Elites. I just wanted to… thank her."

She gazed out the window and absently twisted the leaf around her finger. Leo noticed. "Ah, I see what's going on here."

Kellybean's voice went high with forced nonchalance. "What do you mean? There's nothing going on here."

"Whatever. I see the way you're pining over that plant girl."

"No pun intended?"

"Pun *completely* intended." Leo gave her a playful nudge. "Don't even try to tell me you don't have a green thumb."

A blush prickled through Kellybean's ears. "Is it that obvious?"

Leo laughed. "You've got it so bad you can barely think."

Kellybean mewled and rubbed her eyes. "Gah. You're right. I'm sorry. I shouldn't have let them open for Swaggy. I shouldn't be obsessing over her at all. I know she's bad news. And I know better than to let my personal life interfere with my job."

The notion sparked a memory in Leo's mind—a smashed fotoclip in the bottom of a box in Kellybean's office. Her and a Ba'lux girl, both in WTF uniforms. *Kellybean & Pyrrah 4-eva.*

"Because of what happened on the *Opulera*?" he ventured.

"Yeah." Kellybean's face remained neutral, but her puffed tail betrayed her nerves. "I guess WTF probably briefed you on… the incident."

Nope! I was just blatantly snooping in your things!

"The incident. Yes." Leo nodded. "But I'd prefer to hear your version of it."

"My version…" Kellybean blew out a long breath. "Well, I was the *Opulera's* entertainment director. I was dating the hospitality chief. To my surprise, she was also dating a few showgirls."

"Ouch."

"And yoga instructors."

"Dang."

"And maintenance bots."

"Wow. I'm sorry."

Kellybean shook her head. "When I found out it destroyed me. The prospect of having to keep working with Pyrrah... to see her smug orange face every day... It was... upsetting." Her fur ruffled. "After that, I vowed I'd never get involved with a coworker again. Especially one who didn't respect me."

Leo nodded, fitting the pieces together. "And you're afraid that Verdaphyte girl doesn't respect you."

"I'm afraid she doesn't respect anything."

On stage, Jassi had straddled the microphone stand and was thrusting her hips, pounding the mic into Stobber's face in a comically obscene pantomime he clearly wanted no part of.

"Yeah, I see the red flags. But sometimes people surprise you."

Kellybean gave a quizzical look. "What are you saying?"

"I'm saying, if you like her so much, it can't hurt to get to know her. Give her a chance to prove herself." Leo shrugged. "And if it doesn't work out, you never have to see her again after this cruise."

"Captain!" Kellybean's eyes widened. "Are you suggesting I fire Murderblossom if things don't work out between me and Jassi?"

"Of course not. I'm suggesting you fire Murderblossom because they're the worst band I've ever heard."

The musicians brought their song to a chaotic finale. Jassi ripped the microphone out of its stand. "We're Murderblossom! You've been a terrible audience! Go suck a bag of stamens!" She dropped it with a screech of feedback and strutted off the stage.

Kellybean groaned. "Yeah, there's no way this is gonna work out."

"Probably not." Leo watched Kellybean as she crossed to the door. "Are you gonna go talk to her anyway?"

"No. I'm going to introduce Swaggy Humbershant, Jr."

Leo grinned. "And then you're going to talk to her?"

"It seems like a bad idea."

"It totally does. But I think she'd respect you if she got to know you."

"Why do you think that?"

"Because you're a force to be reckoned with."

A toothy smile spread on Kellybean's face. "I am, aren't I?"

***

Jassi's woody fingertips ravaged the strings of her guitar as she wailed into the microphone. "Green leaves three! Let it be! All bark, all bite! Half girl, half tree!"

She raked back her scalp foliage, wet and sticky with sappy sweat under the hot stage lights. Behind her, Stobber shredded on his double-necked bass keytar and Hax drummed like a pair of sticks attached to an off-balance paint shaker. But Jassi wasn't paying attention to them, or to the crowd, or even the giant sucking space butthole squatting overhead. She was playing this show for an audience of one.

Her leafy brows lowered as she squinted through the irritating flash of stage lights. Kellybean was in the booth talking to the idiot captain, but Jassi barely noticed him. All she saw were big yellow eyes. Slinky feline hips. A uniform polo full of mammal parts...

The song crashed to a conclusion, but Jassi's hands played three more chords on auto pilot before she realized the boys had finished. She wagged her whammy bar, bending her last note in a ridiculous crescendo before letting it drop. The noise of the band was immediately replaced by the booing of the crowd. Jassi ripped the microphone out of its stand. "We're Murderblossom! You've been a terrible audience! Go suck a bag of stamens!"

She dropped it with a screech of feedback and strutted off the stage. Stobber and Hax followed her, and they all left their instruments in a heap backstage before proceeding to the bar. It was a tropical-style thing made of bamboo and thatched straw. Jassi grimaced. Meatworlder architecture was so gruesome.

She banged a wooden knuckle on the wooden bar top and shouted at the bartender. "Beer!"

"Two vodka tonics and a methrum chaser," Stobber barked.

"One can of synthetic lubricant," Hax added. "But only if you have low-carb. I don't want to get all bloaty."

The bartender hustled off to grab their drinks. Jassi slumped back against the bar on her elbows. On the other side of the deck, Kellybean pounced onto the stage and picked up the microphone in a single, graceful movement.

"All right, *Americano Grande*! Let's hear it for Murderblossom! Weren't they great?" She kept smiling, even as the crowd booed and shouted insults. "Now we're going to take it down a notch and set the mood for you romantic souls out there. Please put your arm appendages together for the velvet tones of Swaggy Humbershant, Jr."

The audience pattered applause as an old, gray-striped Geiko with a tentacle pompadour and a sequined jacket swept onto the stage. He caught Kellybean by the waist and the two of them turned in a perfectly choreographed spin, ending in a low dip with her kitty leg kicked out, toes and claws in a dancer-perfect point. Her cruise-uniform skirt rode up, revealing a mile of fluffy white thigh.

Jassi groaned. "Man, what I wouldn't give to put some grass stains on that."

Stobber glanced at the stage and snuffed. "Shix, Jass. You're still making panty nectar over that uptight Gellicle?" He shrugged. "I guess it makes sense."

"Yeah?" Jassi sneered. "What makes sense?"

"You and a cat." He grinned. "'Cause I know how much you love—"

"All right," Jassi barked. "Take your low-hanging fruit and stick it up your poop chute, Johnny Comedy."

"I don't get it," Hax said.

Stobber opened the storage drawer in Hax's hips, pulled out a datacassette, and swapped it out for the one in his tape-deck chest. "Check out the folder called 'Boring Tax Stuff.'"

Hax cocked his head. "Boring Tax—"

"Trust me."

He hit play, and Hax's eye screen frizzed out as he accessed the data. Jassi slugged Stobber in the arm. "Oi! Quit storing your spank bank in the drummer, ya creep."

The bartender returned and set a tray of drinks on the bar. Stobber reached for his tabloyd to swipe a payment, but only found bramble-scratched arm.

"Gahdamn it." He turned to Jassi. "I lost my tabloyd in the gas hole. This round is on you."

"Ugh, fine." She pulled her crinkled device from the back pocket of her leather pants and swiped it at the tray's paypad. "I hope ya choke on it."

Stobber shook his head. "Why you gotta be so rude to me when I'm about to make your dreams come true?"

Jassi sucked a breath and clasped her hands. "You're gonna quit the band?"

"Har de hucking har har." Stobber grinned, baring his

broken yellow teeth. "No. I'm gonna hook you up with a friend of mine who's gonna help you score with Miss Kitty-boo-boo." He pulled out a vial of green pills. "I call him the pharmaceutical cupid."

Jassi sneered at him. "You and your friend can huck right off. I don't need to drug women to get in their pants."

"Yeah, I can tell by the way you're sitting here whining and nursing yer bluebells." Stobber shook out a capsule and dropped it into one of his two cocktails. "Why you gotta do everything the hard way? One sip of this and she'll be randy and ready. You just take her back to your room and get right to it."

"I'm gonna get right to kicking your nuts out your nostrils if you don't—"

"Hey guys! Great show!" a bright voice said. "Your set was really... unique!"

Jassi whirled around to find Kellybean standing behind her, smiling and fidgeting nervously. She quickly raked her fingers through her scalp leaves, straightening her pink wave.

"Uh, yeah. We're a bunch of real unique motherhuckers." She leaned back on the bar, putting herself between her scraggly bandmates and the Gellicle. "So, what brings you here?"

Kellybean's smile dimmed. "I work here."

Jassi snorted a chuckle. "Here to the bar. You've made it perfectly clear you don't drink on duty."

"Maybe I could just once," Kellybean said flirtatiously. "In the right company."

Stobber grabbed his two vodka tonics. "Well you ain't never gonna find a better drinking partner than Jassi." He set the drinks on the bar between the two women and stepped back with a showy flourish. "Enjoy. I won't wait up for you."

Jassi slugged him in the face. He staggered and played it off with a pained chuckle as he hit the stop button on Hax's tape deck. The robot's screen flickered back into eyes, and he blinked and focused on Jassi. "Why don't you just eat ice cream? The mechanics are the same and that comes in chocolate."

"This is a later conversation," Jassi hissed. "Actually, it's a never conversation. Huck off, the both of you."

She shoved her bandmates, and Stobber plodded off with Hax rolling at his side. Jassi took a cleansing breath and turned back to Kellybean. The hospitality chief was perched demurely on a stool, sipping Stobber's drink.

"Ah shix," Jassi muttered.

"Is everything okay?" Kellybean asked, nodding to the retreating band members.

"Yeah, they just had to go play in an open airlock." Jassi eyed the glass in Kellybean's paw. "Everything okay with you?"

"Better than okay." Kellybean licked her lips. "Booze tastes different when you're on duty. The naughtiness gives it a little extra zing."

"Yeah, that's what you're tasting, all right. Naughtiness." Jassi reached for the glass. "You know what? Don't drink that. I don't want to get you in trouble."

Kellybean pulled it away with a giggle. "It's too late for that. You've already corrupted my work ethic." She grabbed the other tumbler and held it out. "Don't make me drink alone."

Jassi looked at the glass. Up Kellybean's slender arm. To her face. Her seductive smile. Her yellow, come-hither eyes.

"Oh, huck me," she muttered. She took the glass and shot the entire thing in one gulp. Kellybean finished her drink and bit her lower lip with a pointy canine.

"Hey," she purred. "Do you want to get out of here?"

Jassi's eyes ticked from Kellybean's smoldering gaze to her tainted tumbler and back again.

"Yes, I definitely do."

***

Leo leaned against the rail, taking deep breaths of the crisp evening air. High above, stray space rocks bounced off the invisible bubble of the artificial magnetosphere, making aurora-like sparks of green light. Beyond the shield, the Blue Hole churned and tumbled like a raging electric sea, but Leo no longer feared it. Familiarity had made the anomaly hauntingly beautiful, and the honey-smooth crooning of Swaggy Humbershant, Jr. had made it downright romantic.

On the deck, a few blue-white pin spots swept lazily over couples slow dancing cheek-to-cheek as the old Geiko worked his magic. Kellybean had left with the Verdaphyte girl almost an hour ago. Love was in the air.

He wished Varlowe were here.

The thought caught him off guard. Why did he wish that? Why did soft music and slow dancing call her to mind? He shook his head. Because the night was going well. Obviously. He just wanted her to see how he had turned things around. Wanted her to know Madame Skardon's contest was in good hands.

Yes. That was definitely it.

"Enjoying yourself, Captain?"

Leo jumped at the booming voice behind him. He whirled to find Burlock staring him down like a half-mechanical ghoul.

"I am, actually." He stood straight and gestured across the dance floor. "And so are the guests."

"Not the ones in the infirmary bleeding out their ear holes."

Leo paled. "Oh my gosh, I forgot about… Is everybody okay?"

"Doctor Waverlee has it under control. Everyone will make a full recovery. But I need to conduct an investigation into what happened."

"Is that really necessary?"

"It is," Burlock growled. "Injuries like that don't just happen spontaneously. When I find out who's to blame, I will personally tear him, her, zer, or bur a new sphincter."

Leo squirmed. He wasn't about to throw Kellybean under the hovercoach. So she made a mistake. Everyone makes mistakes.

"Let's just let it slide this time. No harm, no foul." He considered it and grimaced. "Or, I guess, no permanent harm, no permanent foul?"

Burlock's brow lowered. "Your cavalier attitude toward the safety of the people on this ship disgusts me. But I shouldn't be surprised you don't care about the passengers. You poisoned the gahdamn executive board."

Heat prickled up Leo's neck. "I told you, it was an accident."

"You're just lucky they've all recovered."

"They have? How do you know?"

"The admiral called me personally before we entered the dead zone. The entire board has been discharged from the hospital on Halii Bai and they're en route to Nyja. We'll rendezvous with them on the dock tomorrow morning."

"Oh, that's great!" Leo let out a relieved breath. "I'm so happy everyone is okay."

"For now. But I've assigned an extra duty shift to the infirmary in anticipation of your next screw up."

"There won't be a next screw up," Leo growled.

"There'd better not be. If this were the Imperial Navy you'd have been relieved of command and put out an airlock by now."

Leo's hands balled into fists. "Look, Burlock. I know I haven't been perfect, but I've had enough of this attitude out of you." He tapped a finger on his scorched cap. "I'm the captain of this ship, and I've got everything under control."

"Do you?"

"I do! And from now on it'll be smooth sailing all the way to Ensenada—"

A rock the size of a softball hit the deck at his side, smashing a hole clean through the wood. Leo squeaked and tumbled back. Burlock barely flinched. The music trembled to a stop. Another rock splashed into the pool. A clump of ice crashed through the roof of a cabana.

"What?" Leo's eyes widened. "What's happening?!"

Spastic, stuttering winds blasted across the deck in seemingly random directions. All around them, the normally transparent forcefield wavered and rippled with pale, sickly green.

"Everyone get inside!" Burlock bellowed. "The magnetosphere shield is failing!"

The commander ran off into the crowd, leaving Leo staring upward in horror. The shield was failing. Radial cracks peeled open across its mottled green surface, explosively venting the ship's atmosphere like rips in a hot-air balloon. Clods of ice and rock sailed through the gaps, smashing to the deck.

A withered, fuchsia-striped Geiko shrieked over the chaos. "Help me! Horman, help me!"

The elderly woman clung to a rail as the whipping gusts plucked at her dress, threatening to toss her overboard. Her husband struggled through the panicked crowd. "Hold on, Clerm! I'm coming!"

The desperate scene snapped Leo out of his horrified reverie. He darted forward to grab the woman, but was too late. She lost her grip and shot into the air toward one of the sucking rips in the forcefield. But before she went through it, a jet of spider web hit her square in the chest. Leo turned to see Dilly flick its wrist and reel in the captured passenger like a yo-yo.

"Yes!" Leo gasped. "Good work, Dilly!"

The Dreda's head swiveled as it scuttled across the deck, firing off rescue lines and reeling in survivors from all of its forelimbs at once. It held Clermytha to its face and let out a spittle-infused screech.

"Please do not panic," its collar said.

The woman wailed in terror, uncertain if being in the spider's grasp was a more or less certain death than being sucked into space.

Burlock charged past, dragging a Lethargot with his mechanical hand and palming a Krubb's domed head with the other. He raced to the open archway of the Rushmore Concourse and tossed them through like sacks of dirty laundry. As soon as they were inside he grabbed Leo's arm. "Get inside, you idiot! With the rest of the useless idiots!"

"Stop!" Leo shouted, grabbing at the metal fist clamped around his bicep. "Let go!"

"Shut up and get inside! I'll deal with you later, after I've cleaned up your mess!"

"My mess? I didn't do any—" Leo's shoulder threatened to dislocate as Burlock manhandled him toward the entrance. The heat of his anger sizzled through the cold of the rapidly escaping atmosphere. "Damn it, Burlock! Let go of me! That's an order!"

Burlock paused as the command registered, then released Leo with a shove. "Fine! Die in space for all I care, *Captain*."

A steady wind blew from the Rushmore Concourse's archway as the inside atmosphere rushed toward the lower pressure outside. The gale whipped Leo's captain's hat off his head, flinging it overboard.

"We'll talk about your attitude problem after we get everyone inside! Now go help somebody!"

Leo shoved Burlock, but the commander didn't move. He

didn't even sway. He spoked through a clenched jaw. "Aye, Captain." His massive boots clomped over the ravished deck as he continued grabbing screaming tourists and muscling them inside.

A Verdaphyte man staggered with disorientation, his brown leaves ripping off and fluttering away on the wind. Leo took his arm and helped him to the concourse. Once the man was through the doors, hospitality crew on the other side launched into action, ushering him to safety.

Leo felt a sudden rush of accomplishment. He'd rescued a passenger. An innocent soul had been pulled back from the edge of the abyss to live another day because of his—

"Pardon me," Dilly said.

Leo stumbled aside as it scurried through the door, carrying six screaming passengers in its arms and dragging four more by a braid of webbing slung over its shoulder.

"Show off," Leo grumbled.

He rushed back out between the creaking stage and the boiling pool. His head throbbed and his joints tightened as the temperature plummeted. The magnetosphere had almost completely collapsed, taking the atmosphere with it. Inside the ship, crew members slammed airtight hatches, sealing it off. The broad arch of the Rushmore Concourse narrowed as its massive emergency doors began to slide closed.

Leo struggled to draw breath as he frantically surveyed the deck. Not far away, Burlock was doing the same. The first officer rushed toward the captain.

"That's everyone!" Burlock shouted.

"Are you sure?"

"Yes! Now get your arze inside the gahdamn—"

A hunk of ice the size of a grapefruit smashed into Burlock's back. It exploded on impact, violently throwing him to the deck.

"Burlock!" Leo's shriek voided his lungs, and he clumsily fell at the commander's side. "Are you all right?"

The hulking Ba'lux lay face-down, muscles trembling and servos twitching. His uniform was torn open, revealing a sparking crater in his robotic shoulder that turned into a bloody gash where metal met flesh. Leo pulled him upright. Burlock seemed to want to cooperate, but his stunned body lacked the coordination to comply.

Leo's lungs felt like they were turning inside out as he struggled to yank the Ba'lux to his feet. With gasping effort, he worked himself under Burlock's organic arm and staggered toward the concourse door. The power of Leo's adrenalin burn fought against the weight of the semi-conscious officer and the gale blasting from the slowly closing arch. Burlock stumbled without direction.

"Come on..." Leo choked. "Almost... there..."

A sticky gray spider web launched from inside the ship and slammed against Burlock's barrel chest. In a moment too quick to register, the commander launched through the archway, reeled in by Dilly's spinneret. Leo stumbled and fell as Burlock was ripped out of his arms.

The door was nearly closed. Just a sliver of space barely wider than his shoulders remained. The escaping atmosphere raged through the narrow gap, a deluge of wind against Leo's body. Doctor Waverlee appeared in the break, screaming bubbles into her helmet. "Grab my hand, kid!"

She leaned through the door and stretched her stubby arm as far as she could. Leo's jaw clenched and his muscles burned as he reached for her webbed glove. Pressurized air rammed itself up his nose. His vision went fuzzy. He lost feeling in his limbs.

Everything went dark.

CHAPTER THIRTEEN

Leo floated on a sea of fluffy black nothing. Sounds filtered through the gauze of reality. Unhappy sounds. Screams of confusion and cries of anguish. He didn't want to go toward the sounds, but he felt himself rising to meet them. His eyes tingled as they slowly cracked open. Four faces came into focus. They were human. One had a mustache. But they were all gray. And huge. And made of stone.

He snorted and sat up as the enormous statue of Queen asserted itself in his consciousness. He was on the Rushmore Concourse, lying on a patch of grass in the artificial park. Dozens of aliens were sprawled around him. Hundreds more rubbernecked down at them from the rails of the upper levels as medical staff buzzed about, tending to the injured.

"Well, look who's awake."

Leo turned to see Burlock perched on a bench behind him. A thick, constricting wrap of autogauze was looped around his chest and shoulder like a bandolier, chemically repairing the impact crater on his back.

"What happened?" Leo croaked. "Is everyone okay?"

"No casualties. You got lucky, MacGavin."

Before Leo could express his relief, someone cut him off.

"You got lucky too, old man." Doctor Waverlee set down her medical bag and groaned as she crouched at Leo's side. "The shaved Gellicle saved your orange hide out there."

Memories pushed through the haze in Leo's oxygen-starved

brain. The ice slamming into Burlock's back, and the weight of the man's augmented body as Leo had ushered him to safety. He smiled through cracked lips. "I kinda did, didn't I?"

Burlock scowled. "You were... not useless."

"Enough with the macho nonsense." Waverlee pulled an instrument from her bag and ran it over Leo's body, taking some kind of measurement. "I saw the whole thing. Leo carried you like a little baby."

The commander's eye narrowed. "Aren't there patients elsewhere you need to treat?"

"Nobody more important than the captain." Waverlee looked at her instrument and let out a satisfied glub. "So, kiddo. What are you gonna do with your blood debt?"

Leo blinked. "Excuse me?"

"You know, the Ba'lux honor thing." She waved at Burlock. "You saved his life so now he's basically your slave forever."

Leo turned to Burlock. "Is that true?"

"It's a gross oversimplification," the commander growled. "And you didn't save my life. I could have made it inside on my own. Technically, I owe you nothing." He crossed his arms and looked away with a pout.

"Well, I'm just glad you're okay. We can work on your gratitude issues later."

At the edge of the park, Kellybean staggered in from an adjoining corridor, holding the wall for stability. Her fur and clothes were rumpled as if she'd just rolled out of bed after a dreamless night. Her wobbling legs gave out, but Dilly swept in to catch her and escort her to Leo and the others.

"Doctor Waverlee," Dilly said. "Lieutenant Commander Kellybean requires medical assistance."

"I don't. I'm fine." Kellybean swayed. "I'm probably fine."

Waverlee's old body creaked as she stood up. "Well, in my

professional opinion you look like crap. Did you get caught in the vacuum with the rest of 'em?"

"Vacuum?" Kellybean asked dreamily. She blinked at the makeshift infirmary and sucked a breath as if seeing it for the first time. "Wait, what happened here?"

"Magnetosphere failure," Dilly noted. "With full loss of atmospheric containment."

"I..." Kellybean smoothed down her ruffled fur. "I don't remember that happening."

"You had already left," Leo said.

Kellybean pressed her paws to her temples. "Ugh. I don't even remember leaving."

"Hoo boy," Waverlee muttered. "Let's have a look." She pulled a device from her bag that looked like a thermometer with a suction cup on one end and mashed it to Kellybean's forehead. It whirred and pinged. "Yep, your blood is lousy with drugs."

"Drugs?" Dilly gave Kellybean a disapproving glare. "It expects better of you, Lieutenant Commander."

"I didn't take any drugs! I just had one drink with..." Kellybean's eyes widened. "Oh no."

Leo stumbled to his feet. "What? What's wrong?"

"Nothing. Forget it." The feline's claws extended. "If you'll excuse me, I need to go find a certain Verdaphyte and teach her a lesson about respect."

She turned to storm off in a rage, but her legs dipped out from under her. Dilly clutched her and held her upright. Before she could make another attempt, Praz Kerplunkt scrambled up to them, flanked by two Lethargot technicians. One of them pushed a hovering auto-crate.

"Praz!" Leo snapped. "What the hekk is going on? What happened to the magnetosphere?"

"I'll tell you what happened!" Praz shouted. "It crashed!"

"Crashed?" Kellybean gasped.

"Crashed," Praz confirmed proudly.

"Technically it hasn't crashed," one of the Lethargots said.

"The dynamo's gone into emergency core lockdown," the other added. "It's meant to prevent catastrophic failure if somebody tampers with the system."

Praz whirled on them. "Shut up! I'm the talking one!"

"Wait, I thought the machine room was secured," Leo said. "Who could have tampered with it?"

"How am I supposed to know? We have absolutely nothing to go on!"

"We actually do have a clue," a Lethargot said. He pulled the release lever on his auto-crate and it split open and folded in on itself, revealing a waist-high chunk of burned wreckage. "The bots skimmed this out of the plasma shell."

A second set of lenses flicked over Burlock's mechanical eye as he scrutinized the object. "Do we know what it is?"

Praz snuffed indignantly. "Of course we know what it—"

"Negative," a Lethargot said.

"No idea," the other agreed.

"We're still working on it," Praz grumbled.

Leo barely registered their bickering. He stared at the debris. It was a blackened shard as long as his arm, curved and etched with ridges. It wasn't hard to visualize it as part of a cylindrical drum.

"Oh crap."

Burlock's brow lowered. "Do you have something to say, Captain?"

"Nothing that's not incriminating," Leo mumbled.

Kellybean's ears flicked. "Leo, have you seen this thing before?"

"Kinda? There was more to it last time, but…" He scratched

the back of his neck. "Okay, this is the thing that was crippling the engines after we left the Jaynkee Spacedock. I found it in the machine room when we went to investigate."

"What did you do with it?" Dilly asked.

"I unhooked it from the power junction and it fixed the engines." Leo smiled weakly. "Let's all just take a moment to remember that I fixed the engines. That was awesome, am I right?"

Burlock crossed his arms. "And what, exactly, happened to this unknown piece of malicious tech after you disconnected it?"

"It kind of got away from me."

"Got away *how*?" Waverlee asked.

Leo looked at the floor. "Got away like, rolled off a catwalk and plunged into the plasma shell."

"It *what*?" Praz shrieked. "Are you kidding me? No wonder it shut down! You can't just go throwing random junk into the magnetosphere dinosaur!"

"Dynamo," a Lethargot corrected.

"It's not a garbage disposal!" Praz continued. "It's a sensitive device only understood by the top engineering minds in the field, like me!"

"So this was all the American's fault?" a raspy voice asked.

Leo blinked away from Praz to see Clermytha, the old Geiko woman, eavesdropping nearby. And she wasn't alone. Her husband and a cluster of other injured passengers had gathered around the senior staff.

"Wait, we don't know that!" Leo said defensively. "The problem could have been caused by anything... heavy... dropped from a great height... into the machinery..."

He stopped talking.

"This whole 'Captain American' thing isn't cute anymore!" Horman shouted. He leaned against Clermytha, trying to keep the weight off his bandage-wrapped leg. "We all could have died because of his incompetence!"

A rumble of agreement rolled through the gathered crowd of walking wounded. Hax thrust a plastic finger at Leo. "That man killed my friends!"

"What?" Leo chirped. "I didn't!"

"I can't find them, so therefore they are dead! You caused the disaster wherein they got lost, so by transitive axiom, you killed my friends!"

"I'm not sure your logic is entirely—"

"He's a savage!" Horman snarled. "He doesn't care if we live or die!"

"This was an accident!" Leo cried. "I do care!"

"I don't care if you care!" Clermytha shouted. "We're getting off this terrible ship at the next stop! While we still can!"

"And I demand a full refund!" Horman added, pointing at his leg. "With extra compensation for pain and suffering!"

The angry passengers roared with agreement, looking like they were one second away from grabbing their torches and pitchforks. Leo's heart raced as he felt Madame Skardon's contest slipping through his fingers. If the passengers left, the cruise was over. If the cruise was over, so was Varlowe's presidency. If Varlowe's presidency was over, Eaglehaven was the galaxy's biggest doodie depository.

"No no, stop!" He raised his palms. "Let me sort this out! Please! We can still have a great cruise to Ensenada Vega!"

"We can't, actually," Burlock said.

Leo whirled on him. "Yes we can!"

"No, we can't." New malice seethed in the first officer's voice. "The magnetosphere's shell doesn't just hold the atmosphere and deflect debris. It's our primary radiation shield. We literally can't go on without it."

Horman gasped. "Are you saying the ship has no shielding?"

"We'll be fried to a crisp!" Clermytha wept. "We're doomed!"

Burlock raised an authoritative, calming hand. "We are not doomed. We're just going to have to abort the cruise and abandon ship at the nearest habitable planet."

"And how far away is that?" Horman asked.

Hax's eyes scrambled as his tape deck shuttled. "At this vessel's maximum speed, we should reach Nyja in twelve hours."

"We won't survive another twelve hours!" Clermytha stabbed a blue finger at Leo. "Not with the American in charge!"

The mob shouted in agreement. Leo felt himself going lightheaded with panic. "Wait! Maybe I can fix the dynamo! Then everything will be okay! Just give me another chance!"

Burlock shook his head. "You've had your chance, MacGavin. And you blew it. Over and over again. And now this ship is in real danger. Because of you." His eye lens twitched. "The only way we're getting to Nyja safely is with me in command."

"Finally!" Praz cried. "Somebody said it!"

Burlock's expression went cold. "Captain, for the safety of all souls on board, I demand you step down and abdicate control of this vessel to me immediately."

"What? No!" Leo cried. "Burlock, listen. I know this looks like it was my fault, but..."

He tried to think of a but. There was no but. Burlock's voice lowered. "You're in over your head and you know it. Everyone knows it. The time for fun and games is over. Step down."

"I can't. You know I can't. If I give up, Eaglehaven will be destroyed. I have to protect my home world."

"And I have to protect this ship." Burlock sighed. "All right, I guess we're doing this the hard way." He turned to the others. "I formally invoke the removal clause against Captain MacGavin. I put it to the senior staff for a vote."

Kellybean's whiskers twitched. "You can do that?"

Burlock nodded. "It's in the WTF charter. We can relieve him of command with a simple majority."

"I vote against the dirt monkey!" Praz said. "Lock him up!"

"Oh, come on," Leo squeaked.

Waverlee shook her head. "Kid, you've put more people in the infirmary in two days than most captains do in a whole career."

"Your vote against him is noted," Burlock said.

"Against? That was a vote in favor! I'm usually bored out of my mind down there." Waverlee jabbed Leo. "Keep 'em coming, disaster boy! I like a challenge!"

Burlock snorted. "Well I vote against him, obviously." He turned to Kellybean. "What say you?"

"I say he stays. He may not be perfect, but he's trying his best." Kellybean glared at the others. "Just like all of us."

"Bah!" Praz muttered. "Mammals always vote on party lines."

"All right, that's two and two," Burlock said. "One vote left."

Silence fell as everyone turned to Dilly. The Dreda's pitted eyes showed no emotion as it spoke through its translator collar. "Safety of passengers and crew is its primary objective. Ship would be safer with Commander Burlock in charge."

Leo gasped. "No! Dilly, please—"

"Sorry, sir. Is not personal." Dilly's mandibles clicked. "It votes to remove Captain MacGavin."

"Boo-yah!" Praz cheered. "Don't let the airlock pinch your butt on the way out, hairbag!" He ripped the captain's badge off Leo's chest and pinned it to Burlock's.

"Wait," Leo pleaded. "No!"

The new captain adjusted his badge and nodded to Praz. "Lieutenant Commander, get that magnetosphere back online ASAP. Do whatever it takes."

"Aye, *Captain*! We're on it!" Praz and his Lethargot techs took off for the machine room. Burlock barked orders at the rest of the crew, now fully under his command.

"Waverlee, I want all these guests fully recovered by the time we reach the Nyja Spacedock. Dilly, help the doctor."

They acknowledged and herded the angry tourists away.

Kellybean's fur ruffed. "This is so not fair! Leo didn't do anything wrong!"

Burlock scowled at her. "Lieutenant Commander, go clean yourself up and prep to disembark the guests at Nyja."

"But—"

"That's an order! And it had better go better than your trip to Halii Bai, or you'll be packing your bags too. You are dismissed."

Kellybean's whiskers drooped as she raked back her disheveled hair. "Yes, sir."

She cast an apologetic glance at Leo before scampering away, leaving him alone with Burlock.

"Collect your things, MacGavin. As soon as we dock you'll be on the next shuttle back to Eaglehaven. I wouldn't want you to miss the admiral's big renovation." A sinister smile pricked his lips. "I hope you have a good air freshener."

Leo didn't respond. There was nothing he could say. He just stood there, paralyzed, staring at his badge on Burlock's chest.

He wasn't the captain anymore.

He'd lost the contest. He'd lost Varlowe's presidency. He'd lost his home.

Just like that, he'd lost everything.

CHAPTER FOURTEEN

Dull metallic *thuds* vibrated through the bulkheads as rocks and ice pelted the *Americano Grande*. Leo stood in an elevator, staring numbly at the wall as it rocketed upward. Apparently when he'd destroyed the magnetosphere dynamo he'd also managed to knock out the credential lock on the lifts. He could finally access the command level on his own. Now that it was too late to matter.

He'd been hiding in his stateroom for hours, sulking and watching space debris thud against his balcony like a murderous hailstorm. Part of him wanted to open the airtight door and walk out into it. Just let a clod of ice take him out before the ship got back into comms range. Before Burlock could tell the board he'd been stripped of command. Before Admiral Skardon's smug victory. Before Varlowe's heartbreak. Before Eaglehaven was deluged with dung.

But after a good wallow he had pulled himself together. He was ready to beg. He was ready to grovel. He was ready to kiss whatever part of Burlock required kissing. To save the galaxy's last bastion of humanity, he was willing to sacrifice his pride. Or what little was left of it.

The elevator pinged and the door slid open on the command lobby. Leo took a deep breath and marched out, steeling himself for what he had to do.

"All right, Leo. Put on your 'force to be reckoned with' face. We're doing this!" He swiped his tabloyd at the bridge's lockpad.

It farted an error tone. Apparently some of the locks were still working. He sighed and thumped a fist on the metal door. "Hey, it's Leo! Hello? Guys?"

A moment later the entryway slid open, revealing Swooch's slouchy form. She smiled and blinked her half-lidded eyes. "Oh, hey bud. Come on in."

Leo marched onto the bridge to face his former crew.

Every station was abandoned.

"Where is everybody?"

Swooch returned to the helm and slumped into her seat. "They're all off in a meeting. I guess there's some kind of big emergency or something. I don't know. Above my pay grade."

Leo winced as fist-sized hunks of ice pounded the window glass like frozen birds against a windshield. They didn't seem to bother Swooch. Nothing seemed to bother Swooch.

"Oh. Okay then." Leo shuffled awkwardly. "So... I guess I'll just come back later."

"Nah, you should hang out, bruh. I made pizza clumps."

Swooch grabbed a plate off her console that was loaded with what looked like pre-chewed masses of Chicago deep-dish. Leo averted his eyes and noticed a series of alerts flashing across Swooch's panel. "Wait, what's happening here?"

"Not a whole lot." She nodded out the window at the supermassive Blue Hole spinning off the bow. "This part of space is pretty low-maintenance. Just don't run into that thing and you're golden."

"No, I mean..." Leo gestured at the blinking screen. "What is happening *here*?"

Swooch glanced at her panel, as if noticing it for the first time. "Oh, this? It's nothing. It's just upset 'cause the engines blew out."

Leo choked. "Blew out?!"

"Yeah. They're stone-cold dead." She waggled the steering yoke. Nothing happened. "I put in a help-desk ticket with Praz, so I'm sure he's on it."

"Why are you sure?" Leo squeaked. "What has Praz ever done to make you think he can fix a dead engine? Or identify one?"

"Hey, I don't judge. Everybody's got their own vibe." Swooch poked at the unresponsive panel. "Still, I should probably call down again. Before it's too late."

"Too late for what?"

"To turn."

Leo looked out the window at the gaping gravity well dead ahead. "Oh shix! We're headed for the Blue Hole!"

Swooch raised her palms in a calming gesture. "Yeah, yeah. Don't get all worked up. We won't go into the accretion disc for another..." She checked her console. "Twenty minutes."

"Twenty minutes?!"

"Give or take." The Geiko yawned and stretched. "Plenty of time for the dudes downstairs to work it out. So..." She lifted her plate with a grin. "Pizza clump?"

"Damn it, Swooch!" Leo thrust a finger at the window. "You just said all you had to do was not run into that thing!"

"So?"

"So... *you're going to run into that thing!*"

"Ah." Swooch snorted a laugh. "That's funny."

"Aagh!" Leo clutched his hair. "Can you stop being so infuriatingly chill?"

He shouldered her aside and grabbed the yoke. It was slack in his hands. He dialed dials and slid sliders. Nothing happened. "Oh no. It's hosed. It's super hosed."

"Yep," Swooch said from under his armpit. "S'what I said."

In a panic, Leo flicked the switch for the deep-space comm link. Another warning joined the blinking mess on the panel.

"Comm inoperable while in Blue Hole dead zone."

He pounded a fist on the console. "Damn it! We have to... I don't know... Do something!"

"Oh! I know this one." Swooch sauntered to the MonCom station and tapped a pad. Instantly, the dim, nighttime lighting turned red and an earsplitting klaxon echoed through the ship. She smiled. "Is that better?"

"Yeaghh!" Leo clapped his palms on his ears. "Worse, actually! Turn it off!"

"No problemo."

The Geiko hit the panel again and the alarms silenced. Leo raked back his hair and pulled a deep breath. "Okay. Stay calm. Just find Burlock and—" The door clanked open and Burlock stormed in, followed by Comfit, Quartermaster, and Dilly. Leo blinked. "Dang, that was quick."

"Hey, look who brought the party!" Swooch dropped into her seat and pumped her hands in the air. "Woot woot!"

"What in blazes is going on here?" Burlock roared.

"Short version? Engines are busted." Swooch flicked a finger toward the gaping space maw outside the window. "We're gonna hit that thing."

"Gah! Swooch!" Comfit hissed. "You literally had *one job*."

She raced to her console as Quartermaster slipped behind his and Burlock settled too comfortably in the captain's chair. Behind them, Kellybean darted through the door, still clutching the disembarkation plans she'd been working on in her office.

"I heard the alarm and I—" Her claws dug into the carpet as she saw the bow pointed straight into the nightmare space storm. "What's happening?!"

"We're going to crash into the Blue Hole!" Leo cried. "We don't know what to do!"

Dilly raised a claw. "May it make suggestion?"

"Yes, please!"

"Do not crash into Blue Hole."

"Thank you for your insight, Lieutenant Commander." Burlock turned to Comfit. "Report!"

"Engines are completely unresponsive." Comfit tapped at her consoles. "I can't even run diagnostic scans on them."

Quartermaster hammered his keyboard. "I'm reading spontaneous, catastrophic failures across multiple systems."

"How could this happen?" Burlock asked.

"It can't!" the EngTech cried. "All these systems have redundant backups! A direct torpedo hit couldn't take out so much so quickly!"

"All right, people I need answers! What's it gonna take to keep this ship from going into that gravity well?"

Swooch licked her greasy fingers and shrugged. "A miracle?"

"Can confirm," Comfit said.

Terror curdled Leo's gut. "We have to evacuate."

"We're not going to evacuate," Burlock said. "I've never lost a ship under my command and I'm not about to start now."

"What are you going to do? Get out and push?" Leo shouted. "We need to get the passengers in the lifeboats and abandon ship before it's too late!"

"Just in case you've forgotten, you are no longer the captain. You no longer have a say in command decisions. In fact, why are you still here?" Burlock looked at the others. "Someone remove this rodent from my bridge."

Kellybean crossed her arms. "Look, Burlock, I can see you're enjoying your exciting new power trip, but Leo is right. We need to get the passengers to safety!"

"Apparently what we need is a refresher on job descriptions." Burlock pointed to himself. "Captain. In charge of command decisions." To Kellybean. "Hospitality Chief. In charge of shuffleboard tournaments." To Leo. "Nobody. In charge of nothing." He turned his empty gaze to the rest of the bridge crew. "Anyone else need clarification on their duties?"

"No, sir!" Comfit, Quartermaster, and Dilly said as one.

"*Doodies,*" Swooch giggled.

"Damn it, Burlock!" Leo snapped. "The engines are out! We're headed for a gravity well! Every living thing on the *Americano Grande* is going to die horribly if we don't evacuate right now!"

Burlock sighed. "Are you quite finished?"

"Depends. Are you gonna pull your horn crown out of your hind end?"

"All right, now you're finished." Burlock waved a hand at Dilly. "Take this noisy ape to the brig."

"Aye, Captain." Dilly flicked a wrist, firing a stream of web at Leo's chest. He gagged as the wind was knocked from his lungs. The Dreda reeled him in and scuttled for the door, but Kellybean jumped in its way, arms spread.

"Whoa, whoa! Stop!" She turned to Burlock. "What are you doing? You can't just lock him up for disagreeing with you!"

"I'm the captain. I can do whatever I want. Do you have a problem with that, Lieutenant Commander?"

"I do, actually," Kellybean said. "You're the captain, not the king of the universe! I think you need to stop throwing your weight around and listen to reason."

"And I think you need to join the former captain." Burlock snapped his fingers at Dilly. "Take her into custody. For gross insubordination."

"As you wish, Captain."

Kellybean hissed as Dilly scooped her up in its forelimbs. Burlock waved it toward the door. "Lock 'em up and keep 'em quiet. I've got a ship to save."

CHAPTER FIFTEEN

Leo and Kellybean grunted and struggled to free themselves from the chitinous vice-grip of Dilly's arms as the security chief scuttled down the corridors toward the brig.

"Dilly, stop! Please!" Leo pleaded. "We have to evacuate the ship, before it's too late!"

"You are not captain," Dilly's collar intoned. "It no longer takes orders from you."

Kellybean wriggled her feline body and scratched her claws on Dilly's exoskeleton. "This isn't about orders! It's about the lives of everyone on board!"

"Captain Burlock will fix problems."

"How can you be so sure?" Leo gazed into two of Dilly's eight horrible eyes. "Dilly, you said your primary duty is to protect the passengers and crew."

"It is."

"Then why are you arresting us when all we want to do is keep everyone from being crushed into a singularity? Because that's what's gonna happen when we go into that gravity well!"

"Captain will save ship."

"But what if he can't? What if nobody can?" Kellybean said. "You heard Quartermaster. Catastrophic failures across multiple systems! Are you willing to gamble the lives of everyone on board on Praz Kerplunkt's engineering prowess?"

Dilly's steps slowed. "It agrees passengers are in danger. But what can it do?"

"You can let us go," Kellybean said. "So we can start the evacuation."

"It must bring you to brig. It cannot defy orders."

"Okay, you're a good soldier. I get that," Leo said. "But what if we just happened to escape?"

"Escape?"

"Sure! You could tell Burlock we overpowered you and got away in the scuffle." The Dreda's insectile face made the closest thing physiologically possible to an incredulous smirk. Leo frowned. "Fine. Maybe not that."

Dilly's determined stride came to a full stop. It let out a resigned sigh that whistled across its misshapen jaw, then lifted Kellybean toward its face. "The Gellicle must claw its eyes out."

Kellybean's whiskers twitched. "I'm sorry, what?"

"Its eyes are most vulnerable area. If you claw its eyes, escape story is plausible."

"But won't you, you know, go blind?"

"Is small price to pay for lives of thousands."

"Or, alternately," Leo said, raising a finger. "We could all work together on this, save everyone, and keep all of our eyes intact." He shrugged. "Just spitballin' here."

The spider clicked in torment. "It cannot disobey order."

"Dilly, the order is wrong and you know it," Leo said, not unkindly. "If you don't know it in your head, you know it right here, in your heart."

He rapped a knuckle on Dilly's breastplate. It shook its head. "You are incorrect."

Leo slumped in defeat. "So that's it then? You're locking us up? You're choosing orders over conscience?"

"No. You are incorrect." Dilly tapped a claw on its chest. "Heart is not right here." It tapped its behind. "Heart is in dorsal abdomen."

"Oh. Okay." Leo frowned. "I think maybe you missed the point I was making."

"It did not." Dilly's arms unfolded, gently setting Leo and Kellybean on the carpet. "Lives of passengers and crew are most important thing." It nodded at an emergency panel in the wall behind a protective pane of smoked glass. "You will begin evacuation. It will accept consequences."

"Wow, really?" Leo said. "I mean, awesome! Thank you, Dilly!"

Kellybean rested a paw on one of Dilly's enormous legs and smiled. "You've done the right thing." She turned and raised her arm to the lockpad on the secured panel. Nothing happened. She gasped and clutched her bare wrist. "My tabloyd is gone!"

Leo spun and looked at the floor. "Did it fall off?"

"Probably? I don't know." She rubbed her temples and groaned. "It's been a rough day."

"Let me try."

Leo tapped his band and a puffy heart popped out.

"Call Mommy!"

He pulled his sleeve over the hologram. "I got nothin'."

They both turned to Dilly. The Dreda's head fell back on its shoulders with a screeched groan.

"Expletive deleted," its collar said without emotion. It raised its own tabloyd to the panel. The lockpad flashed green and the glass slid away. Dilly unfolded a hand and gave a sarcastic flourish at the evacuation controls. "Can you issue announcement, or must it do that too?"

Leo snorted. "No, I've got it from here. Thanks, Chief."

The panel was littered with switches and dials, but one stood out from the rest. A big red button surrounded by yellow and black warning stripes labeled "Initiate Evacuation." Leo steeled himself and pushed it. Immediately, rows of bright lights blazed to life along the floors and ceilings, blinking in sequence toward the muster stations. The evacuation alarm echoed through the decks as Leo lifted the microphone to his mouth and squeezed the button.

"Hello, everybody. This is your... well, I guess I'm not the captain anymore, so..." He cringed at the sound of his own voice booming through the ship. "Look, I'm really sorry to ruin your evening and all, but we're having a little problem with the engines. Actually, it's kind of a big problem, so..."

"Give me that," Kellybean snapped, grabbing the mic. "Attention all passengers and crew. This is not a drill. Proceed to your emergency muster stations immediately to abandon ship. I repeat, proceed to your emergency muster stations. This is not a drill."

She clapped the microphone back into the panel. Leo nodded. "Right. Well done."

"Come on, let's get those boats filled and launched while we still can." Kellybean pulled a drawer from the emergency panel and yanked out three retinal scanners and three bright yellow vests labeled "CREW." She handed a big one to Dilly and a smaller one to Leo. He looked at the label and frowned.

"Technically, I'm not crew anymore."

"You're officially deputized." Kellybean slipped into her vest. "Welcome back to the crew of the *Americano Grande*."

Leo smiled weakly. "I hope it works out better this time."

"I wouldn't consider it a long-term position." Kellybean turned on her scanner. "To the muster stations, people. Let's get to work!"

***

Kellybean stood at the round door of an emergency lifeboat, ushering panicked passengers inside. As each one passed she scanned their visual organs to confirm and log their evacuation status. The device registered each evacuee with a green light and bright *ping*.

"That's right, move all the way to the end of the row. Don't worry, there's a seat for everyone."

She turned to scan the next passenger—a Ba'lux with a puffy ski jacket and a scarf wrapped around his face. He tried to hustle past Kellybean, but she stepped in his way.

"Whoa, there. I need to scan you to make sure everybody is accounted for." She lifted her scanner to his eye and it lit red with a rude *buzz*. "Sir, are you sure this is your assigned muster station?"

"Yes! I don't know! Let me on!"

He tried to shove past, but Kellybean caught him by the arm. "Sir! I'm sorry, but you need to report to the lifeboat that—" The scarf fell away from the man's face. Kellybean's eyes narrowed. "Praz Kerplunkt, what do you think you're doing?"

"I'm trying to evacuate! Get out of my way!" Praz struggled, but Kellybean held him, now with claws out. "Ow! Quit it!"

"You're supposed to be fixing the engines! Or the dynamo! Or anything!"

"What's the point?" Praz squealed. "This ship is totally hucked! We need to get out of here! Come on!"

He tried to wrestle Kellybean onto the lifeboat, but she hissed and shoved him away. "You're the chief engineer! Go fix something! Now!"

Praz stumbled and took off down the corridor. Kellybean turned to her next passenger. The moment they locked eyes, her muscles reflexively tightened.

"This is the worst cruise we've ever been on," Clermytha Gwapwaffle whined. "And you're the worst hospitality chief!"

"And we know what we're talking about!" Horman said.

"We're Platinum Elite Class!"

Kellybean forced a smile and took the man's withered blue hand, helping him limp through the door on his injured leg. "I do apologize for this unexpected turn of events, sir. As always, your safety is my primary concern."

As soon as Horman was settled in his seat he slapped Kellybean away. "Look at my leg!" he snarled, pointing to the bandages. "It looks like I just got back from the war! Except in the war, I didn't get hurt so bad!"

"And you people ruined my dress!" Clermytha tugged at the spider silk still clinging to the fabric from when Dilly had saved her life. Her lip quivered. "And I never did get my box lunch!"

"And we paid extra for that!" Horman added.

Kellybean harnessed them into the last two seats and ducked through the low doorway back out into the concourse.

"Again, I do apologize," she said, peering in through the door. "Your feedback is important to WTF cruises, so please put all of your complaints in writing, stick them inside a pair of cactuses, and stuff them up your withered blue buttholes!"

Clermytha squealed. Horman gasped. "You furry savage! I'm reporting you to—"

"Bon voyage, bishes." Kellybean yanked the launch lever and the doors slammed shut. With a dull *thump* against the hull, the Gwapwaffles were fired into deep space at twice the speed of sound. A shudder ran through her body. "Wow, that felt good."

***

Leo looked through a porthole window at the glowing back end of a lifeboat he had just launched. It was his third so far. Sixty guests he'd personally rescued. If he couldn't save Eaglehaven, he could at least save some lives here.

He rushed along the concourse to the next muster station. A

group of passengers were ready to be loaded into the lifeboat, but the Krubb crew member had yet to open its door.

"What's the hold up?" Leo asked, thumping a palm on the hatch. "Let's get these people on that boat."

"I can't get the door open!" the Krubb squeaked. She yanked the release lever up and down but nothing happened. Leo put his face to the tiny window, mounted too high for the Krubb to see out of. Outside was nothing but the spiraling storm cloud of the Blue Hole.

"It's gone. You already launched it."

"I did not!" the Krubb said indignantly.

"Are you sure?"

"What do you mean 'am I sure'?" She jabbed a long arm at the guests. "Do you think it slipped my mind to put the passengers on it first?"

A panicked rumble ran through the gathered crowd.

"Wait, hold on," a Ba'lux woman gasped. "Our lifeboat is *gone*?"

"Oh shix, we're all dead!" a Screetoro screamed from his trumpet-bell mouths. *"Deeeeaaaaad!"*

The alien's wailing voice sent a shock of panic through the already terrified passengers. A Simishi woman sobbed into her helmet and a Verdaphyte man dropped leaves from his scalp like autumn came early. Leo raised his hands.

"It's okay! We can squeeze you all into other boats!" He waved a hand toward the next station. "Come with me!"

He dashed down the concourse to another group of guests in front of another closed door. A Lethargot girl in a housekeeping uniform and a yellow vest stooped to peer out its window.

"Why aren't you loading your boat?" Leo barked.

The girl lazily raised a hand to point out the porthole. "Boat's gone."

A Gellicle man mewled in fear. "What do you mean gone?"

The Lethargot shrugged. "Like, I dunno. Not there."

A voice cut through the gathering chaos, screaming like wind over bamboo. "Captain! Captain, over here!" Leo looked up to see a Verdaphyte man darting toward him with an unfolded tabloyd. The crewman caught his breath and stammered. "Something's gone wrong, Captain."

"Technically I'm not the captain anymo—"

"The lifeboats, sir! Some are missing!"

"So I've heard. Don't panic. We'll figure something—"

"Actually, a lot are missing." The Verdaphyte swiped his leafy fingers on his device. "There was corrupt code in the internal sensors. The evacuation system has been misreporting false nominal status since we left Jaynkee!"

"Say it in normal words!" Leo barked. "Where did the lifeboats go?"

"They didn't go anywhere, sir. They were never loaded onto the ship to begin with."

Leo's hands went clammy and his throat went dry. His voice came out in a hoarse rattle. "Do we have enough lifeboats to evacuate everyone on board?"

"Not even close, sir."

A wave of hysteria crashed through the passengers. Leo raised his hands. "No no! It's okay! I'm sure this is a mistake!"

"It's not. You can check for yourself."

The plant man tapped his tabloyd to the one on Leo's wrist and they both lit blue with a syncing chime. Leo blinked in confusion. "Wait, did that actually work?"

He yanked his band off his arm and unfolded it. For the whole voyage it had only showed two apps—"Call Mommy" and "Cruise Itinerary." Now there was a third icon. A folder next to a green message. *New data received. Documents folder unlocked.*

He tapped the icon and the screen filled with information. At the top was the Verdaphyte's report. Below it were dozens of other files.

"What the… Where did all this come from?"

The crewman peered at the screen and raised a puzzled brow. "Sir, did you have your documents folder hidden behind a child lock?"

Leo didn't answer. He barely even acknowledged he had asked his question out loud. He just stared. These weren't his files. But whose were they?

His fingers trembled as he flicked through them. Staffing requests and entertainment contracts. Reports on Ba'lux digestive toxins. Operational specs for a certain cylinder-shaped mystery device.

"Oh shix," he whispered.

"Sir?"

"Shix!" Leo shouted. "It wasn't an accident!"

"What wasn't an accident?"

"Any of it!" He turned and bolted down the concourse. "I've gotta tell Burlock!"

***

Jassi felt the roll of ocean waves heaving against her gut in the darkness. A siren worked its way into her ears—bold and authoritative but stopping just short of being panic-inducing. Her eyes cracked open and she found herself floating backwards down a corridor. Not floating. Being carried.

She snorted and shook her head as reality rushed in. Her body was thrown over Stobber's massive, bramble-scratched shoulder and he was plodding down a concourse of panicked tourists. She tried to twist out of his grip, but her vines felt slack on her twigs.

"What the huck?" she croaked. "Put me down, shixhead."

"There she is. Finally." Stobber chuckled. "Gahdamn, Jass. How much did you have to drink?"

Jassi planted her palms on her eyes. "I don't remember."

Stobber whistled. "That much, huh? Yer lucky I found your dumb arze."

Something tickled under Jassi's chin. She rubbed it away. Her hand came back sticky with drool and covered in white fur. A memory sparked. Then another. Flashes. Passion. Then darkness.

"Where's Kellybean?" she asked.

"Kellywho?" Stobber grumbled.

"Kellybean! The Gellicle!"

"Hooray! You're alive!" a digital voice cheered. Jassi looked up to see Hax speeding up behind Stobber, his eyes aglow with joy. "I was so worried! Where have you two been?"

"Lookin' for you, wingnuts," Stobber grunted. "Come on, we're all getting out of here."

"Yay! Together forever!" Hax chirped.

From her vantage point atop the towering Nomit, Jassi suddenly became aware of passengers gathering at the muster stations. "Wait, what's going on here?"

Stobber stopped walking and set Jassi down at the back of a group being hustled into a lifeboat. "I dunno. Looks like the American captain screwed the pooch. We gotta abandon ship."

A frenzied Simishi crew member in a yellow vest rushed over with a scanner. "I need your optical organ! Now!"

Stobber bent down and widened his enormous, salad-plate eyes. The Simishi scanned him with a green light and bright *ping*. "Stobber, Sikkolas. Get in!"

The Nomit crouched and squeezed himself through the door and into the lifeboat. Hax rolled up eagerly. "Me next!"

One of his eyes winked out and the other expanded to fill the screen. The crewman scanned it. "Haxkit Electronics model 132, serial number: FFEA97?"

"That's my name, don't wear it out!"

Hax's tires bumped over the edge of the door and he settled into the seat next to Stobber. The Simishi turned to Jassi and impatiently waved a webbed hand. "Come on, come on!"

Jassi shook her head. "I... I can't."

"What do you mean you can't?" Stobber said.

"I can't! I have to find Kellybean."

"Are you kidding me?" Stobber snorted. "Get in the boat!"

The Simishi shoved his scanner in her face and it pinged. "Kiktrash, Jassilyn! Move it!"

"Get offa me!" she roared, shoving him away. "I'm not leaving without Kellybean!"

"Why not?" Stobber said. "She had no problem leaving you!"

"The huck you talking about?"

"I found you passed out in a bar! Alone!" He shook his head. "That furry bish hucked and chucked you, Jass."

Jassi squinted at him. "Seriously?"

"Yes, seriously! Get in the gahdamn boat!"

"Listen to your friend!" the Simishi glubbed. "Move it!"

"Jassi, please. Come with us." Hax reached out a plastic hand. "Best friends, right? Together forever?"

His eyes turned pleading. Jassi put her fingers to the sticky cat saliva on her neck. She tried to imagine Kellybean ravishing her then dumping her unconscious body in a bar. She couldn't remember any of it.

She took Hax's hand.

"Together forever, buddy."

***

Kellybean loaded passengers into a lifeboat with an ache of relief. This was the last of her assigned muster stations, which meant her work was technically done. There was one seat left on this boat, and it was reserved for her. But she couldn't bring herself to board.

She had unfinished business.

Her fingers flicked across the screen of her retinal scanner and scrolled through the names in the shipwide register. There were still a lot of people to evacuate. But the person she was looking for was not among them.

Kiktrash, Jassilyn had abandoned ship. Kellybean wasn't surprised. Abandoning seemed to be her jam. Jassi had already abandoned Kellybean in her own bed.

Her blood boiled at the memory of waking up in a twist of blankets, still strewn with crinkled leaves. Trusting Jassi had been a mistake. Her claws twitched. Now she was ready to evacuate. Ready to track down that treacherous plant and show her what happens when you disrespect a Gellicle.

Kellybean tapped the panel next to the lifeboat's door, prepping the auto-launch sequence. But before she could step inside, a horrible rattling, clanking noise caught her attention.

She turned just in time to see a battered yellow maintenance bot barreling down the concourse. Its front side was smashed completely flat, and an ax stuck out of its head. Almost before Kellybean understood what she was looking at, the bot plowed into her. She mewled in pain as it clumsily snagged her in its four arms and ran straight into the wall.

The robot fell apart upon impact, leaving Kellybean sprawled on the floor with the air pounded from her lungs. Her vision swam through a possible concussion, but she managed to focus on an orange figure rushing up to the lifeboat.

"Praz!" she gasped. "What did you do?"

"I fixed something!" he said proudly.

Praz leaped through the hatch and the door slammed shut behind him. With a dull thump against the hull, Kellybean's lifeboat launched without her in it.

"No!" Pain surged from her smashed legs as she struggled to her feet and kicked her way through the bot debris. She reached the window just in time to see her boat swoop away to rendezvous with the rest of the escape fleet. "Damn it, Praz! That was my seat!"

"Kellybean!" a voice shouted. She staggered around on her bruised legs to find Leo sprinting up to her. He scrambled to a stop, gasping for breath. "We've been sabotaged!"

"What?"

"The poisoning! The engines!" He slapped at his tabloyd. "It's all right here! Somebody did it on purpose!"

"What?! Who?"

"I don't know! But we need to tell Burlock! Come on!"

Leo bolted down the abandoned concourse, dodging around overturned café tables and discarded luggage. Kellybean hobbled after him.

But as soon as Leo made it to the first corner, someone stepped out to meet him. Burlock's fist hit Leo's jaw like it had been fired from a torpedo tube. Leo's head twisted on his neck and he hit the wall then the floor in rapid succession.

"Leo!" Kellybean mewled.

Before Leo could stand, an orange hand closed around his throat and hauled him off the deck.

"You stupid, gahdamned *fool!*" Burlock roared. "What do you think you're doing?"

"Burlock!" Kellybean hissed. "Let him go!"

She screeched and pounced at him, claws out. With a powerful swing of his cybernetic arm, Burlock smacked the feline out of the air mid-lunge. She sailed across the corridor and hit the opposite wall with a sickly *thwack* before falling to the floor in a heap.

"Kell... Bea..." Leo gagged.

He scrabbled and thrashed but couldn't break free of Burlock's tightening grip. The Ba'lux seethed with rage as he pointed out the window. "You two idiots doomed all those passengers!"

"No." Leo gasped. "We... saved... them."

"You ignorant mammal! What do you think is going to happen to them?"

"Picked... up. Rescue ship."

"What rescue ship? We're outside the shipping lanes, millions of miles out of comm range in any direction!" Burlock turned Leo's choking, purple face toward the window. Clods of rock and ice continued to pelt the glass. Far in the distance, the glowing specks of the lifeboat engines were barely visible against the raging storm of the Blue Hole. "Those boats don't have shielding for a debris cloud like this! They'll be smashed to bits within an hour!" He banged Leo's skull on the bulkhead, rattling his brains. "Feel that? That's eighteen inches of reinforced chromasteel! They were safer on the ship, you gahdamn idiot!"

The fight went out of Leo as Burlock's fingers crushed his windpipe. His vision darkened and his muscles unspooled.

"I... didn't... know..."

"You didn't have to know! *I* knew! That's why I didn't order an evacuation! Your little mutiny has condemned every soul on those boats to die a grisly death in the vacuum of space." Burlock's voice turned icy. "So I condemn you to the same fate."

He hauled Leo to the nearest airlock like a lethargic rag doll.

"Stop..." Leo whispered. "Burlock..."

His hands swatted limply and clumsily at Burlock's chest and face, but the Ba'lux didn't even flinch. He tapped the pad on the airlock, and the inner door slid open. Kellybean tried to stand but crashed to the floor, her battered legs and concussed head both working against her.

"Burlock!" she cried. "Stop!"

"Quit your mewling, cat!" Burlock roared. "I'm putting you out next!"

"I don't think so," a gravelly voice muttered.

Burlock spun to see a ragged Verdaphyte girl with a magnum of champagne hefted over her shoulder like a baseball bat.

"Cheers, motherhucker."

Jassi's long muscles whipped the bottle around and smashed it into the side of Burlock's head, shattering the glass. His skull let out a gruesome *crack* and his prosthetic sparked against the bubbly deluge. He roared and stumbled back, dropping Leo to the deck.

"Jassi!" Kellybean gasped. "What... how... *you!*"

"I know." Jassi wagged a brow. "Speechless, right?"

Burlock wiped the booze out of his eye and glared with murderous rage. "Looks like it's time to cut the grass!"

He drew back his mechanical hand and three serrated blades unsheathed from his fingers with a *schling* of metal on metal. But before he could swing it forward, his arm was caught by a plastic hand.

"You can have this back when you're ready to play nice."

Hax stabbed a screwdriver into Burlock's lethal prosthetic, spinning it with drill-like speed. The metal arm fell off at the elbow and dropped to the floor. Burlock swung his stump at Jassi, but she dodged. At the same time, her boot swung up and connected with his crotch like she was kicking a field goal. Burlock howled and fell to his knees, and Jassi followed up with a vicious uppercut that knocked his implant right out of his skull. The crescent of his organic head trembled as he keeled over and crashed lifelessly to the deck.

Kellybean struggled to her feet. "You killed him!"

Hax stuck out a finger and plugged it into one of Burlock's cranial sockets. His eyes frizzed out then came back into focus. "He'll be fine. But his reproductive capacity has been reduced by a factor of seven percent."

Leo coughed and rubbed his crushed throat. "You... you saved me! Why did you save me?"

"I didn't." Jassi thumbed at Kellybean. "I saved her. You just got in the way."

"Well, thanks anyhow," Leo mumbled.

Kellybean stared at Jassi. "But... you were scanned off the ship. You evacuated!"

"Almost!" Hax said cheerily. "She grabbed my hand and I thought she was going to get in the boat, but then she pulled me *out* of the boat!" He clasped his hands. "Surprise twist! So dramatic!"

Jassi shrugged at Kellybean. "I couldn't leave. Not until I knew you were okay."

Warmth percolated in Kellybean's chest, drawing a hint of a dreamy smile to her face. But before it could bloom she stomped it out with a scowl. "What do you care if I'm okay? You certainly didn't care when you drugged me at the concert."

Jassi cringed. "It wasn't me! It was Stobber!"

"Hey, where is Stobber?" Leo asked.

"He stayed on the lifeboat," Jassi growled. "Huck that guy."

"No, huck you," Kellybean said choking out the expletive. "You're the one who took advantage of me!" Her claws came out. "You violated my trust, Jassi!"

"I..." Jassi raised her hands and quirked a brow. "Did I?"

"Yes you did!"

"How?"

"What do you mean *how?*"

"Like, literally. How? What did I do?" Jassi clutched her head. "I have no idea what happened after we left the concert."

"I'm sorry," Leo said. "I don't mean to interrupt, but maybe this argument isn't our highest priority right now."

"Oh, so sorry to trouble you with our tiresome female ladyproblems," Jassi said. "Please, mansplain exactly what's more important."

"Somebody sabotaged the engines and we're currently coasting toward a gravity well with no hope of escape, we just staged a full-on mutiny and nearly murdered the captain, there aren't enough lifeboats to evacuate everyone left on board, and it doesn't matter anyway because the boats we've already launched are going to be smashed apart by debris, leaving the passengers to asphyxiate in the vacuum of space."

Jassi's eyes rolled. "Fine, we'll put a pin in the ladyproblems."

Leo's laundry list of catastrophe settled in Kellybean's mind. "Oh my gosh. The lifeboats! Burlock was right! We can't call for a rescue ship to collect them!"

"Don't worry," Hax said. "A ship will be passing by soon."

"No, it won't," Leo groaned. "We're millions of miles outside the shipping lanes!"

"Nonetheless, a ship will be passing by soon." Hax cocked his head at the window. "That one, specifically."

Everyone peered through the glass at the distinctive red flare of ion burners in the distance. The vessel's shape was blacked out against their blinding glow, but whatever it was, it was enormous. A manic grin spread on Leo's face. "It's a ship! There's a ship! We're saved!"

"Not necessarily," Kellybean said. "The Blue Hole seriously

wangs up external sensors. They probably don't even know we're here."

Leo rushed off down the concourse.

"Then let's go make sure they do!"

CHAPTER SIXTEEN

Leo raced onto the command bridge, followed by Kellybean, Jassi, and Hax. Every console blinked errors and screamed warnings, but they were all abandoned except for the helm.

Swooch spun in her chair and raked a hand through her long scalp tentacles. "Hey hey! It's Not-Captain Leo! Good to see you, buddy. I thought Burlock would have killed you by now."

"It's good to see you, too," Leo said, ignoring the rest. "Any progress on the engine repairs?"

"Nah. Still boned." Swooch put a finger on the yoke and gave it a flick, sending it into a useless spin. "But check this out." She pointed to the window. In the corner was a box reading *200x magnification*. It framed a ship that looked like an enormous metal lionfish with an ion burner stuck up its butt.

"It's the *Opulera*! It's Varlowe!" Leo's heart swelled with relief. "Somebody open a comm channel!"

Swooch shook her head. "I already tried. They're not talkin'."

"No?" Leo peered at the magnified view in the window. The *Americano Grande's* tiny lifeboats were queued for landing in an open shuttle bay on the Ba'lux ship. A few were already inside. "Clearly they know we're here. Why wouldn't they answer us?"

Kellybean swiped on the MonCom panel and a glitchy rectangle appeared in the corner of the panoramic window. "Interference from the Blue Hole is scrambling comms. We can't get a link."

"Lemme take a look," Jassi said.

She stepped behind the MonCom console at Kellybean's side. Kellybean crossed her arms and pulled back, annoyed. "You think I don't know how to use a comm panel?"

"No, I think your system is all hucked up." Jassi poked at the readouts. "You got the power, you're just using it wrong."

"I'm using it exactly the way it was designed—"

Kellybean yelped as Jassi slammed the point of her woody elbow into a groove at the lower edge of the console and wrenched her arm. With a sharp *pop*, the seal broke and the panel hinged open.

"Hey! Don't wreck that!" Leo cried. "We need it!"

"Cool yer balls. I'm not wrecking anything." Jassi held up a hand. "Hax. Wrench me. Three-quarter inch."

"Coming up!" Hax opened the drawer in his hips, plucked out a wrench, and hurled it to Jassi. It hit her woody palm with a *clack* and she dug into the exposed panel.

"These big starships have stupidly wide comm beams. You got power to waste, so you do, blasting your shix over half the galaxy. If you put all that juice into a tight beam and actually aim the damn thing..."

She fitted the wrench on a component and gave it a twist. At the same time, the distorted image on the window resolved into a WTF logo with a blinking message. *Ship-to-ship network established. Awaiting remote connection.*

"Whoa!" Leo said. "You fixed it!"

"Duh." Jassi flicked a hand at the *Opulera*. "You can chat your meaty face off as soon as they pick up the call."

"That's awesome! Thank you so—"

Leo choked as a strand of spider web as big around as his arm hit him in the back. Before he could pull a breath he was yanked off his feet and into the arms of Dilly, standing hunched in the doorway. A second strand hit Kellybean and reeled her in beside him. The security chief dangled them in the air, clenching them in its spindly fingers.

"Dilly!" Leo gasped. "What are you—"

The Dreda's glowing eyes flared in anger as it screeched in Leo's face, showering him with sticky drool. "You said you wanted to save passengers, but you put them in danger," its translation collar said calmly. "You tricked it into helping you."

"We didn't trick you!" Kellybean mewled. "It was a mistake!"

Leo's head bobbed in agreement. "It was a good deed gone horribly wrong!"

"Oi! Spider!" Jassi cracked her knuckles. "Put the kitty down or you're gonna be in for a world of—"

Dilly fired a net of webbing that blasted Jassi off her feet and slapped her brutally against a bulkhead. Hax gasped.

"Jassi! I'll save you!" He raced to her, but another burst of silk wrapped his arms and bound his tires. He wobbled and crashed to the floor. "Actually, never mind."

They both thrashed and struggled against the sticky strands. Dilly's eyes turned to Swooch. "Anything to add, Lieutenant?"

Swooch shrugged. "Nah, I'm chill."

"Good work, soldier," a voice growled. "I guess you can follow orders after all."

The spider scuttled aside, revealing Burlock towering in the doorway, with all of his cybernetic implants restored. Dilly bowed submissively. "Yes, sir. It apologizes for insubordination. Will not happen again."

"See that it doesn't." Burlock marched onto the bridge. "Comfit, open a channel to…" He glanced at the empty stations. "Where are my MonCom and EngTech?"

"Oh, they're long gone," Swooch said. "As soon as the shix hit, Comfit split. Quartermaster even faster." She snorted a chuckle. "Dang, listen to me. I'm like a rapper."

Kellybean wriggled in Dilly's hand. "Let us go!"

"Burlock!" Leo cried. "Somebody sabotaged the cruise! I have evidence! My tabloyd—"

"Silence them!" Burlock snapped.

Dilly whirled Leo and Kellybean in its arms, neatly binding each of them in webbing from their ankles to their noses. They shouted muffled curses as Dilly set them down on their feet like a pair of exhumed pharaohs. It pointed to the comm view on the window. "Connection is in progress, Captain."

Burlock raised his voice to the glass. "This is Captain Rexel Burlock of the *WTF Americano Grande* hailing the *WTF Opulera*. Do you copy?" Nothing happened for a long moment. "Damn it, *Opulera*! Do you copy?"

"Yes, Burlock, I copy."

The comm rectangle flickered and resolved into an orange face. Admiral Skardon was in his formal robes, standing in front of what looked like an enormous window overlooking the Blue Hole. As the picture came into sharper focus, a lifeboat flew through the window, sparking red as it passed through the glass. Leo realized it wasn't a window at all, but the gaping door of a shuttle bay with an atmospheric containment field.

"Admiral Skardon." Burlock snapped to attention. "I've never been so happy to see you, sir."

"I wish I could say the same," Skardon replied. "We came as soon as we got your distress call."

Leo thrashed his head and worked his jaw, coaxing the webbing down over his chin. "We didn't send a distress call!"

"Of course you did," the admiral said. "We received it while en route to Nyja and immediately set an intercept course at maximum speed. Luckily we were in time to start collecting your lifeboats before it was too late." He gestured over his shoulder at the busy shuttle bay behind him. "Quite a fortuitous turn of events, eh? Me, being here with this regal Ba'lux ship to rescue the survivors of Varlowe Waylade's catastrophic American-style cruise." He rubbed his hands with delight. "She will never live down this humiliation."

Burlock nodded. "Yes, sir. It's been a shix show over here, to be honest. But I don't understand how you're responding to a distress call."

"What's to not understand? You called for help and we answered."

"But we really didn't call for help," Burlock said. "We've been in the Blue Hole's dead zone for hours. It's not possible you could have received a deep-space comm from—"

"He didn't get a distress call!" Leo shouted. "He knew someone was going to wreck the engines! He sent the saboteur!"

"Shut your blasphemous mouth!" Burlock roared. "Or I'll have Dilly bite your gahdamn head off!"

Skardon tutted. "I'm disappointed, Burlock. It seems the monkey figured it out before you did."

The color flushed from Burlock's face. "Wait. MacGavin is *right*? You put a saboteur on your own ship?"

"Not on *my* ship." Skardon chuckled. "On *Varlowe's* ship."

"But why?"

"To protect my interests, of course. It was a foregone conclusion that the American couldn't captain that monstrosity all the way to Ensenada Vega, but the stakes were too high to leave it to chance. So I sent in my own little agent of chaos."

"Yeah, I know," Leo said. "I found all your secret files."

Skardon snuffed. "You did not."

"I did! Look!" Leo wrestled both arms from between the strands of his binding and swiped his tabloyd. A holographic heart sprang from his wrist.

"Call Mommy!"

"Gah!" He stuffed his hands behind his back. "Well... they're on there! Trust me!"

"They are not. Your device is useless. I should know. I'm the one who ordered it." Skardon grinned mischievously. "The real captain's tabloyd has unlimited access to all areas of the ship, as well as every system. I gave it to my agent, who used it to wreak havoc without ever being detected."

Burlock's jaw trembled. "Sir, I don't understand. You can't honestly have sabotaged—"

"Praz Kerplunkt!" Kellybean shouted. She spat a wad of gnawed-up spider web on the floor and hissed. "Oh my gosh! You made that idiot the chief engineer so he'd have access to the engines and magnetosphere dynamo!"

"Praz?" Skardon giggled. "Are you kidding me? Praz is a nincompoop. I wouldn't count on him to tie his shoes, let alone sabotage a ship." He grinned. "No, my saboteur was not on the senior staff."

"Whoa," Swooch said. "Was it Comfit?"

"No."

"Quartermaster?"

"No."

"Was it me?"

"No!"

Swooch scratched her head. "Does anybody else work here?"

Skardon pinched his eyes. "Let me make it easy for you."

The picture became all hand as the admiral reached out and adjusted the camera angle. When he pulled his fingers away, the view resolved to a few parked lifeboats and one very smug looking Nomit slurping a tall-boy of blue beer.

"S'up, dickweeds?" Stobber said.

"Ha!" Jassi crowed. "I knew it!"

Kellybean gasped. "You knew Stobber was the saboteur?"

"No! I knew he was a lyin' wuss! He said he hacked the ticketing system to get us on the excursion, but he just used an all-access tabloyd." She snorted a laugh at Stobber. "You can't hack software for shix, you traitorous fartknocker!"

Stobber scowled. "Yeah? Well at least I can hack hardware without hucking it up!"

"No you can't," Jassi barked.

"He can, actually," Skardon said. "If it's simple enough. I made sure of that before I booked Murderblossom for this cruise."

"That was *you*?" Kellybean said.

"It was," Skardon mused. "When I recruited Mister Stobber, I surreptitiously added his band to the entertainment roster. Being a musician was the perfect cover for him to slip this past security."

He flicked the tabloyd on his wrist and another window appeared on the glass wall, showing a tech schematic of a device in the shape of a waist-high cylinder.

"Hey!" Hax cried. "That's my bass drum! The one Stobber bought me then lost!"

"That's no drum," Leo said. "It's the thing I destroyed in the machine room!"

Burlock just stared, his eye lens twitching. "It's a parasitic capacitor. Ba'luxi Prime Navy tech. Back in the war we used those to disable enemy ships."

"Ah, so there is something left in your hollowed out brain," Skardon said smugly. "I liberated a para-capacitor when I left the service. Kept it hidden away for a rainy day." He glared at Stobber and sighed. "It was such an elegant plan. The Nomit was supposed to smuggle it on board as part of a drum kit, then use the captain's credentials to sneak into the machine room and clamp it to a power junction."

"Which I did!" Stobber said defensively.

Leo's mind flashed back to when he first met Praz in engineering.

"Look at the lockpad logs!" He had whined. *"Captain! Captain! Captain! He's been in here more times than I have!"*

"Wait," Leo said, blinking back to the present. "So that gizmo was draining power from the engines the whole time?"

Stobber sipped his beer petulantly. "It wasn't supposed to. It was supposed to kick on and blow them out when we got to the Blue Hole. But something hucked it up."

Leo remembered finding the device, and the error message flashed in his mind's eye. *Surge detected. Core corrupted. 15% efficiency.*

"Praz must have accidentally activated it when he was wrecking consoles in engineering," he guessed. "But the surge damaged it too much to kill the engines. It only weakened them!"

Burlock sucked a sharp breath. "That explains why the nav thrusters went out when we left Jaynkee." He turned to Stobber in a rage. "We barely missed a rogue iceberg! You almost killed us all!"

"And way too soon," Stobber grunted. "I hadn't even gotten Skardon and the other bigwigs off the ship yet."

"You did not get executives off ship," Dilly noted. "Board was medically evacuated by doctor."

Burlock pointed to Leo. "After the chimp poisoned them with his disgusting American cuisine."

"Pfft, whatever," Stobber said. "*I* poisoned them. Or at least I set it up. It was easy. And cheesy."

"The huck is that supposed to mean?" Jassi asked.

Skardon snuffed at her. "As everyone knows, Ba'lux physiology is very sensitive to certain types of dairy."

"Everyone knows that?" Leo asked incredulously.

"I did," Kellybean confirmed. "And I personally checked over the menu for the Captain's Welcome Dinner. The only dairy was the cheese on the nachos. Gouda is on the safe list!"

"It is," Stobber agreed. "Which is why I stole all of it."

Leo's mind reeled back to his encounter with the chef, and the Geiko's reaction to his criticism of the "American nachos."

"If you're going to be a pedant about it, yes, we were out of gouda cheese so I used muenster."

He raised a brow. "They were poisoned by muenster cheese?"

Skardon nodded. "Highly toxic and strictly banned in the kitchens of Ba'lux ships. But on an American ship…"

"So I didn't poison them at all!" Leo cried. "You set me up!"

"And you nearly ruined it by changing the menu," Skardon snapped. "And then you went and destroyed the para-capacitor." He shook his head. "You're a bigger thorn in my side than I ever expected, MacGavin."

"Back at ya," Leo grumbled.

"Wait, I don't get it." Jassi nodded at Leo. "If the hairbag wrecked the sabotage drum…" She nodded at Stobber. "How did shix for brains still blow out the engines?"

Stobber snorted. "They were supposed to burn out during the concert. When they didn't, I knew something was hucked up. So I had to go demolish 'em by hand." He shrugged. "Wasn't even hard. All the systems are wide open once you get past the secure doors."

"And how did you manage that?" Jassi asked. "Because I know your dumb arze can't fake credentials, and you lost your sugar daddy's tabloid back in the gas pit."

"I stole a new one from a senior staff member," Stobber said. "And you helped."

"Jassi!" Hax squealed. "How could you?"

"I didn't help!"

"Stobber!" Hax squealed. "You fibber!"

The Nomit raised a broad hand. "All I'm sayin' is, I never could have drugged the Gellicle without you."

Kellybean glared at Stobber. "You drugged me and stole my tabloyd?"

"That makes no sense," Jassi said. "Why did you get her all horny so you could mug her?"

"Horny?" Stobber asked.

"Yes, horny! The second Kellybean swallowed your stupid sex drugs she was all over me!"

Kellybean's ears blossomed red. "Can we not talk about this?"

Stobber burst out laughing. "They weren't sex drugs! They were just standard, run-of-the-mill tranquilizers." He grinned at Jassi. "You of all people should know!"

"How?" Jassi growled. "How should I know?"

"Because I put 'em in your drink too, idiot. The plan was for you to lure her away from the crowd for a little kitty coitus, then you'd both black out and I could steal her tabloyd with no witnesses." He shrugged. "And I could get a show out of it."

Kellybean's whiskers twitched. "You watched us?!"

Stobber grinned. "I even recorded it. Check it out." He pulled a minicam from his back pocket and flicked its controls.

"No!" Kellybean screeched. "Don't show it!"

A video window popped up on the glass, showing a jerky handheld shot tracking down a hallway of stateroom doors. Kellybean and Jassi were shoulder to shoulder, arms slung over each other, feet shuffling and bouncing over the carpet as if they were on the twelfth stop of a pub crawl.

"Okay, Beans," Jassi slurred. *"Almost home. Keep it moving."*

"Oh, I'll keep it moving," Kellybean moaned. *"Moving into your pants!"*

She lurched against Jassi, slamming her into the wall. Jassi groaned as Kellybean pressed against her body, licking her neck with long, clumsy strokes of her little cat tongue.

"Stop," Jassi said drowsily. "Stop it. I've gotta get you into bed."

"Yeah ya do," Kellybean purred.

"Inta your bed. Alone. You gotta sleep this off. You've been drugged." Jassi gestured limply at the camera. "That shixhead gave you drugs."

Stobber's grunt of laughter was too loud, too close to the minicam's microphone. Kellybean nuzzled her furry head against Jassi's wet neck.

"You're my drug," she whispered.

Jassi's knees wobbled. "Well, I am a quarter catnip on my mother's side."

On the bridge, Jassi thrashed against the webs gluing her to the wall. "What the huck? You said they weren't sex drugs!"

"They weren't!" Stobber said. "That's all her! After one drink!" He snorted. "That kitty cannot hold her liquor."

Kellybean looked at the floor and muttered under her breath. "This is why I don't drink on duty."

The video glitched and flickered, then resumed inside Kellybean's stateroom.

"Okay, we're here," Jassi mumbled. "We're at your place."

"Finally!" Kellybean cooed.

Her claws came out and Jassi yelped as Kellybean grabbed her and threw her onto the bed.

"Don't," Jassi yawned. "Stop it. Staaa..."

Her eyes drifted shut and her head tipped back with a snore. Kellybean pawed at her for an uncomfortably long time before she collapsed and fell off the bed.

Behind the camera, Stobber chuckled. "*And* scene. *C'mon, Jass. We got work to do.*"

A massive hand reached into the shot and grabbed Jassi's limp body. A smaller hand plucked the tabloyd off Kellybean's wrist. The video glitched again, changing the scene. Now the minicam was lying on its side in an engineering conduit. Jassi was big in the foreground, sprawled on the floor and snoring like a sawmill. In the background, Stobber ripped hunks of circuits and bundles of wire out of the walls and ceilings like he was trying to dig his way out. Music echoed faintly down the corridor, laced with a smooth, crooning vocal. The video stuttered and turned off.

Leo blinked as the quiet voice resolved in his head. "That's Swaggy Humbershant, Jr.! This was filmed during the concert!" His eyes went wide. "*You* were the one who took down the magnetosphere dynamo!"

"Guilty." Stobber slipped his minicam back in his pocket. "That was an accident though. I was only trying to huck up the engine. I didn't mean to ruin the concert."

Jassi sneered. "Yeah, it's a real party foul to spoil the entertainment when you're just trying to murder everyone."

"Oh no, not everyone." Skardon shook his head. "That simply wouldn't do. The ridiculous American ship had to go, but the passengers had to live." He smiled proudly. "Imagine the news feeds. Thousands of survivors of Varlowe Waylade's deadly folly, plucked from the jaws of death by the steady hand of Admiral Rip Skardon amidst the regal grandeur of the *WTF Opulera*."

Leo crossed his arms across his bound chest. "So that's it? You doomed this ship just to make people like you?"

"Of course not! I'm not a homely pre-teen!" Skardon snapped. "I did it to realign the brand. To destroy Varlowe's inane legacy and bring back traditional Ba'lux values under my reign as president!"

Burlock's jaw clenched "Respectfully, sir, this is madness. I don't like this American ship any more than you do, but there are still hundreds of souls aboard. And we're out of lifeboats!"

"By design, Burlock. All by design." Skardon flashed a sinister grin. "I had the dock workers remove half your escape craft before you left Jaynkee."

Dilly's mandibles flexed angrily. "You intend to kill us to keep your secret?"

"Certainly not. I intend to kill you because you're the worst crew in the galaxy."

Swooch chortled. "Sick burn, bro."

"We may be a little rough around the edges," Leo admitted. "But worst in the *whole galaxy*? I don't think so."

"You are, MacGavin. Trust me," Skardon said. "Each member handpicked by me. I saddled you with the worst of the worst of the entire WTF fleet. Dead weight to cut. Garbage to incinerate. All of you."

"Dude," Swooch chuckled. "That is a next-level sick burn."

Kellybean scowled at her. "I'm sorry, do you not understand what's happening here? He just said he put you on this ship to die."

Swooch shrugged. "Nobody lives forever, right?" She rubbed her belly. "Anybody else hungry?"

"Nobody else is hungry!" Jassi snapped. "What's the matter with you?"

Skardon smoothed down his robes. "That's an interesting subject, actually. You see, young Miss Swoochatowski suffers from a rare neurological condition known as Spicoli Syndrome. She is physically incapable of experiencing fear. Medically unflappable." He turned to Swooch. "Which is why she was dishonorably discharged from the Geiko Prime Supernova Strikeforce."

The helm officer nodded and slouched in her chair. "I went

down behind hostile enemy lines. Bad guys got ahold of my fighter. The commanders got pretty bunched up about it."

Hax tipped his head. "You were shot down?"

"Nah. I stopped for tacos."

"She's relaxed to the point of being a liability," Skardon said, a hint of regret in his voice. "She's a damn good pilot, but it's not safe to leave her on the bridge unattended."

"So we've noticed," Leo grumbled.

"Then there's crabby old Doctor Waverlee who can't tell a heart attack from a hemorrhoid." Skardon waved at Dilly. "And that horrible Dreda security chief."

Dilly's eyes flashed. "Do not accuse it of being derelict in its duties."

"Not at all," Skardon said. "If anything, you're too good at them. A beast like you should be cracking heads in a maximum security prison for the criminally psychotic."

"So what are you saying, sir?"

"I'm saying you scare people shixless. You're a monster with no business rubbing your multitude of elbows with passengers on a luxury cruise liner. But we can't very well fire you for that. Equal opportunity protections and all."

"So you chose to exterminate it instead."

"It was the easier solution," Skardon admitted.

"But you did fire me!" Kellybean cried. "I didn't even work for WTF anymore! Why would you hire me back just to kill me?"

"Are you serious?" Skardon asked. "You burned down three decks of the *Opulera!*"

"She *what*?" Leo turned to Kellybean. "I thought you left because of a bad breakup!"

"I did! I was upset and I had a drink. And then another drink." Her nose twitched. "And then I kinda set fire to my ex's office."

"Dang," Jassi muttered. "We've gotta get you in a program, girl."

Skardon's lips pulled tight. "Pyrrah was furious she'd been dumped by a lesser being. Frankly, so was I. It turns my stomach to think of a filthy mammal treating my niece with such disrespect."

"Hey, *she's* the one who treated *me* with..." Kellybean's eyes widened. "Wait, Pyrrah is your niece?" She cringed. "I did not know that."

"You defiled my ship. Worse than that, you defiled my family's honor," Skardon seethed. "Firing you wasn't enough. I want you *dead*."

Burlock blinked helplessly. "This isn't like you, sir. You don't punish failure with murder." He raised his metal hand and tapped on his metal brow. "When I failed you in the siege of Rankorrdar, you rescued me. You gave me these implants. You didn't leave me to die for my mistake."

"There was no mistake on Rankorrdar. Everything went exactly according to plan."

Burlock's eye lens flashed. "Sir?"

"You were set up to fail. And when you did, I swooped in to evac your team." Skardon grinned at the memory. "Each of you were loyal to the Imperial Navy, but after that day, you were loyal to *me*. Personally. Five blood debts. Five savage grunts to do my dirty work, forever."

"You sent my team on a suicide mission?" Burlock roared. "On purpose?!"

"And I've sent you on countless suicide missions since, but you always manage to come back, eternally loyal and eager to do my bidding."

Burlock took a menacing step toward the admiral's image. "I do have a bad habit of surviving suicide missions." He flicked his fingers, unsheathing his blades. "And when I survive this one, I think you'll find my loyalty has somewhat faded."

"Well then, I guess it's time to finish the job I started on Rankorrdar." Skardon glared into the camera. "You are dismissed, soldier."

The admiral swiped at his tabloyd and a high-pitched whine filled the bridge of the *Americano Grande*. Burlock wailed in agony and fell to his knees. His skull sizzled at the edges of his cranial implant. Tendrils of black smoke seeped through the seam between flesh and metal.

"Burlock!" Leo screamed. "No!"

He tried to rush forward to help, but his legs were still bound in Dreda silk. With a wild kick, he launched himself at Burlock. In one awkward movement, he grabbed the prosthetic, yanked it free, and gave it a desperate heave. The implant sailed across the bridge and burst in a sharp *pop* of yellow pyrotechnics.

"Ooh! Pretty," Swooch cooed.

Leo crashed to the deck. Burlock toppled over, smoke still pouring from his voided skull. Dilly wailed in anguish.

"Commander," its collar said calmly. "No."

On the screen, Skardon's expression drooped. "Aww, you ruined everything, you stupid ape. I was about to say, 'Did I blow your mind?' It was going to be hilarious."

"How can you make jokes?" Dilly said, cradling Burlock's lifeless body. "You killed the commander."

Skardon shrugged. "You'll all be dead in a few minutes."

Kellybean wriggled and clawed through her bindings. "You can't just leave us here to die!"

"We kinda already did," Stobber said. "And now I gotta find a new drummer and guitarist for Murderblossom."

"Huck you," Jassi said. "I gotta find a new bass keytar player for Murderblossom. It's my band!"

"It is not!" Stobber barked. "I'm the lead motherhucker!"

"Nobody cares!" Leo cried.

"For once, MacGavin is right. Nobody cares. About any of you." Skardon grinned at Leo, still lying on the floor, half bound in silk. "You poor, pathetic creature. My only regret is that you won't be around to see me become president of WTF cruises and begin the demolition of Eaglehaven." He swiped at his tabloyd, pulling up the hologram of the placid blue-green globe. "I can't wait to start painting the town brown."

"You lousy jerkhole!" Leo pushed himself upright against the captain's chair. "I thought you Ba'lux were supposed to act with honor! Do you think killing a bunch of innocent people to win a contest is honorable? What would your mother think of all this?"

Skardon snorted a chuckle. "My mother is a withered old fool who's far outlived her usefulness. As soon as your asinine ship is destroyed, the senile crone will cede full control of WTF to me. No one will ever know about my, shall we say, temporary lapse of integrity."

"Well then, I guess you win. Good for you. You bested us all. But there's one thing I still don't understand." The captain's chair squeaked as Leo grabbed its arm and forced himself to his feet. "How did I end up with a tabloyd with kid credentials?"

Skardon cocked his head. "I already told you, I had personnel make an unaccompanied minor device for me, then I swapped it for the captain's before Varlowe gave it to you."

"Ah. I see." Leo nodded. "So you asked them to make an unaccompanied minor tabloyd for you?"

"Yes! What's your point?"

"Nothing. It's just, I think they literally made it *for you*. They synced it to your WTF account. That's why it downloaded your documents and your contact list."

Skardon smirked. "Those both should have been restricted.

Children's tabloyds are completely locked down except for the emergency contact app."

"Remind me, what's the name of that app?"

"Call Mommy!"

Leo smiled. "Oh, I already did."

He pulled back his sleeve and a holographic call in progress beamed out of the band on his wrist. Its heart-shaped bubble contained the wrinkled, sagging face of Madame Skardon.

And she was miffed.

"Mother!" The admiral's eyes widened and he adjusted his robes. "Hello. Uh... how long have you been listening?"

"Long enough to figure out how to make it a conference call."

The old woman mashed a withered finger on her band and three more bubbles appeared above hers, containing Willijer, Kersa, and Varlowe. Their expressions ran the gamut from appalled to furious.

Stobber snorted a laugh and clapped a hand on Skardon's back. "Oh man, you are so hucked."

Skardon turned to the cluster of orange heads above Leo's wrist. "I assure you, this isn't as it seems. I can explain everything at the next board meeting."

"You can explain it now," Varlowe growled. "To our faces."

Skardon whirled to see the WTF executive board enter the *Opulera's* shuttle bay, each with caller bubbles floating around their arms. His mother was in the center, rolling in her rickety, powered chair. She dropped the call, sending a ripple of popped bubbles across everyone's wrists.

"So..." Madame Skardon seethed. "I'm a 'withered old fool,' am I? Or was that 'senile crone'?"

The admiral winced. "Some of my remarks may have been taken out of context..."

Varlowe crossed her arms. "You just explained, in detail,

precisely how and why you're murdering an entire WTF crew. What are we taking out of context, exactly?"

Skardon stabbed a finger at Stobber. "It was the Nomit's idea! He made me do it!"

"Pfft, whatever." Stobber chugged his beer. "I don't even know this arzehole."

Madame Skardon eyed her son. "Have you not a single shred of honor or dignity left? This contest is over. Varlowe wins."

Varlowe pumped a fist. "Yes! Thank you, Madame Skardon!"

"But *Moooooom!*" The admiral's shoulders slumped and he pointed out the shuttle bay door at the doomed ocean liner. "The ship didn't make it to Ensenada Vega! You said if—"

"Quit your whining, you snotty little whelp! You cheated and now you're getting what's coming to you." Madame Skardon waved a hand at Varlowe. "This one may be terrible at running a business, but at least she's honest about it."

Willijer scrolled on his tabloyd. "Additionally, pursuant to the charter, Rip Skardon is hereby removed from the board, due to a comprehensive list of felonies." He pushed up his glasses. "Committed, attempted, and still pending."

"Blast you and your blasted charter!" Skardon screamed. "You're not getting rid of me that easily!"

He thrust his hands into his robes and came back with two Imperial-Navy-issue pulse rifles.

"Varlowe!" Leo cried. He instinctively moved to protect her, but he was on the wrong side of the screen and several thousand miles of open space.

Varlowe's eyes narrowed defiantly at Skardon's guns. "Put those away! Are you insane?"

"I'm not insane! I'm just highly motivated for advancement!" Skardon raised his weapons. "And I'm going to be the next president of WTF, even if it has to be over your dead bodies!"

"Skardon, stop!" Leo screamed. "You don't have to do this!"

"I do now! Because of you!" Skardon aimed a gun at Varlowe's head. "If you'd have just died quietly like you were supposed to, your little girlfriend could have lived!" Spittle flew from his mouth. "You did this! Their blood is on your hands!"

Dilly stood over Burlock's body. "There will be no more bloodshed. Stand down, Admiral. While you still can."

"You're in no position to make threats, you eight-legged—"

Dilly cut him off with a deafening screech.

"No translation available," its collar intoned.

Skardon's head whipped to the side as he was smashed in the jaw by a jet of spider web. A second blast nailed him in the chest, followed by three more across his body. Stobber yelped and tried to scramble away, but a barrage of webs wrapped his legs, slamming him to the deck and sloshing his brew.

"Careful, man! There's a beverage here!"

Leo gaped at the feed as ten Dreda security officers scuttled in and swarmed over their screaming prey, binding them in the most brutal way possible. He turned to Dilly in shock. "Your drones are on the *Opulera*! How?"

"Its duty is to protect passengers." Dilly nodded at the shuttle bay full of *Americano Grande* lifeboats. "Would be careless to launch boats without security."

"Dang," Leo muttered. "You *are* good at your job."

Varlowe scrambled toward the camera, filling the view with her frenzied face. "Don't worry, Leo. We're sending the lifeboats back for your crew!"

Leo looked up from the call to the Blue Hole looming in the window. "Better make it fast. I don't think we have much time."

"I've already got pilots gearing up. But you have to evacuate before you cross into the accretion disc. After that, there's no chance of—"

The hull rumbled and the floor jerked as if the *Americano Grande* had been broadsided by a tsunami. Everyone who wasn't tied down tumbled to the deck as the comm went dead. Klaxons blared and searing blue lightning sizzled across the window.

"What happened?" Leo screamed.

Swooch stretched and yawned. "No biggie. We just crossed into the accretion disc."

CHAPTER SEVENTEEN

Arcs of searing white lightning lashed the *Americano Grande's* exterior decks as the ship coasted into the Blue Hole's unstable accretion disc.

Everyone on the bridge had been cut free of their spider web bindings and taken positions at the consoles. Swooch remained at the helm, Kellybean had commandeered MonCom, Jassi was at EngTech, and Hax parked himself at the auxiliary console at the rear. For lack of anywhere else to go, Leo perched squeamishly in the captain's chair.

The window was opaque with boiling swirls of blue gas, laced with blinding streaks of unbridled cosmic power. Impacts of high-velocity rock pitted the impervious glass. The comm link still floated on its surface, showing nothing but rolling fuzz.

Kellybean tapped at her panel. "I can't connect to the *Opulera!*"

"The comm array is down," Jassi said. "When we hit the storm it put up a blast shield."

"Can you force it open?" Leo asked.

"No problem!" Hax said. "But it will destroy the array and trigger a feedback cascade large enough to fry the ship's internal atmosphere."

Leo nodded. "Maybe just leave it closed then."

In the back corner of the bridge, Dilly was crouched beside a medical gurney that held Burlock's unconscious body. Doctor Waverlee fussed over him, wiring him to the bed with a series of electrodes. Her gills wrinkled inside the water-filled bubble of her helmet as she probed the scalded mass of his head.

"Hoo! I'm glad I can't smell that!" She grabbed the gurney's diagnostic lid and tried to close it, but the bottom thumped down on Burlock's barrel chest before it latched. "Ugh, shoulda brought the big bed."

Jassi sneered. "Why even bother saving that jagoff? He was ready to kill us all five minutes ago." She looked out at the storm hurling rocks at the window. "Plus we're all about to die anyway."

"We are not," Dilly said. "Captain will think of plan."

Hax blinked. "That seems unlikely, considering most of his head blew up."

Dilly rested a hand on Burlock's shoulder. "Not this captain. It meant real captain."

It turned to Leo. Leo's eyes widened. "Who, me?"

"It was mistake to remove you from command. Magnetosphere failure was not your fault. Nothing was your fault."

Leo scratched the back of his neck. "Well, okay, true, but—"

"No buts! You're the captain!" Kellybean mewled, slashing a claw at the window. "And we're going into a gravity well! So put on your big boy pants and give some orders!"

"Right! Orders!" Leo chirped. "Okay! Somebody figure out what we have to do to fix the engines!"

"Damage report, coming up!" Hax swiped on his screen and a three-dimensional wireframe hologram of the ship appeared above his console. Its decimated systems were laid bare in color-coded layers, laced with blinking error messages. "Hmm. I think we can get the engine pods back online, but we'll need to repair at least two of these systems." He pointed to flashing areas. "The ion governor and the linkage to the photon boiler."

Leo turned to Jassi. "Can you reroute around the damaged circuits?"

"How am I supposed to do that?" Jassi asked.

"I don't know!" Leo admitted. "That's a thing you engineering people always say! 'Ooh, there's a system failure, I'll have to reroute around the damaged circuits.'" He turned to Swooch. "Am I right?"

Swooch nodded. "It's their favorite go-to."

"I can't reroute into nothing." Jassi rapped a knuckle on her console. "This isn't a blown plasma conduit or some shix. Those systems were torn out by a motherhucker who wanted them to stay broken."

"Jassi's right," Hax said. "Wanton destruction is apparently Stobber's only technical skill. He didn't leave thru-circuits in any critical junctions. It'll all have to be manually patched."

"So let's do that," Leo said. "We can do that, right?"

The robot held his hand to the holographic diagram and his fingers twitched open and closed like calipers, measuring distances. "We can do that!" he said brightly. "I'll need about seven hundred feet of cable, connected to components over three decks."

"Awesome!" Leo cheered. "Do we have that much cable?"

"According to the ship's manifest..." Kellybean poked her console and frowned. "We do not have any."

"Dang it!" Leo crossed his arms and looked at the floor, defeated. *Think!* There had to be some other way to... He blinked at the shredded Dreda webbing still littering the deck. "Wait! I just remembered something!"

Waverlee kneeled on the lid of Burlock's gurney, bouncing up and down on his chest like she was trying to close an overstuffed suitcase. "You're about to go into heat! Gah! Mammals are so gross!"

"What? No! Just so much no!" Leo snapped. "Dilly, when we got to the Murderblossom concert you tried to unplug a speaker and electrocuted yourself, remember?"

"Yes." Dilly's gray face wrinkled. "Is not good memory."

"Yes it is! Because it means Dreda webbing is electrically conductive."

Kellybean's head cocked. "Wait, are you suggesting we use Dilly's silk as cable?"

Leo turned to Dilly. "Would that work?"

Dilly flicked its wrist, firing a web at Burlock's gurney. As soon as the strands bridged the gap between the edge of the lid and the contacts on the bed, a white spark blasted Waverlee off the top with a bubbly yelp. The diagnostic panels lit up as the connected electronics whirred to life. Dilly nodded.

"It would work." It scuttled to Hax. "Come along, robot. We have repairs to make."

It grabbed Hax and stuffed him under its arm. Hax cheered as Dilly raced off the bridge. "Wheee! New lab partner!"

Waves of lightning sizzled across the window as rocks and ice peppered the hull. Leo turned to his crew. "Any chance we can get that magnetosphere shield back online before the storm obliterates us?"

"I'm sure Praz is all over it," Swooch said.

"Praz abandoned ship!" Kellybean cried.

"Oh." Swooch shrugged. "Then no."

Kellybean hopped down from the MonCom console. "I can go take a look. But I'm gonna need someone who's a genius with hardware. Someone I can trust." She threw a coy glance at the EngTech station. "Do you want to get out of here?"

Jassi grinned. "Yes, I definitely do."

***

Alerts buzzed and warnings flashed across screens in the primary machine room. Beyond the windows, the dynamo chamber was quiet and dark. The enormous orb of its iron core sat dead still in a ring on the floor with its plasma shell pooled in a moat around it. Kellybean pawed at a glitching console as Jassi lay underneath, yanking out its wiring.

"There's one thing I still don't understand," Kellybean said distractedly. "If you knew Stobber put something in my drink, why didn't you tell me?"

"Apparently I did. But we were too blotto to remember." Jassi stripped a wire with her teeth and spat out the insulation. "I hauled you out of there to sleep it off 'cause I didn't want you to get in trouble. I know you have a reputation to uphold and all."

A blush ran through Kellybean's ears. "That was very gallant. I'm sorry I accused you of disrespecting me."

Jassi shrugged. "I'm sorry I formed a band with the biggest arzehole in the galaxy." She twisted two wires together and Kellybean's flickering console resolved to clarity. "Boom."

"Nice!" Kellybean leaned in and studied the screen.

Jassi climbed to her feet and waved at the darkened dynamo. "So do you actually know how to start that thing?"

"Maybe?" Kellybean tapped the interface. "I've got a level-one engineering certification, but the dynamo is really high-end stuff. Hopefully the help files are—"

She hissed as a hologram burst from the top of her console. It depicted an orb of black iron the size of a basketball with two big googly eyes.

"It looks like you're booting the dynamo!" the sphere shouted.

"Ack!" Jassi snapped. "What the shix is that?"

"I'm Core-y! I'm the magnetosphere dynamo interactive assistant! Would you like help?"

"Yes!" Kellybean said. "How do we power up the dynamo?"

"I'd be happy to guide you through the process. But first, would you like to install updates?"

"No."

"Are you sure? Regular updates keep your system running at optimal—"

"It's not running at all!" Kellybean snapped. "Just tell me how to turn it on!"

"Technically, it is on," Core-y said brightly. "A system failure has put your dynamo into emergency core lockdown."

"Fine! How do we fix it?"

"First you'll have to initiate the suspensor beams through the stabilization interface."

Kellybean's screen changed to a diagram showing the iron core resting on the deck with six beam emitters surrounding it—three on the floor and three on the ceiling.

"Thank you!" She tapped each one in sequence and the lights dimmed as a deep mechanical rumble thrummed through the deck plating. In the dynamo chamber, the three lower emitters kicked on, blasting the enormous sphere with blue light. It trembled in its base, but didn't move. Errors flashed over Kellybean's console. "What's wrong? I did what you said!"

Core-y tried to answer, but his hologram blinked and glitched.

"I don't get it," Jassi said. "We should have enough juice for this, unless..." She unlatched a wall panel and peered inside at a row of twitching gauges. "Shix! The whole ship has been running on backup batteries since the primary power links were severed." She waved at the core. "It's enough to keep the air warm and the beer cold, but no way it's gonna be able to get that thing's heavy arze off the deck."

"Okay. Plan B." Kellybean's tail thrashed as she pulled up a

GALAXY CRUISE: THE MAIDEN VOYAGE   225

list of all ship systems. "Maybe I can steal enough power to lift it, but it's going to mean turning off almost everything."

"What if we only turned off one thing?"

Kellybean shook her head. "Nothing pulls enough power by itself to—" Jassi pointed to one checkbox. Kellybean's eyes widened. "Oh my gosh, Jassi. You're a genius."

***

On the bridge, Doctor Waverlee fussed over Burlock's bed, poking at the control panels and adjusting levels of medication and healing currents.

"Is he going to be all right?" Leo asked.

Waverlee shrugged as lightning sizzled across the window. "Well, he's not gonna die of old age, that's for sure."

Leo turned to the only bridge station still occupied. "Swooch, any word from Hax and Dilly?"

"Nope. Lemme see if I can get 'em on the horn." She leaned over her console and flicked through a crew directory with an agonizing lack of urgency. "Haddonfield... Haggis... Hasselhoff... Ah, Hax."

She poked the screen and an outgoing call popped up on the front window. A second later it resolved into a video feed of Hax in an engineering conduit.

"Thank you for calling Hax!" the robot said. "I'm sorry, but I am not available to take your call right now."

Swooch turned to Leo. "Sorry, bro. He's not there."

"Clearly he is. I can tell by the way he answered the call."

"I didn't say I'm not here, I said I'm not available," Hax clarified. He shouted off screen. "Good work, Lieutenant Commander Marshmallow Hug Dilly Dilly! Now do breaker L-770 to conduit 118-9."

"Acknowledged," Dilly's collar said.

"What's happening?" Leo asked. "How are your repairs coming along?"

"Oh, just dandy! Check it out."

Hax turned his camera around to reveal a corridor tall and wide enough to drive a hovercoach down, extending into darkness in both directions. Its walls were lined with sparking wreckage and leaking pipes, torn apart in swaths the size of enormous Nomit hands. But the technological carnage was mostly hidden behind an elaborate and systematic spider web that stretched from wall to wall, ceiling to floor, knitting the ruined components together.

Dilly slapped a spinneret on breaker L-770 then flicked its wrist toward conduit 118-9, throwing out web like a fisherman casting a line. The instant the strand made contact, both ends sparked and the bridge lights brightened with a pleasant *whirrr* of power.

"Yes!" Leo said. "Whatever you're doing, do more of it!"

The wall behind Hax slowly drifted downward, as if he were in an invisible elevator. "We're almost finished. Just a few more connections and the engines should—"

He squeaked and his eyes frizzed as his head banged against the ceiling. All around the corridor, loops of webbing floated like seaweed in calm shallows. Leo jumped out of his chair.

"Hax! What did you do—"

Before he could complete his thought, a fist of nausea punched his stomach, as if he'd just gone over the peak of a roller coaster. He yelped and swung his arms as his feet failed to connect with the deck. In front of him, Swooch gently floated out of her seat like a balloon.

"What's happening?" Leo shouted.

Waverlee tumbled through the air and caught hold of the MonCom console. "The artificial gravity is off!"

"Gah! Another system failure?"

The doctor peered at the screens. "No! Somebody turned it off. On purpose!"

Leo thrashed wildly as he drifted toward the ceiling. "Why would somebody do that?!"

***

The weightless iron core of the magnetosphere dynamo floated in its chamber, slowly drifting from side to side as its suspensor beams erratically pulsed and trembled.

"To the left!" Kellybean shouted. "The left!"

Jassi had six wall panels hanging open, exposing their sparking innards. She twisted a power modulator inside one and a single beam grew brighter, shoving the ball to one side.

"No!" Kellybean shook her head, thrashing her bob in a floating wave. "Sorry! *My* left!"

"Gah!" Jassi kicked off the wall and flew like a dart to the other side of the room. She cranked another modulator, tipping the sphere the other way. It drifted against the anemic force of the flickering beams and settled in the center of the space.

"There! Stop!" Kellybean crouched in her bolted-down seat, toe claws dug into the upholstery. "That's it! The core is aligned!"

"Huck yeah!" Jassi cheered. "Let 'er rip!"

Kellybean mashed her panel, but nothing happened.

"It looks like you're igniting the plasma sphere!" Core-y the interactive assistant said.

"Yes! Why isn't it working?"

"The sphere can't be ignited without a boost from the engines," Core-y explained. "The system has insufficient power."

"Still? Come on!" Kellybean hammered her thumb on the pad. "Just ignite, you stupid ball!"

"Ah ah ah! You don't have enough power." Core-y wagged side to side condescendingly. "Ah ah ah! Ah ah ah!"

"Please!" Kellybean cried. "Gah damn it! I hate this hacker crap!"

Jassi whipped her rumpled tabloyd from her back pocket and dialed a call. "Hax! Get your shix together! We need those engines powered up!"

***

Dilly sailed through the engineering conduit, patching pipes and connecting junctions. But Leo wasn't watching the video feed of the Dreda. He was looking past it, through the bridge window, eyes wide in unbridled terror.

The gaping pit of the gravity well loomed in front of them like a planet-sized, polished black marble of nothing. Just a complete and total absence of something, leaving only pure, unadulterated nothing. Enormous boulders caught in the raging storm funnel tumbled into its ravenous maw. As one crossed its event horizon it seemed to pause for a moment before stretching out like an infinitely long noodle and then vanishing in a crackling red fizz of obliteration.

Leo tugged at his collar and whimpered. "Hax? Please hurry."

"Don't worry, Mister Captain!" Hax said from the feed. "Just one more... Oh! I have another call."

He tapped his screen and Jassi appeared in a second window next to him. "Hax! Get your shix together! We need those engines powered up!"

"Well, aren't I the belle of the ball?" Hax turned to Dilly. "Ready, spider friend?"

Dilly slung a web between a sizzling crystal and a knot of torn wires. "Final connection complete as directed."

"Then we are good to go!" Hax cheered. "You may fire the

engines when ready, Captain!"

"Swooch!" Leo shouted. "Do it! Do the thing!"

"Right on." Swooch's stubby legs kicked off the ceiling and she did a slow end-over-end rotation in the air, making a soft, butt-first landing in her chair. She fastened her seat belt and grabbed a set of keys stuck in the helm console. "Let's rock and roll, brah."

She cranked the key in the ignition and the video feed from the engineering conduit strobed like a thunderstorm. Hax screamed as Dilly swept him away from the wriggling blue energy blazing through the spider-web wiring. With a deep groan and a gut-churning rumble, all four engine pods thunderously ignited at once.

All around the ship, lights brightened and music echoed through concourses as systems that had been in standby mode woke up. On the bridge, half the console alerts blinked out. The other half still screeched warnings about the gravity well dead ahead.

"Swooch, get us out of here!" Leo shouted.

"You got it, dude."

The helm officer planted a palm on the steering yoke and languidly cranked the wheel as she stood on the accelerator pedal. Blazing arcs of white-hot exhaust belched from the thrusters, incinerating a mile-wide swath through the storm as the ship did an abrupt 180-degree turn.

***

The machine room lurched to one side, sending the core drifting perilously out of alignment. Kellybean clawed at her console. "It's shifting! We're losing it!"

Jassi floated near the ceiling, gripping fistfuls of tied-together cable and hose in both arms. Her makeshift belts were looped around the beam-strength modulator wheels in six different panels circling the room. She grunted and tugged the belts, remotely manipulating the wheels like clothesline pulleys.

"I can't balance them all! The gain is too unstable to—"

A thunderous bass note rattled the windows as the six flickering suspensor beams suddenly blasted to full power.

"Engines online!" Core-y's hologram intensified as a smile spread across his face. "Dynamo systems energized! Ready to ignite plasma shell!"

"Do it!" Kellybean cried.

A green "start" button appeared on her console and she smashed it. Core-y's cartoony sphere began to revolve as a gooey dribble of red plasma crept across his surface like an apple being dipped in toffee.

At the same time, a blinding magenta light seared through the windows. Kellybean threw a paw over her eyes, squinting against the brightness. Fixed firmly between the enormous, blazing columns of the suspensor beams, the iron core accelerated to a blur of speed. As it did, raging streams of superheated, hyperconductive plasma surged upward from the moat and clung to the ball, creating a liquid shell slowly rotating in the opposite direction.

Jassi shuffled off the belts and drifted across the room. "It's working! Holy shix, it's working!"

"We did it!" Kellybean cheered.

Core-y's face disappeared in a blur as he spun himself to oblivion with a joyous, "Wheeeeeeeee!"

***

On the bridge, the pounding hailstorm of rocks against the window went silent as a wave of energy surged off the hull, pushing back the storm in a perfect sphere of protection. Leo's ears rang in the newfound silence as he gaped at the ball of green aurora blazing a quarter-mile off the bow.

"Yes! The magnetosphere is up!"

Waverlee grunted as she wrestled with Burlock's weightless gurney. "But the gravity is still off!"

Jassi called out from her comm window. "Oh, that's us. Hold on."

She grabbed a slider and Kellybean sucked a breath. "Wait!"

Jassi shoved the control all the way up. A thunderous clatter rang through the ship, as everything from flatware to grand pianos to crew members became reacquainted with the deck. Leo dropped into the captain's chair. Burlock's gurney crashed to the floor, and Waverlee slapped down on top with a dull *thwump*.

Kellybean winced at Jassi. "Standard procedure for reinstating gravity is to turn it up slowly over a period of five hours."

Jassi snuffed. "It's sweet you think we're gonna live that long."

Leo gazed out the window at the bow of the ship. It was pointed toward the edge of the storm, but the safety of open space wasn't getting any closer. In fact, it was creeping farther away. He sprang over to Swooch. "What's wrong? Why aren't we leaving the accretion disc?"

"I'm tryin'. Every thruster is maxed out full-forward but we're still getting pulled in." She shrugged. "Gravity wells are the worst."

"Show me."

"Right on. Activating rear-view."

Swooch's long fingers tapped her console and a holoscreen sizzled up behind Leo. He turned to look and a screech caught in his throat. Beyond the blaze of the engines, the crushing black void of the event horizon inched ever closer behind them, sucking them toward oblivion.

Leo whipped back around, eyes wide and cheeks pale. "I regret looking at that."

On the comm screen, Hax waved a hand. "Oh, hey captain! I just thought you should know, these repairs are only effective for a limited time."

"How limited?"

"Surprisingly limited."

Hax turned the camera to reveal an inferno blazing through the engineering conduit. White lightning and yellow flame surged through the webbing, turning the strands to cinders. Connections snapped and shorted against their neighbors as Dilly raced up and down the corridor, firing off webs from all of its upper limbs, trying to control the damage. A trembling hiccup rumbled through the engine pods.

"Dilly! Don't let those engines burn out!" Leo shouted. "That's an order!"

Before Dilly could reply, a power junction exploded in the conduit. The bridge lights flickered and all the comm feeds blinked off the front window.

"Dilly!" Leo threw himself into his chair and poked at the buttons. "Somebody get that connection back!" An incoming call popped up on the window and Leo mashed the button to answer it. "Dilly! Are you all—"

"Leo!" the face in the link interrupted. "Are you all right?"

Leo's brain locked up as it violently switched gears.

"Varlowe?" he cried. "How did you—"

"I've been trying to call! Your comms just came back up!"

Leo realized the comm array must have lowered its blast shield when the magnetosphere came online. The picture sizzled with distortion, but he could make out Varlowe surrounded by crew on the lavish command bridge of the *Opulera*.

"We're in trouble!" Leo cried. "We can't escape the gravity well!"

"Don't worry, we're gonna pull you out."

Varlowe turned to the *Opulera's* helmsman. The Ba'lux officer checked his console and spoke with authority. "*Americano Grande*, prepare for link-up. Fire your mooring beams, full power, vector four-two-niner on my mark."

Swooch nodded. "You got it."

The Ba'lux gave the order and a dazzling green beam blasted off the bow of the space ocean liner. It pierced the shield and blazed into the sea of storm. A shudder ran through the deck and a message blinked on the window. *Link-up successful. Fortifying beam integrity.*

A pulse thumped off the beam, searing a corridor through the accretion disc. In the window's augmented view Leo saw the *Opulera*, five-hundred miles away and safely beyond the edge of the storm. At the midpoint between them was a knot of clawing energy where the two ships' mooring beams knitted together.

"Pull them out!" Varlowe ordered.

A screeching rumble pulled through the *Americano Grande's* bulkheads as the beams tightened. Leo clutched Swooch's chair. "Is it working?"

Swooch shook her head. "Nah. Still drifting backwards."

Leo turned and shouted at the Ba'lux helmsman on his screen. "*Opulera!* Full reverse! Now!"

The helmsman obeyed the command and both ships shuddered as he pushed the engines to maximum power. The *Opulera's* Simishi navigator raised a brow at his partner. "Since when do you take orders from mammals?"

The Ba'lux elbowed the fish and hissed, "Show some respect!

This is the captain who outsmarted Admiral Skardon!"

"No way," the Simishi whispered. "That was an *American*?"

Leo scowled. "Human, actually. We're called humans."

"Humans. Huh." The Ba'lux considered it. "I guess we have a lot to learn about your people."

"We all do," Varlowe said. "And we'll get to learn it straight from the source." She turned to Leo with a tense smile. "I've already canceled Skardon's stupid demolition order and filed a motion with the Four Systems Council to have your world designated a protected cultural site."

Her smile passed to Leo. "So Eaglehaven is saved?"

"Now and forever. You did it, Leo. So let's get you home to celebrate! I can't wait to—"

She stumbled as the video feed bucked and flickered.

"What was that?" Leo cried. "What happened?"

Waverlee scrambled behind the MonCom console and poked a screen. "The *Opulera* just hit the edge of the accretion disc."

"No!" Leo turned to Swooch. "Can you boost power to—"

The ship violently lurched as one of the engine pods sputtered out. Swooch clicked a toggle switch off then back on. Nothing happened. "Pod four is smoked." She flicked the switch again. "Better call Praz."

"We can't call Praz! Praz is—"

"We're still drifting backwards!" Waverlee's webbed hands furiously pounded the MonCom console. "The gravity well is less than a hundred miles away!"

Leo turned to Varlowe. "Pull harder!"

Varlowe shouted at the *Opulera's* helmsman. "You heard the captain!"

Behind her, a stout Ba'lux in a WTF command uniform raised a finger. "Technically, *I'm* the captain. So—"

"You stay out of this!" Varlowe barked.

Leo tumbled back into his captain's chair as the deck lurched under his feet. Swooch clicked another switch on and off. "Aw, man. Now number three is out."

"Less than fifty miles to the event horizon!" Waverlee blubbed. "And we're speeding up!"

"We're losing position!" the *Opulera's* helmsman shouted. "They're pulling us in!"

Swooch tapped a finger on her panel. "Ooh, number two is not looking good." She glanced at Leo. "Last call, buddy. Smoke 'em if you got 'em."

"No!" Varlowe wailed. "Listen to me, Leo! We're getting you out of there! You're going home a hero! You're gonna make that girl regret dumping the savior of Eaglehaven!"

Leo jolted at the non sequitur. "What girl? What are you talking about?"

"The girl! The one who dumped you and sent you running off to space! Remember?"

"Oh, that girl." Leo rubbed the back of his neck. "Yeah, we were never technically dating, as such."

Varlowe cocked her head. "But you said she broke your heart!"

"She did." Leo blew out a breath. "She was a regular at my karaoke gig. I had a huge crush, but I was too shy to tell her. We never actually spoke. She married some other guy and I ran away feeling sorry for myself."

He shook his head at the memory. It seemed like it was something from another life. A simpler life with simpler, stupider problems. Alerts screamed at him from the arms of his chair. Proximity warnings and system failures. Reminders of problems far worse than an unrequited crush.

Varlowe's empty eyes turned sympathetic. "Well, I'm sure your experience as a WTF captain has made you more confident." She bit her lip. "If you cared about a girl now you'd tell her. You wouldn't just let her go."

The *Opulera* shuddered as it was dragged into the deadly electrical storm. Flying debris sheared a cluster of solar sails off its hull, smashing them to bits. Leo laid a hand on an armrest control as he gazed into Varlowe's eyes.

"Sometimes the best way to tell someone you care is by letting them go."

He disengaged the mooring beam.

The *Opulera* blasted backwards into the safety of open space.

The *Americano Grande* plunged into the gravity well.

CHAPTER EIGHTEEN

Time stopped. Existence accelerated. Leo couldn't feel his body. At the same time he could feel it being unraveled to the edges of eternity. Light pulsed. Colors swirled. Consciousness expanded. Leo was no longer Leo. He was greater than Leo. He was a being of absolute, everlasting illumination drifting in the celestial—

A thunderclap like an open-palm slap to reality threw him from the captain's chair. His knees and elbows hit the deck. Leo sat up, reeling at the very idea of having a corporeal form. He blinked his wet eyes and forced focus through their crude, organic cameras. He was on the bridge of the *Americano Grande*. He was alive. He leaped to his feet.

"Aagh! What the shix just happened?!"

Nausea curdled his belly. To his left, Waverlee glubbed bubbles into her helmet as she peeled herself off the MonCom console. Behind him, Burlock's collapsed gurney gave off sickly electronic beeps indicating some form of life. To his front, Swooch slouched at the helm. "Dude. What a rush!"

"We're alive," Waverlee said. "Stars and gas, we're alive!"

She hopped out of the MonCom station and rushed to Burlock to check his stats. Leo's gut and mind continued to reel as he blinked out the window. The Blue Hole was gone. In its place was a velvety black space pinpricked with stars. In the distance, a grotesque spiral of blazing orange storm vomited a cloud of energy into the cosmos.

"Is everybody all right?" a voice mewled.

Leo didn't turn as Kellybean and Jassi rushed onto the bridge, followed by Dilly and Hax.

"It is unharmed," Dilly said.

Hax gave a double thumbs up. "All systems go!"

A knot formed in Leo's belly as he gestured to the monstrous space geyser outside the window. "Could somebody please tell me what that is?"

"Whoa!" Kellybean pounced into the MonCom pod and pulled up sensors. "It's... weird! It's got all the same properties as the Blue Hole, but the opposite. It's like an..."

"Orange Hole," Leo said.

"I was going to say obtuse, negatively charged gravitational anomaly." Kellybean shrugged. "But sure, let's go with Orange Hole."

"Who cares what it is?" Jassi said. "Where the huck are we?"

"Hold on. Lemme check." Swooch tapped the navigation panel and brought up a star map on the cracked front window. "All righty. So here's the galaxy. This is Ba'luxi Prime." An indicator popped up. "And here's Gellico, and way over here, that's Jaynkee."

"Those are all great answers to the question 'Where the huck *aren't* we?'" Jassi said. "I asked where the huck *are* we?"

"Oh yeah." Swooch messed with her console. "Okay, got it."

She pinched her panel and the star map zoomed out. And out. And out again. Worry creased Leo's brow. "Please tell me we're not outside the Four Prime Systems."

"A bit. As far as I can tell, we're somewhere around..." Swooch continued to zoom out until the border of the map came into view, including the copyright notice of the Geiko Star Cartography Institute. When it would zoom out no further, Swooch stood up, crossed to the back of the room, and pointed to a spot on the wall. "Here."

"Holy crap," Leo whispered.

Kellybean checked her sensors. "She's right! We're beyond the boundaries of known space!" She looked up, eyes dilated. "Not just beyond what's been explored, but beyond what we can see with our largest orbital telescopes. Do you know what this means?"

"Yes!" Hax said. "Nobody use your tabloyds or you'll get dinged with roaming charges!"

Kellybean ignored him. "We're the first ship to ever navigate an interstellar wormhole!"

Leo scratched his head. "So... the Orange Hole is the exit from the Blue Hole?"

Hax got behind the EngTech console and clicked some switches. "Yes, sir! That's definitely where we came from."

"Okay, great," Leo said. "So is it possible to go back through it to get home?"

Swooch nodded. "If we adjust the—" Without warning, the orange deluge of ejecting cosmic mass roared backwards into the tear in space like a reverse geyser. When the last of it had vanished, the void sucked in its own edges, pulling itself inside out before disappearing with a *pop*. Swooch blinked. "No, it's not possible."

"What happened?" Leo cried.

"It's gone," Hax said.

"I know it's gone!"

"But it's like *gone* gone." Hax tapped at his screen. "Sensors don't see any trace of it. It's as if it never existed."

Waverlee laughed. "Well, ain't that a kick in the gills?"

Panic tightened Leo's throat. "But if it's gone, how are we going to get back home?"

"Dunno." Swooch dropped into her chair. "Oh, hey. I'm getting something. Check it out."

She twisted a dial and a dark mass appeared on the scarred window.

"What is it?" Leo asked.

"Looks like a ship. And it's coming in fast like zoom zoom, bro."

Swooch tapped the helm and a sector of space magnified on the window, bringing a strange vessel into focus. It was like a pair of enormous Bowie knives mounted side by side, the blades black and marred with uneven ridges as if it had been scorched in a campfire. A halo of blazing orange ringed its rear end, bending the light of the stars behind it.

"I don't like the looks of that," Leo said. "Power up weapons."

"Sorry, I can't do that," Hax said.

"Why not?"

The robot shrugged. "There aren't any weapons."

"This is a luxury cruise ship," Kellybean added. "We've got no defenses."

"None?" Leo asked.

"There's an archery range we could pillage if we get really desperate."

"Okay, good to know. Actually, not good to know. Very disheartening to know." Leo's eyes stayed glued to the ship as it approached at ludicrous speed. "Can you open a comm channel?"

The hospitality chief pawed at her screen. "Channel is open."

Leo straightened his uniform and stood in front of his captain's chair, projecting his voice at the window. "This is Captain Leo MacGavin of the *WTF Americano Grande* to the alien... pointy, burned-up looking thing. Do you copy?" A video link opened on the glass, rolling with static. A dark shape loomed in the center. Leo squinted and turned to Hax. "Could you make that more clear?"

"Righto!" Hax adjusted his controls and the image resolved. Leo yelped and flinched.

"Could you make that less clear?"

Everyone gaped at the creature staring back at them from the window. The face was mostly teeth of varying size and sharpness, arranged in a circular hole in what looked like a lump of pale, fleshy clay covered in pasty goo. Three things that might have been eyes were lined up across its forehead, looking like sucking pink sphincters. Its body was a collection of greasy, crustacean-like limbs, jointed at painful-looking angles. The alien leaned forward and its hideous mouth expanded, screeching with a noise like an accordion being beaten to death.

"Holy shix." Jassi grinned. "I think I found my new bass keytar player."

With a nauseating blink of its wet, puckered eyes, the creature bellowed and howled, waving its forelimbs and slashing them at the air. Leo cleared his throat and waved. "Yes! Hello! So... this is awkward. I don't suppose you speak Quipp, do you?"

A shudder ran through the alien captain's blobby head and it turned and brayed at a few other abominations perched on a ring of stools around it. The crew members opened their circular mouths and howled at each other, their teeth jiggling in their soft skulls. Several of them stuck their arms into divots in the walls and began levering them up and down.

Kellybean eyed her panel warily. "I don't want to freak you out, but I'm reading a big power surge on that ship."

Rivulets of orange energy poured through the crevices on the alien vessel, running toward bristling arrays of cannons.

"Ah crud," Leo grumbled. "Swooch, get us out of here!"

The helm officer cranked the yoke and accelerated. The blobby alien bellowed and a barrage of weapons fire sizzled through the magnetosphere, grazing the *Americano Grande's* exterior decks.

"Stop!" Leo shouted. "Don't move! Nobody move!"

Swooch froze the ship in an awkward half-turn away from the battleship. The alien captain sprang off its command stool, eyes clenched in constipated rage. It pointed a claw at Leo and bayed savagely. Three more energy bolts sizzled past the window.

"I don't understand!" Leo shouted. "Listen, we're not your enemies!"

"Their weapons are at full power!" Kellybean said. "They've got targeting beams locked onto our engines!"

"We need to move!" Jassi said.

"If we move they'll shoot us!" Leo argued.

"If we don't move they'll shoot us!" Hax cried.

"What's the call, Cap'n?" Swooch drawled.

"I don't know!" Leo admitted. "I don't know what they want or—"

"SNEEEEEEEEEERRRRRRRRRRRRRF," a voice wailed.

Everyone on the bridge flinched away as Dilly bellowed at the comm. The glowing gem at the throat of its translator collar had turned from its usual gold to a dull blue. The alien captain stopped blustering and blinked its fleshy eyes. Dilly continued. "Aaaort. Heeeeeeerrrrrrrrg. Heeerrrrnnn."

The blob tipped its head and made a noise like a broken party favor. Dilly repeated the sound and the alien seemed to calm.

"Whoa, you chilled that dude right out," Swooch said.

"You speak grease crab alien," Leo asked. "How?"

Dilly cranked the gem back to gold. "Its collar has learning mode. Is crude translation, but it can understand little bit."

"What did you tell that guy?"

"It told alien we are not threat." Dilly blinked. "Probably." The pasty blob scuttled toward its screen and let out a spittle-filled wail. Dilly returned the aggressive posturing and cranked its gem to blue. "UUUUUNG. Heeeep heeeeep. Uuuuut."

Everything went silent on both ships. The energy cannons sparked and pulsed, bursting to fire. The alien captain's round mouth constricted. Leo held a tense breath. Swooch yawned.

A savage bark sounded from the monster's throat, repeating with such furious passion it shook its whole body. Leo's pulse raced as he took a step back.

"What's that?" he hissed. "What's it saying?"

Dilly turned the gem. "Is not saying anything. Is laughing."

"Laughing?" Waverlee asked. "At what? Did you actually manage a joke?"

"It reported we are unarmed pleasure vessel." Dilly cocked its head. "Is not joke. Is truth."

The other aliens surrounding the battleship captain hooted and brayed excitedly to each other before the leader raised its claws to quiet them. It barked an order and the energy canons powered down and retracted into the scorched black hull. The circle of its mouth broadened as it addressed Dilly with a series of howls. It tipped its head expectantly. A tense silence fell over both crews.

"What?" Leo whispered. "What did it say?"

Dilly turned the gem in its collar back and forth.

"Is rough translation, but alien basically said..." It shrugged. "They want to come over and party with us."

CHAPTER NINETEEN

The sounds of bellowing voices and barking laughter filled the storm-ravaged decks of the *Americano Grande*. The fleshy crab aliens from the battleship—Mashtaplops, as Leo understood it—were apparently having the time of their lives. In the two days since first contact, the remnants of Leo's WTF crew had reassembled a few makeshift cocktail bars and learned to mix drinks strong enough to smooth over the language barrier.

Leo looked down from the scorched rail of an upper-level sundeck, breathing in the artificial sea air and feeling the warm glow of a star no human being had ever seen. But he wasn't in an exploratory mood. He scrolled through his tabloyd's final sync of Skardon's files and pulled up the order to demolish Eaglehaven. The status was now stamped through with a big red CANCELED, but the hologram of the spinning globe remained. He'd saved his beautiful, blue-green moon from destruction. It was a bittersweet victory, all things considered.

A dark shadow fell across him and he quickly swiped the form away. Burlock settled at the rail, looking out over the reveling Mashtaplops.

"Hideous sons of bishes, aren't they?"

"I'm sure they think the same about us," Leo chuckled. "How are you feeling?"

"It's good to be whole again, I'll say that much."

Leo glanced up at the Ba'lux's cranial implant. The metal was blackened and scarred with fresh welds, but otherwise intact.

"I had the Lethargots put it back together while Waverlee was putting you back together. It should have all the same functionality it did before." He shrugged. "You know, except for the explodey parts."

Burlock's scratched eye lens twitched. "Yeah. About that." He rested his hands on the rail. "I just wanted to say th..." He choked. He paused. He grimaced. "Thank you."

"It was nothing."

"It was not nothing. You saved my life." Burlock's jaw muscles tightened. "When Admiral Skardon tried to terminate me, he terminated my blood debt to him. And in the same moment, you picked it up."

Leo shook his head. "That's not necessary. Really."

"Do not presume to understand Ba'lux honor, MacGavin. I owe you a blood debt."

"So you're not mad that I staged a mutiny against you?"

"I staged a mutiny against you first."

"What can I say? Everything I know about command I learned from you."

Burlock snorted a laugh. "You know, when my implant was gone and I was stuck on that gurney, I couldn't move or speak, but I could still see and hear. I was aware of everything going on around me. I saw you command under fire."

"And?"

A long moment passed.

"I'm not unimpressed."

Burlock handed Leo the captain's badge. Leo accepted it with a grin. "So... we're friends now?"

Burlock turned and strode away.

"Let's not push it, Captain."

***

Down on the Piñata Deck, a small, out-of-the-way lounge was packed claw-to-claw with scuttling Mashtaplops. The aliens whooped and swayed in what appeared to be total bliss, which made no sense, considering the mind-wrecking noise coming from the tiny stage.

Jassi shredded on her guitar while Hax drummed, neither of them making any effort to form a melody with the other. Jassi windmilled her arm across her strings over and over until the noise threatened to shatter the bottles behind the bar, then threw finger horns and shouted at the audience.

"Thank you! We're Murderblossom! And you're a bunch of disgusting crabs with butthole eyes who can't understand a gahdamn thing I say!"

The crowd whooped and rubbed their forearms together in a gesture Kellybean presumed was their version of applause. She waved at the stage as Jassi hopped off, getting her attention. The briefest look of surprise flashed across Jassi's face, and she swung her guitar over her back and swaggered over to Kellybean's table, followed by Hax.

"Heya, Beans. Funny seeing you here." Jassi smoldered and tipped her head toward the stage. "What'd ya think?"

"I think you're better without Stobber," Kellybean said.

"So you enjoyed the show?" Hax asked.

"I think you're better without Stobber," Kellybean repeated noncommittally.

Jassi sighed at the cheering crowd. "We finally get some groupies and they're a bunch of sphincter-faced jelly turds."

"One of them gave me its room key!" Hax cheered.

"You're only excited because you don't know what that means." Jassi rapped a knuckle on Hax's plastic casing. "Hey, why don't you go to the bar and fetch us some drinks." She gestured to herself. "Beer." She gestured to Kellybean.

"Milk," Kellybean said. "Just milk for me, please."

"Oooh, calcium rich," Hax said. "Good choice!"

He rolled away and Jassi slumped into a seat. "So... I haven't seen you around much since the whole repeated-near-death-experience thing."

Kellybean groaned. "Ugh. Do you know how hard it is to be the chief of hospitality when you have to plan activities for a bunch of gooey crabs you know literally nothing about? It's been a nightmare." She raked her paws through the bob of her hair. "To be honest, I kinda miss when we were just trying to keep the ship from exploding."

Jassi leaned in and met Kellybean's eyes with unexpected tenderness. "I kinda miss that, too."

"You know, it could be like that every day." Kellybean gave a coy smile. "Not the exploding part, but the part where we're together. If you're into it."

"I am," Jassi said breathily. "I so am."

"Awesome! Then I officially extend the offer."

She put a small, flat box on the table and pushed it toward Jassi. Jassi eyed it with confusion and flipped it open, revealing a WTF badge with three yellow chevrons. "What's this?"

"It's Praz's badge." Kellybean smiled. "The *Americano Grande* needs a new chief engineer. How would you like to join me on the senior staff?"

Jassi waved her hand and wrinkled her nose. "Bah. No way. I'm not some fancy-pants starship engineer. I'm just a spaceport gearhead."

"Our last chief engineer wasn't even that." Kellybean's eyes turned pleading. "Come on, Jassi. You've got mad skills. And you already know this ship's systems better than anyone else. The Lethargots are lost without a leader. Will you do it for them?"

"No way."

Kellybean put a paw on Jassi's hand and gazed through her lashes. "Will you do it for me?"

Jassi sighed in defeat. "You really want this?"

"I do."

"Then I guess I just got myself a new job."

Hax rolled up to the table with their drinks as Jassi picked up her badge. "Ooh! Shiny! What's that?"

"A new pain in my arze," Jassi grumbled.

"Oh, come on. This is going to be fun!" Kellybean gave Jassi a cheeky salute. "Welcome to the senior staff of the *WTF Americano Grande*, Lieutenant Commander Jassi Kiktrash."

"Wow!" Hax said. "That sounds so much more dignified than 'repeat offender Jassi Kiktrash.'"

The tiniest smile played at the corners of Jassi's lips.

"It does, doesn't it?"

***

Leo sat at the head of the table in a glass-walled boardroom overlooking the Rushmore Concourse. The damaged furniture of the artificial park had been cleared away and most of the water was back in the pond. Every café was full of Mashtaplop revelers eating and drinking and generally raising a ruckus.

"This nonsense needs to stop, and it needs to stop now." Burlock pointed at the ongoing party below. "It's one thing to make a gesture of goodwill to save our skins, but those things have been at it for two full days!"

A general rumble of agreement rolled around those seated at the table—Burlock and Waverlee to Leo's right, Kellybean and Jassi to his left, Dilly crouched at the other end.

"Not to be grim," Kellybean said, "but they've already eaten half the food on board. We only had enough on hand to get us to Ensenada Vega. Four days worth of perishables."

Dilly nodded. "Chances of survival are bleak. We have no resources."

"That's not true," Leo said. "We have the greatest resource of all. The crew."

Waverlee shook her head. "Even if we resort to cannibalism, we'll run out of crew in three, four months, tops."

"Wow, that is so not what I meant." Leo stood up and paced in front of the windows. "Look, Skardon thought this crew was the worst of the WTF fleet, but we've already proven him wrong. We pulled together when it mattered. When he tried to kill us, we survived. And we're going to keep surviving."

"And how do you propose we do that?" Burlock asked.

Leo's eyes glimmered. "By doing what we do best."

"Injuring the passengers?" Waverlee said.

"Shoddy repairs?" Dilly ventured.

"General reckless endangerment?" Kellybean suggested.

"No!" Leo snapped. "By hosting amazing cruises!"

Jassi snorted. "I wouldn't even put that in the top ten."

Leo pinched his eyes. "You guys, I'm serious." He took off his tabloyd and unfolded it, pulling up a roster of the people left on board. His device had been much more cooperative since Hax had broken the child lock. "We still have a lot of deckhands, and cabin stewards, and entertainers, and kitchen staff, and more. We've easily got enough crew to keep running cruises."

"But why?" Dilly asked. "What is point of running pleasure cruises here?"

"The same as it was back home," Leo said. "We show people a good time. They pay us for it. We buy more supplies. We live another day. And repeat. For as long as it takes." He lifted his chin and puffed his chest. "I promised Varlowe Waylade I'd get this ship to Ensenada Vega, and I'm gonna do it. So who's with me?"

He grinned and held out a fist for a show of solidarity that failed to materialize. Waverlee crossed her arms. "Look, kid. I don't mean to put grit in your oyster, but we're a bajillion light years from the Four Prime Systems. Even if this ship could somehow make it to Ensenada Vega, we'd all be dust and bones by the time it got there."

"Yes, but the Blue Hole brought us here in like, five seconds. What if there's something else out there that can take us back just as fast? We'll never find it if we just give up." Leo swiped on his tabloyd, bringing up Skardon's demolition order and its vibrant hologram of Eaglehaven. "We all have something to go back for, right? Close your eyes. Picture it in your mind. Do you want to give up on ever seeing that thing again?"

An annoyed grimace pricked Burlock's face. "I never give up on anything." His eye lens clicked as he turned to the others. "MacGavin's plan is terrible, but I got nothing better. I'm in."

"Thanks, Burlock." Leo considered it and teetered his hand. "Thanks-ish."

"Well, I believe Leo can pull this off." Kellybean grinned at him. "The captain is a force to be reckoned with."

Leo returned her smile. "I guess I am, aren't I?"

"I don't give two shix about going back." Jassi kicked her boots up on the table. "But if Kellybean's in, I'm in."

Leo cocked his head. "I'm sorry, are you on the senior staff now?"

Dilly clicked its mandibles. "Captain's plan will maximize life spans of remaining crew. It is in favor."

"I guess we'd all be dead already if not for the kid's cockamamie schemes," Waverlee said. "We're gonna have to work our fins off, but let's do it." She jabbed out a webbed fist. "For the things worth going back to!"

This time everyone stuck in a limb, bumped fists, and

repeated the rallying cry. "For the things worth going back to!"

Leo gazed at the hologram of the demolition order, but his eyes weren't on the revolving globe. They had drifted to the signature on the cancelation line, and the accompanying identicard photo of Varlowe. He smiled.

"For the things worth going back to."

THANK YOU!

Hello, reader!

Thank you for joining me on the maiden voyage of the *Americano Grande*! I hope you had fun and didn't get lost in space.

If you enjoyed this book, could you please do me a favor and leave a quick review? Your positive word-of-mouth does so much to sway potential readers. Let them know what you think!

Here's a web page with easy, direct links to review sites:
oldpalmarcus.com/review-gc-book-1

As a token of my appreciation, you can get a free ebook novella, *Galaxy Cruise: Language Barrier*, at this website:
canabypress.com/gc-language-barrier

And then you can head on over to **GalaxyCruise.net** to get book two—*Galaxy Cruise: Royally Screwed!*

Thanks for your support. I appreciate you!

Your old pal,
— Marcus

THANK YOU, TOO!

Thank you to everyone who helped me to get this crazy cruise out of my head and into this book.

To my beta readers—Christopher, J.J., Jer, Joy, Julia, Karen, and Victoria—thank you for pointing out all the things that sucked so I could fix them. And thanks to Mr. Senecal, my ninth-grade English teacher, for still being interested in what I'm writing thirty years later.

Thank you to Craig Martelle and 20BooksTo50K for teaching me how indie publishing works, and to William Van Winkle and the PNW Author Meetup Group for your wisdom and support.

Thanks to Jon Lundy for the awesome 3D model of the *Americano Grande* that's on the cover of this book, and to Maria Semelevich for showing me how to build a galaxy around it.

Thank you to my amazing Advance Review Crew for sharing the love across retail and reader sites. I appreciate you more than you'd be comfortable hearing about.

And most of all, thank you to my wife, Amanda, for never letting me give up. You are my favorite thing in the known universe.

ABOUT THE AUTHOR

Your old pal Marcus Alexander Hart is an award-adjacent novelist, self-proclaimed karaoke star, and default awesome dude. He has been a roller-derby skater and a real-life quidditch player. He once won an overnight road rally in a fake ice-cream truck. Marcus lives in the Pacific Northwest with his wife and two imaginary children.

For more nonsense, visit OldPalMarcus.com.

Printed in Great Britain
by Amazon